The King's Voice

Karen Peradon

National Library of Australia Cataloguing-in-Publication entry

Creator: Peradon, Karen, author.

Title: The King's voice / Karen Peradon.

ISBN: 9780994284501 (paperback)

ISBN: 9780994284518 (ebook)

Target Audience: For young adults.

Subjects: Fantasy fiction.

Dewey Number: A823.4

Printed & Channel Distribution

Lightning Source | Ingram (USA/UK/EUROPE/AUS)

To my Dad
who was the first writer I ever knew.

PART ONE

PART TWO

PART THREE

GOAERO
Shadowlands
River Lek
Quelta
River Lichen
Naharancan Plains
Blulupia
Carbinia
Casino
Lake Lantaba
Mount Or
Fuschian Jungle
Brook River
Pashanka River
Biron
Pashanka
Cortly
Wryan Waterway
Clarissa Crowcrone
Arfan
Anishka
Mortlock Range
Spode
Vandret Falls
Lake Vanish
N

PROLOGUE

Many Moons ago, when the Sun was a mere starlet she danced through time wearing robes of violet with iridescent ribbons flowing from her hair. She was the maiden of the galaxy and flirted with whoever she came across. She ran rings around Saturn and threw meteors at Pluto, she blew volcanos at Uranus and played hide and seek with the Moon. But there was something about Mars which attracted her. She teased him with circles that made him dizzy, she blew him kisses that made him soggy. Until, one day, Mars exploded and thundered:

"Why do you tease me so, Glow-Maiden? Come here and be my wife!"

So she ran to him in delight but her passion scorched him and he tossed her far, far away and turned his back on her. As her love burned, her sandy tears flowed, along with small drops of Mars' glowing embers which floated down and landed on a little rock. The rock grew bigger and bigger with Sun's sandy tears until it became a teardrop shaped planet which she named Goaero.

The Sun's tears, now called Sun Sand, are buried deep down in the centre of the planet. It carries a miraculous property that bestows life and turns everything it touches white. The Sun watches over her child, protecting, warming, nourishing, and the inhabitants of this sometimes beautiful, sometimes stark land revere her and her power. She circles her offspring, patrolling its shores, favouring the southern green face, leaving the bulbous end of the planet in perpetual darkness.

It is said that once peoples from the dark nether regions trespassed on the land and fought savage battles for the lush warm pastures. But the crones created Shapeshifter Territory, a defence that soon put an end to these invasions. This is the perimeter of Goaero, a dangerous place where the sea meets land. There are few who brave this region where only five portals allow entry. Hence only the mad or outcast were found there. But these stories became myths, and as far as Goaerons knew, they were the only inhabitants on the planet and thus they refer to their country as Goaero.

She whispered to the dove sitting in the palm of her hand, intently moving her lips and gently running her little finger down its breast. She checked the note was securely tied around the slender leg, slowly raised her hand and gave a little flick. The bird flew up and away, whisked off by air currents. It glided over the mountain ranges out over the stark frozen expanse of the River Lek, across the blue misty forests and then up again flapping hard to the tip of the great Mount Or before landing softly on the slumped shoulders of a still man.

PART ONE

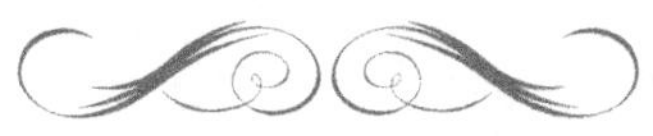

Chapter 1

MALLORY IN THE JUNGLE

The jungle ceiling was a mosaic of leaves in overlapping shades of jade and emerald. Each was dripping from the recent downpour, as if the rain was still falling. Steam rose from the narrow pathway toward a clearing. Vines hung down perilously, threatening to garrotte any advancing party. The Fuschian Jungle hissed and purred as birds reawakened from the deafening storm and slowly built up layer and layer of sound until the symphony was back in full swing. It lay like a huge lush blanket to the west of the great Mount Or, fed by the giant cascades that fell from the mountain peak into Lake Lantaba.

With a thundering crash the gentle green ceiling was broken open – momentarily quieting the jungle music again – and a shaft of sunlight hit the leafy floor like a meteor. A body followed shortly behind it with an 'oooph'. A purple shadow rested over Mallory as the silk sheet draped on the branches above, the hanging cords still attached. Droplets landed on his eyelids and he flicked them open. They were green, flecked with golden yellow; they focused and he cautiously moved his head of thick blonde hair from side to side, not only to check it was still connected but also to observe his surroundings.

He looked up and tugged the ropes. The leaves high above waved at him but did not release the parachute that had unceremoniously dropped him. He took the short knife from the sheaf at his belt and sliced himself free.

Mallory looked at his right hand and gently stroked the cuff on his wrist, wiping the drips off the face. He gazed at it for a moment, the briefest glance was all he needed. The two hands stood to attention, pointing in a direction a little to his left. He picked up his brown felt hat, shoved it on his head and leapt up and off into the tangled jungle.

It should have been a struggle to move through the contorted branches, roots and leaves but he seemed to move effortlessly; slicing a vine here, vaulting a log there as if he already knew the obstacles in his path. He passed the mouth of a cave which breathed out a breeze of cool air but Mallory ignored the temptation and went onward through the humidity. He glanced again at the cuff, and then paused. Its mystery unsettled him. Although he didn't know *how* the hands knew north from south, he thought there *was* a logical explanation, but what really puzzled him, and held him in awe, was that when it was worn on the left arm, the compass showed you the direction of that which your heart most desired. Mallory knew what his heart most desired: to serve the king and find his voice.

The compass told him to go no further; the hands spinning aimlessly. He found himself in front of a round, clear pool. He could hear the soft burble of the spring and see a layer of fragile amber leaves resting on the bottom. A glint caught his eye. He bent down and plunged his right arm into the warm water. The old leaves drifted about and Mallory's hand touched a small bottle. He pulled it out, the blue glass shimmered silver to green, as if it were made of water itself. It felt alive, pulsating. Mallory drew out the long, narrow cork protruding from the top and tipped golden sand into his cupped palm. A scrap of parchment fell out with it. He un-scrolled the brittle paper and read:

Tears of grief built this land

The last of which lies in your hand.

Spurned love transformed into a tree

Bearing fruits of wisdom and mystery.

Find the one who seeks a name

And show that we are all the same.

Ask the winged for help to see

That tears can turn to harmony.

The golden sand in his palm tingled. He scooped it back inside the bottle, wedged in the cork and wrapped it up in his handkerchief before tucking it inside the breast pocket of his vest. He looked at the compass and set off once more. As he fought with the unyielding inhabitants of that green underworld Mallory could feel the little bottle thrumming against his heart. It made him feel warm from the inside out which was a pleasant sensation except that soon he began to feel uncomfortably hot and steam began to rise from his skin. He had noticed the cool dripping cave mouth and he hoped the compass was leading him there. He was not sure if this was what his heart most desired but sure enough the cave was to be his next stop. He collapsed into the shade and pressed his cheek against the cold hard rock, breathing in deeply. His hands sizzled when he touched the pulsating vessel and he hurriedly pulled it from his pocket. He examined the bottle. Inside, the parchment had been incinerated to dust and the golden sand sparkled fervently. Bravely, he uncorked the bottle again, for Mallory now had an inkling of what he was dealing with. At the release of the cork a huge feather of flame leapt out burning a hole right through Mallory's hat and turned a streak of hair bright white. He stuffed the cork back in. Tiny orbs of red gold sprinkled down on the black sand in the cave. The sand turned white around each gold pearl rendering the floor a polka dot parquet.

"Sun Sand!" breathed Mallory as he stared in shock at the pellets rotating themselves in front of him.

Mallory was amazed for good reason. Sun Sand was extremely rare – so rare, in fact, it only existed in legend, so rare that the last person to see any was said to be a Quill; a mythical being, a human in most respects apart from a large pair of wings tucked under his arms. This Quill had died five hundred years ago at the age of two hundred and seventy. (They could live longer than Goaerons as they flew high into the sky where they could breathe in the Eternal Mists of Life, which hung above the clouds.) And this Quill had seen the last phial of Sun Sand in a sacred place when he was just three years old. The Quill watched a holy man unstop the urn and the resulting plume of flame had desiccated the whole place.

Mallory was not deemed the 'General's best man' for nothing and he had memorised the verse before he had activated the Sun Sand. And being the 'best man' he pushed aside the magnitude of his discovery and all that it might mean and sat down to try to work out what to do next. He murmured the poem to himself. It didn't seem to make any sense. How was Sun Sand to help restore the king's voice? Which tree bore fruit of wisdom and mystery? Who seeks a name? Winged ones?

By now the wobbling pellets of Sun Sand had sunk down and small plants were growing out of the white sand pools. In front of his eyes the plants unfurled and bloomed into perfect blue Forget-Me-Nots. Mallory crawled forward in wonder and lay down on his stomach to watch the miracle up close. At once he heard a high-pitched buzzing noise. He lifted his head up to look...it stopped. His eyes scanned the cave without moving another muscle; nothing. He cautiously lay back down.

"Mmmmmmmmmzzzzzzz," he sat up bewildered. Again he saw nothing, until he looked closely at the flowers. Head first in a fresh bloom he saw a bee shuffling into the pollen before moving onto the next one. Mallory followed the bee slowly work its way from plant to plant, deeper into the cave.

"Ask the winged ones for help to see," he repeated.

"What can you see, little bee? Can you help me?"

The bee seemed unaware of Mallory, despite his unusual presence in the jungle. He continued to hop lightly from flower to flower, wiggling his stripy bottom, deeper into the mouth of the cave. Eventually they moved beyond the flowers into darkness. Mallory followed with his ears as the bee hummed onwards.

Chapter 2

BRAVINDO AND ENCODA

Mount Or was the pinnacle of Goaero and on it the royal palace was the greatest building in the vast continent. It was built at the peak of the Mount above the country's only city, Carbinia. The turreted palace was separated from Carbinia by a swath of forest which settled itself on a gentle slope. As the slopes flattened out, the spread of white roofed houses untidily formed themselves into a busy metropolis, which dripped down the mountainside to the lake and flatlands many miles below. The city sat like a vast apron on the south face of Mount Or where the Sun always shone her favour. To the south of Mount Or lay a paradise of gentle rolling hills, trickling brooks, fertile farmland and the largest region, Pashanka. In addition to the River Lichen, Lake Lantaba fed two more rivers. The Pashanka River split the region from the plains on the east side and the Brook River spilt out of the lake to the west dividing the wild jungle from farmed land. Bounded by these rivers resided the bulk of the nation. The towns and villages of Pashanka were strewn around the land, laced together with tracks and roads, paths and horse trails, so that the view from the palace was that of a delicate winged moth.

King Bravindo, the ruler of Goaero, was mute. As a boy Bravindo was lively and boisterous with a choirboy's voice. He was popular and clever, a perfect heir for the throne. He and his younger brother Encoda maintained a friendly rivalry as children. They raced on foot through the warren of the palace and on their horses in the dark forest that cupped the northern flank of the grounds and around the many gardens inside the palace walls. The heir to the throne was only slightly bigger than his younger brother but his wit was sharp and he outdid him in most battles. Encoda fronted up to his brother every time and only ceased when all four limbs were bound or pinned down, or when his horse was outrun or when he simply could not find him. Encoda was left with a churning of love, despair, humiliation and admiration towards Bravindo.

When the heir's voice deepened, he all but vanished from Encoda's life as Bravindo began to learn the ways of leadership. He was schooled in kinghood, educated in etiquette, he took lessons in law, studies on his subjects, he was saturated with history, assaulted by protocol and drowned in bureaucracy. Encoda rarely glimpsed him and so was shocked one day when he stumbled upon his brother on the roof of the palace.

Encoda was lonely. He had taken to exploring the palace's lesser-known corners. The turrets that poked the clouds over Mount Or were purely for show and could be accessed through a small hatch, after a knee achingly long climb up narrow winding stairs into one corner of the roof. Here one could squeeze around the ten turrets which were pitched with pocked copper to catch the Sun's beams. On a clear day, one could see the whole of Goaero. Encoda had never encountered anyone else on the roof and so a jagged shaft of fear ran through him when he heard a gentle sobbing. He shuffled as quietly as he could toward the sound and slid his head around one of the towering central turrets. In the middle of the roof there was a small space, large enough to lie down in and there sat a man, crying into his hands. It took Encoda a few moments to realise that this man was his brother. No longer a boy, he had morphed into a broad-chested, angular prince. Encoda's heart raced; he was at once pleased to see him but disturbed by the raw emotion, he was uneasy at being discovered on the roof and discovering another there. He was unequipped with the right words and unprepared for this man, his brother, feeling like a stranger. He backed away and silently slipped down into the palace.

After that day, Encoda saw Bravindo more often. Bravindo took to sitting in the palace orchard. Encoda would sit nearby, not knowing what to say and Bravindo appeared not to notice, or, as Encoda presumed, take no notice. It was on one such occasion, the day of Bravindo's seventeenth birthday that a bird flew down from an apple tree and launched itself at the heir's throat, piercing his Adam's apple, before a horrified Encoda threw a stone at the bird and it flapped noiselessly away. Bravindo clutched his throat as blood oozed between his fingers. For many weeks he lay pale and bandaged, visited by every physician in the land, by crones and magicians. But Bravindo never spoke another word.

The kingdom had never been governed by a mute king. Their father, King Myral deliberated with his council for many long years. They argued, debated and twisted around decisions until the heart of Encoda – whose ear was to the door – also twisted and turned into a small knot. Finally, there were only two seasons before the coronation was due – in Bravindo's twenty-first year – and no decision could be made. King Myral opened the dilemma to his people and asked them who they wanted as king. Bravindo's charm and charisma had struck the citizens and they unanimously voted for him to be their ruler. But his voicelessness had led him into a monastic life – one of few avenues where he could excel – so Prince Encoda was left to vicariously rule the country. Encoda dutifully became his brother's right hand; the king's voice in fact, but his knot continued to twist and turn and feed and grow, waiting for its moment to unravel. Bravindo had never married and bore no heir and Encoda was still a prince and wore no crown.

And so it is many years later, where this story begins. Early one morning when Bravindo was sitting in the palace garden deep in meditation, Encoda was brooding over his brother nearby, as he had done for nearly fifteen years. Suddenly a dove appeared from nowhere and gently alighted on Bravindo's shoulder. Due to his catatonic state Bravindo did not notice the intrusion but Encoda, now alert, crept forward and offered his finger for the bird's perch. The dove hopped on and Encoda noticed a message attached to the bird's leg. He took it and the dove flew into the clouds. Encoda unravelled the parchment which revealed a verse:

A voice was stolen, by a little bird,

Since then not a whisper, a single word

Has framed the feelings that lie inside,

Of loss and love, of passion and pride.

The time has come to release the truth;

Find the one of golden youth

Who will be the key to set you free

And complete the circle of unity.

Encoda quickly left the peaceful garden. He had never imagined the king could regain his speech; an event that would push him from power and into the shadows further. His bitterness swelled. He needed to find this 'one of golden youth' and ensure he never set foot in front of the king; that way the king would never be fully restored to power. In a flash it was now clear to Encoda that he needed to become king and fulfil his ambitions once and for all.

He would need a loyal servant to find the key to setting Bravindo free, a soldier of determination and skill. He summoned his General. The General arrived and, swearing the man to secrecy, explained the mission. The General knew immediately who to send. Encoda finished the meeting with:

"Good, send him to me!"

And so entered Mallory of the Lion's Head Regiment, the General's best man, loyalty and bravery making up for his short stature. Encoda took one look at the steely determination in Mallory's intense stare and knew the job was as good as done.

"There is a youth on the run, he has stolen from the king and must be returned to the palace immediately. He is golden haired and has the key to returning the King's voice. Search the land and bring him directly to me. To me, you understand?"

Mallory nodded and was about to ask more about the thief when Encoda continued.

"You may take this to aid you on your search."

He lifted a lid on one of the throne's armrests and pulled out a bronze cuff which Mallory placed on his wrist.

"This compass will take you to what your heart most desires, the General assures me your heart belongs to your King and country. Need I say more?"

Mallory nodded again, tongue tied as the prince saw him out of the chambers.

As soon as he was alone, Encoda tore up the dove's message and flicked the pieces into the crackling fireplace.

Mallory left Prince Encoda with a thrill beating across his chest. Although the prince had been curt, he felt honoured to be chosen for such a task; to find the key to the King's voice. Despite Mallory's greatest efforts, his loyalty and steadfastness, he always seemed to slip by unnoticed. Here, finally, was his chance to prove himself.

The Fuschian Jungle lay many miles from the palace, beginning at the base of Mount Or and spreading out right to the edge of the land. It would take many days to descend and then skirt the massive Lake Lantaba that was fed by The Cascades. So the General told Mallory he was to collect a kytera from the store. The kytera was a flying machine made of wooden struts and silk wings which enabled soldiers to fly through the air after launching from a high cliff. For a while, the rider could control direction and speed on the wind currents before loosening the struts and floating, like a giant handkerchief, down to the world below.

First, Mallory went to collect his kit. He filled his bag; three changes of clothes, a hat, a knife, a bottle, coins, dried fruit and biscuits. His regiment was in the canteen and Mallory knew he had little time to spare. He lifted his sleeve and stared at the bronze cuff. The thick metal band sat comfortably on his arm with a hoop of curved edges to slip his wrist through. The oval face was flush with the bronze and seemed to be without edges as if it were part of the metal. It shimmered in pale rainbow coloured stripes like an oil slick catching the light. Prince Encoda had explained that what your heart most desired lay in the direction marked ◊ which was etched on north. As Mallory examined it, he saw other symbols around the face which came in and out of focus so that he could not quite work out what they were. He heard footsteps outside and hurriedly packed the last few items and disappeared out the back door of his dormitory.

Chapter 3

THE CRYPT OF MANOLA

The moment the dove had hopped onto Encoda's finger, he saw his chance had arrived. His mind had been working furiously since that moment and although he did not yet have a plan, the challenge thrilled him like a fox hunt. His mind was his steed chasing the fox – the crown – and although the fox was giving him a good run he knew he was likely to catch it at the end of the day; he just needed his wits about him.

As a boy he paid little attention in the lore of kinghood. His big brother Bravindo would be king. But he did know about one secret, very important and dreaded rite of passage every king had to undertake: The Crypt of Manola.

Encoda only knew that the Crypt was a room deep in the bowels of the palace and was rarely opened. Most were blissfully ignorant of its existence, while those who were not would shudder, a dark shadow flicker across their eyes when the place was mentioned. Every king had to enter before his coronation and although Encoda went cold at the thought of it, he knew he must and he hoped it would help him outsmart the fox. So, that afternoon, Prince Encoda told his courtiers he would ride alone into the city. So as not to arouse suspicion, he hinted that a fair maiden was awaiting him. He set off and after cantering for about five miles, he doubled back and took the old road out of town which led to a deserted track curling around the palace walls. Here he stopped at the northernmost point next to an old, low, oak door in the palace wall.

Encoda pulled his horse up to the door. Once upon a time the king's soldiers would patrol this area, but now that peace was so entrenched, the king had kept just one retainer at the Back Door. This old man had been blind for over thirty years and although the door was double locked, old King Myral urged King Bravindo to keep him on in order that he could feed his family of thirteen offspring.

The Prince had taken the keys from The Lockery – his only obstacle now was the blind old man. As he trotted up to the weathered oak door he saw the gnarled figure slumped in the doorway. On hearing the horse's footsteps he struggled up and pulled his hood over his head. Too respectful and afraid to look directly at the Prince, he kept his head lowered. He bowed as Prince Encoda dismounted and remained hunched over. Encoda pulled a large velvet purse from his saddlebag and jingled it provocatively.

"No man came by here this day!" he stated bluntly and tossed the bag at the old man. He swiftly strode past and pulled a heavy key ring from his breast pocket. The metal clank was satisfying as the door swung open to a squat dark corridor.

Once the door croaked shut the old man threw back his hood. But it was not the rheumy ancient eyes of a decrepit old man that stared in wonder at the purse, but those of a brown eyed, smooth skinned, raven-haired young woman.

Chapter 4

KAFIA

It had been a source of great pride and considerable income for Donny Skinner to guard the Back Door of the palace. He knew it was a job for life and while all his old compatriots from the army lived on a steady but unworthy pension, Donny was still able to work, sitting by a door and managing to feed and school not only thirteen children but half a dozen grandchildren too.

Donny Skinner had been in old King Myral's personal division. These special soldiers were known as the cream of the crop, handpicked by his majesty himself to accompany him on royal missions. No real battles had ever been fought. They mainly took part in minor skirmishes with highway robbers. Although Donny was a fine and loyal soldier, he had earned no distinction from his fellows until Brookbank Battle Day.

Brookbank Battle Day is a holiday, a day of celebration, the second greatest day of the year. This day signifies the last day of the Forty Years War. Legend has it the final standoff happened on the banks of the Brook River. The enemy stood on one side, the army of our land on the other. The king had hatched a plan. Early that morning he sent a man to pour a magic potion in the river three miles upstream. The previous night in a rousing and historic speech, he forbade his men to drink from the river with the promise of cascades of wine to follow their victory. But the unsuspecting enemy drank from the river in readiness for battle, filling urns and watering horses. Within minutes the entire army were frozen to the spot, the numbing magic potion reducing them to statues. Every man was slain.

So custom forbids any person to bathe in the river any day of the year except Brookbank Battle Day. On this day every man, woman and child flock to the river and throw themselves into the pristine flow, followed by feasting and celebrating until dawn. The king, of course, always erects his own marquee at the most beautiful part of the river in lush pasture, cradled in a sheltered curve. A sumptuous feast is prepared and carried downstream from the palace on canal boats. One particular year, King Myral was in extra high spirits, having recently welcomed his son, Prince Bravindo, into the world. He was gustily tucking into roast goat when suddenly a rib bone became lodged in his throat. Donny was idly loitering at the entrance to the tent wondering whether he should pursue the Queen's handmaiden or not when he noticed King Myral quiver and turn puce. Donny saw terror grip the king's face and without thinking he ran over to the head table leapt over it like an athlete and gave Myral a short and very sharp thwack between his shoulder blades. The tiny bone flew out of the king's mouth unseen by the guards who promptly apprehended Donny and treated him to a night in gaol. By morning the story had been straightened out and Donny was released to the king's chambers. Now the king would not be a king if he were not proud and strong. If any of his citizens heard of his near-death experience from the sharp end of a goat's rib his reputation would be in shreds. So he sincerely thanked Donny, sadly handed him a small silver phial, a large sack of gold coins and a new set of orders. The king commanded Donny to leave his division and report to the guard at the Back Door. He was to drink the phial of potion that would slowly produce a film over his now sparkling eyes and cause his tongue to become inert and lifeless. Being a bright young man Donny knew he was silenced for life, and accepting his bittersweet destiny he stationed himself faithfully at the door. The years ticked by and Donny turned up to the Back Door loyally. His coffers were dutifully filled every Moon day, until, one day Donny did not return home.

Donny's wife sent his third youngest daughter, Kafia-Lily, to bring him home. But she found him cold and lifeless, slumped by the old Back Door. She managed to pull his frail frame over her shoulders and shuffle home as best she could.

Henny Skinner, Donny's wife, was a canny woman. She had grown fat and lazy now her childbearing years were mercifully over. All her children but Kafia were married or courting. Her family was swelling and she had grown used to her little indulgences afforded by Donny's handsome pay. To give herself time to think she sent Kafia to take her father's place, just for a few days; no one ever passed the Back Door any more. But in the end, the days turned into weeks and the weeks turned into seasons. Kafia had now roasted through Sun season and shivered through Sorry season twice. They had quietly buried the old man with only close family as witness and paid the priest generously for his silence. Kafia, loyal to her mother, dutifully went to the Back Door every day.

In all that time she had never seen a soul and so the appearance of the prince scared her so much she shook under the hefty cloak her father had worn for so long.

Chapter 5

KAFIA TO THE RESCUE

The Prince had not been in this part of the palace. The brothers were never allowed here alone, forbidden to explore outside the palace walls. Once, Encoda, being a curious and mischievous young child had slipped out and peered through the keyhole by the light of the moon but he could see nothing except a velvety blackness. So Encoda did not know that immediately over the threshold, steep steps dropped into darkness. In his hurry to close the door on the old man, he fell like a stone in a well. He cried out as his cheek scraped along the flinty wall, his knee twisted and popped, his chest pounded in fright and agony. He pulled a torch from his belt and lit it. Gingerly he hopped down and round, round and down, deep down until at last he reached another door. The cellar air was dry; the dust flew away from his hopping boot and caught in his throat. He was in pain and he laid his head against the smooth wood but jumped back in surprise; the door felt warm and alive, yielding. He hauled the key out of his pocket, it sat in his entire palm and the weight seemed heavier than it looked. He positioned it into the lock but without moving a muscle the key was suddenly sucked into the keyhole and turned on its own accord. Encoda flinched in surprise but what sent shivers down his spine were the words "*I greet you*", or was it "*I eat you*", which emanated in a sinister whisper from the door.

Encoda was still steadying himself from the fall. Adrenaline armed his body and his mind, now taut with foreboding. The apparently living, whispering door did nothing to ease his pounding heart. But, here he was and he had to find out what was within. He thought about his brother, passively ruling while he, Encoda, did all the hard work. He recalled the adoring public who would cheer and chant "King Bravindo!" with tears in their eyes whilst Encoda was ignored, unseen in the shadow of his brother. He remembered the day his father had not trusted him to be his protégé, to be a leader, and he thought of the dove that had so freely hopped onto his finger and divulged its secret.

Unwilling to touch the door with his hand and unable to use his injured leg, he shouldered his way into the room, one hand firmly resting on his sword. The room was spherical, the air thick and suffocating. He lit the six lamps on each side of the door which hung on ball joints, as if on a ship. As he walked from lamp to lamp he felt a sense of vertigo in the pit of his stomach and each step made him lightheaded. With difficulty he advanced back toward the door and it suddenly creaked and heaved shut. The noise induced another shot of adrenalin which curdled his churning stomach. He slid down the stone wall and tried to curb the nausea which banged in his temples. As he massaged his head, he looked at two round holes in the wall opposite. If they were shelves, they were very deep because he could not see the wall behind, just darkness, and the irregular curve would make it impossible to hold books. He found it hard to look away but pulled his gaze up to the domed ceiling, the smooth rock was etched with an irregular kind of patchwork, his eyes were drawn again to the holes and he noticed a kind of upside down heart shape between them. It then dawned on him that he was in a room that appeared to be the inside of a skull and he was looking at the eye and nose sockets. He stood again making the room tip, the pain in his knee flared up his leg causing a torrent of ugly words to fly from his mouth. The black holes seemed to be watching him as much as he was watching them, and it was now clear that he was standing inside a head that was nodding up and down. He realised he was feeling a kind of motion sickness – that odd feeling of stepping onto a jetty which appears to be solid but is in fact floating around on the water.

Time was passing and Encoda reminded himself of his mission. He was expecting something grander from this feared place, it was sinister indeed but not really too challenging, and there was nothing in it. The oval alcoves were the only place to look and he felt magnetically pulled towards them. As he moved closer he could make out a faint yellow light in each hole. He squinted at the left side. What was it...a candle, an eye, a star? Where was it coming from? The blackness inside the window looked gloopy; he felt it drawing him in. In the yellow light he began to make out a figure, it was facing him, looking at him and he stared back, stepping closer. He could feel the blackness sucking him in; a hungry vacuum. He glanced at the right hole and the light flashed at him, searing a gash of white light into his eye. Alarmed he looked away but his eyes were drawn back to the other side. Then the figure became clear; it was himself, standing, here in this room and he let out a laugh of relief at the reflection. But as he moved closer again he saw his reflection step backwards, swear and grimace in pain, then move around the room un-lighting the lamps. He saw the door open and he went out and he saw himself fall up the stairs, he saw himself throw the bag at the old man and riding his horse back to the palace, he saw his life up to that moment moving quicker now, uncurling before him, flicking like the end of a rope. As he watched, the socket drew him closer until he reached out his hand toward the black and it grabbed hold of him. He felt himself falling into a vortex; his life flashing past him, his emotions reeling into him, his pains passing through him. He was now in the black up to his shoulder and he could see his parents crying over him in his crib. His feet slid across the floor and the side of his chest thumped against the wall. Both arms were now through, he craned his head backward still seeing the panorama of his life, his mother's, father's, his brother's, he saw...

Suddenly something solid clutched him around his waist and yanked him away. He tumbled backward onto a soft body. The room rocked heavily and the lamps swung leaving trails of candlelight in their wake, hissing loudly. Encoda's reeling mind stopped, his left arm was throbbing with purple and swollen fingertips, his right arm ached. He found himself gazing into the eyes of a soft velvet angel whose large pupils stared into his with fear and admiration. After the bubble of shock popped, Kafia winced and wiggled her leg free from the Prince. He mumbled an apology. They stood up, the floor slanted like a seesaw and grabbing each other headed towards the door. Encoda growled at his twisted knee, Kafia supported him through the threshold.

"Wait!" Encoda cried out.

Kafia hesitated; she was keen to leave the creepy vault.

"I have to lock it."

Encoda fumbled for the key with his good hand and slid it into the lock.

"What you see, I saw before, before I saw you watch, you see. What you see, I saw before, before I saw you watch, you see."

The voice slithered like a ghost, repeating it over and over as it spat the key back into Encoda's hand. The door seemed to breathe and Kafia dragged Encoda up the steep stairwell to the Back Door, the words chasing them until they stumbled out and slammed the door. They both fell to the ground gulping in the sweet dusk air.

Encoda had looked into the left eye socket and had viewed his past. Every event in his life had been replayed to him. He had seen it all until Kafia had grabbed him, but it was just dawning on him now that in the peripheries of his vision all events that had been connected to him had played back too, leaving trails of rippling storylines, going on forever, sucking him along in the slipstream. He was the centre of a thousand stories of his existence and they were forcing him into their core. And although the images remained firmly entrenched in his memory, he could not make head or tail of it. He only saw what happened, and if this was the truth or not, his truth would be different from another's.

Chapter 6

MALLORY AND THE BEAR

James Ardent Mallory was born under an oak tree, which was why his childhood nickname was Acorn. It was only when he ran away to join the army did he become known as Mallory. James and Ardent never had a look in. He was born under an oak tree while his mother was looking for truffles. He was always glad that hadn't been his nickname. In fact, according to his father, truffles were far more valuable than his son was and he would never have deserved that name. His opinion was harsh but truffles had kept his family alive for twenty-five generations. They were one of only five truffle families in the land and truffles, known as "Crone's Gold", was a sought after and expensive commodity.

Not anyone could become a Truffle Delver. You had to have the nose. Both of Mallory's parents were from truffle families. It had been an auspicious union; much haggling had taken place, many meetings had been hosted and finally the young couple were married in much splendour and merry making. Soon they bore their first child. His mother had had a vision when Mallory was growing inside her. It was a dream of greatness and acclaim. He was riding into the palace on a white horse with a golden tail and mane. They had pinned great hopes on their son, especially as it became apparent that he was to be their only child. But when Mallory reached the age of sixteen and could still not smell the difference between an old boot and a fresh truffle his father threw him out. Since there was no circus in town, Mallory ran away and joined the army, to serve his country and king.

Mallory had never forgiven his dud nose and so had honed all his other senses. He trained his ears by counting all the sounds he could hear; he could hear twenty different noises at any given time, even in the silent dead of night. His vision was so acute he could tell you the gender of an eagle soaring through the sky. His touch was so sensitive he could tell you blindfolded which flower he held in his palm. He worked so hard at refining these qualities that he gave birth to an extra-sense; the sense of premonition. It wasn't that Mallory could see into the future. No, he would have been a rich man if that were the case. His sense beheld that which would happen in the next few moments. This keen sense made him an invaluable soldier. He knew if an enemy was about to attack, he could hear danger before it arrived and sensed a trap before it caught them. More importantly, he knew if cabbage soup was for dinner – which meant his fellows could find food elsewhere, rather than eat the gut-wrenching gruel. Since his country had been at peace for hundreds of years Mallory's talents were reserved for drills. And since there had been no war, the soldiers were able to choose pumpkin stew and bread rolls from the local canteen, and Mallory remained a lowly officer in an out-of-work army. But now in the cave Mallory was on a real mission and he was able to negotiate the rocks and stalactites, as he had done the roots and branches in the jungle using his extra-sense. He kept his boots dry from the pools of water and the soft glow from the moonworms gave enough light for his keen eyes to see into the dark. The bee's song echoed loudly against the walls and even as it paused for a drink, Mallory could hear its bristling fur.

But then Mallory froze; a flash crossed his mind, the image of a beast so great and he could see it filled the tunnel ahead of him. He knew the beast was territorial, protective of something, and would guard it with her life. He heard the gentle thump of feet and the 'clit-clat' of sharp claws on rock but it was her nose which arrived first, glistening, twitching and seeking out the threat. Her ears were erect, turning this way and that. At last, a pair of yellow eyes rested on Mallory. He swallowed loudly. It was only now the possibility of danger loomed in his mind. Up until now he had been so pleased with himself, so filled with zealous pride that he had not considered he might have to face fear, that he might have to fight, or struggle, that he might even – he swallowed again – die.

The bear roared and rose up on her hind legs and as she came crashing down she bared her teeth. He flung himself against the cave wall, her bulk filled the cave and she seemed to suck out all the air, leaving Mallory's chest heaving. His heart banged in his ears – get out, get out, get out. What was he doing here? He felt so small and weak, how could he overcome this beast? The task ahead was huge. She growled in agreement and lumbered toward him striking with sharp claws. Mallory clutched his grazed stomach, curled himself into a ball and rolled himself back toward the open mouth of the cave. His heart dropped into his belly as if it were trying to get as far away as possible. But his cowardly retreat sickened him. He glanced at the compass, the hands pointed resolutely into the cave. He could scarcely believe his heart's desire was facing this, this terror. But he knew then, in a moment of stillness that his determination to succeed would overcome. The beast roared again and he quivered expecting another swipe from her huge paw. He fumbled for his knife and waved it at the bear but she lunged forward and knocked it from his hand as if it were a blade of grass. He cried out and was about to crawl the last few feet when the drumming in his ears was overcome by the bee's drone. The song grew louder and louder and he felt the presence of the bear retreat. He pulled his head from under his arms. The bee was flying around the bear's head as she uselessly tried batting away the small insect. The buzzing reached a crescendo and Mallory admired the creature's spirit. Again he became aware of his cowardice bracing against his desire and, drawing strength, raised himself once more and defied it. His mind reeled as he tried to find a way to defeat her. He then became aware of the Sun Sand pulsating at his breast and realised this, and his own valour, were his only defence. He stood and squared up to the bear, opened his jacket and drew out the bottle. As he popped the cork, a mighty flame swept through the cave and the bear collapsed back and rolled into a ball. He re-stoppered the bottle and could see her clearly; a now pure white bear cowering on the floor. What he could not see were his own snow-white eyebrows matching the streak of hair from the first uncorking.

More cautious now he picked up his knife and edged past the comatose bear and deeper into the tunnel. Soon Mallory's feet began to stick to the ground. His fingers felt the walls become tacky. The thick, sweet air made his head swim. He felt as if he was moving through treacle. Muddied and muddled, the buzz of the bee was all that cut through the atmosphere, and he followed it. But soon he heard a harmonious humming, like the 'Om' of a thousand chanting monks. The noise vibrated through every bone in his body until he knew not if he could move them. At last, he came to the end of the tunnel. The hexagonal shaped cell oozed an amber liquid which dropped slowly into a pool. Each drop caused a ripple which lethargically moved toward the edge. The bee circled Mallory's head and came to rest on the wall.

Mallory vibrated with the h'om of bees and he struggled to breathe the soupy air. He knew it was going to get dark soon and he needed to move on but the bee had led him here. Furthermore, Mallory's stomach was not only smarting from the bear's claws but grumbling too. He looked down into the honey pool and a flicker caught his eye. A dart of blue, here, then there, and as his sharp eye focused he made out the shape of little fishes darting in the honey.

Honeyfish are no ordinary fish. Despite the fact that honey is the most viscous substance known, these fish can race through it like a marble down a hill. The fish feast on pollen powder that passes through the honefication process untransformed. Pollen, a miraculous substance that aids in the creation of new life, has a close relationship with time. In fact, one could say a grain of pollen is a grain of time. In addition to the honey (which holds a surplus of time) the fish manifest a time reaction. This allows them to move through honey as if it were the salty ocean.

Mallory knew then that his supper was swimming before him and he suspected that on digestion he might find himself a part of that reaction and, possibly, somewhere else entirely. But, he wondered how he was to catch these furiously fast slivers of blue. He knew from childhood that a finger in a honey pot was a no-no. He could almost feel his father's spoon rapping his knuckles. He looked around for inspiration; net, fishing rod, hollow straw?

"OW!" he yelled into the dense unrelenting atmosphere, which made the noise echo in reverse around the cave making him feel queasy. For a brief moment, the h'om ceased. The bee that had led him here had stung him right on the end of his nose.

"What did you do that for?" he muffled from under his clutching hand. His nose throbbed and expanded as he waved his knife to swat the nasty insect. But the bee was already perched on the end of it and no matter how hard Mallory swiped it the bee clung on, casually wiggling its bottom. Mallory was losing his patience, when his extra-sense alerted him to a blade full of honeyfish. He stopped flailing his knife which the bee had now coated with pollen, and wafted it over the honey. All of a sudden a crowd of blue flecks leapt from the water on to the blade. Once out of the pool the little fished moved as if in honey air and squirmed slowly to a halt. The bee buzzed near Mallory's mouth and seemed to be indicating that he should eat. Mallory picked a fish from the end of the knife. It was about the size of his little finger and a few flickers of bright blue still radiated from its body. Mallory ate savouring the taste, a sweet sour explosion on his tongue, with a hint of fizz. The flesh was soft, but not mushy and he was surprised at the lack of crunch; no bones or scales to reduce the experience. He ate the half dozen on the knife and went back for more. The bee had deposited more pollen bait and produced a second bumper catch. Twice more Mallory dipped and he finally felt full, but he was tempted to experience that subtly complete taste sensation one more time. He quickly waved the knife over the honey pool and three more fat fish obligingly leapt on. He savoured the last three, thanked the bee and felt his way back to the cave mouth, careful to avoid treading on the sleeping white bear.

It was dusk as he came out and could just make out a small alcove in the cave wall. He tucked his knife in his waistband, curled up with his head on his bag and went to sleep.

Chapter 7

KAFIA AND ENCODA

"Who are you?" Encoda spluttered, not sure which word of the question to emphasize, making his voice high pitched.

"Kafia. Kafia-Lily Skinner…er, your Majesty."

"I mean, what are you? Why did you…how did you…?"

Encoda's cool demeanour was well and truly broken. Kafia, expecting a thank you, or at least a chivalrous kiss on the hand, was taken aback.

"I was guarding the door, your Majesty."

"You?" he looked around. "Where did the old man go?"

"It was me…I was the old man, your Majesty."

"Enough of this 'Majesty' business! It is supposed to be an old man guarding the door."

"Yes, er, Sir, my father Donny, Donny Skinner, your…"

Encoda was losing his patience and wondered about the relevance of his questioning.

"Enough! Where is Skinner now?"

"In Morpick Cemetery, your...er...honour."

"Oh good heavens I'm not a judge. Morpick Cemetery? Ah, moonlighting is he, well I'm sure the General will not look kindly on that travesty," he threatened.

"He's buried there, sir. So I have taken over."

Kafia smiled. She knew about secrets. When Henny first conceived her, she kept it a secret for three weeks until Donny returned from his tour of duty and the 'official' conception took place. After Kafia was born Donny and Henny kept her a secret for seven days until Brookbank Battle Day. A child born on this day is considered highly auspicious and showered with gifts. More importantly to the Skinners they would receive a large bag of money from the king. As Kafia grew up in a bustling household of schemers and con artists, she became a patient and careful listener. She knew a spilt word could crumble the perfect plan and produce painful recriminations. Soon her siblings would trust her with all their convoluted schemes, deeds and confessions. And before she knew it, she became a Secret Keeper.

Every town and village had two or three Secret Keepers. There had to be more than one to maintain anonymity. Secret Keepers are quiet creatures who tread softly and can weave through places unnoticed. They listen actively without comment or judgement and a mere blink of the eye confirms the secret has been absorbed. Few question the riddles they hear or try to understand them. They just keep them in a box close to their heart.

So Kafia knew Encoda carried a secret; she saw the look, felt it skulking away inside him, poking and prodding, looking for a crack to break out. Kafia knew secrets, she knew they only had one ambition – to be released. They were like little spirals of energy that burned hotter and brighter the longer they were contained. She knew she was a balm, a small release that made them easier to live with. She also knew when a secret was out – she felt a little tug in her chest, followed by a wave of nausea and half a day of hiccups, but it didn't happen very often. Apart from that, secrets didn't bother her. She never gave them a second thought. But she felt a strange stirring as she was looking at the prince.

I wonder, she thought, *I wonder...*

And suddenly it felt like a wind blowing around her heart, she felt little hot pins pricking her insides and she really felt like hiccupping back to front, from the outside in.

"Did you know Josephine Ample kissed Jeremy Fortescue?" she clapped her hands over her mouth. "Sorry!"

Having had no advice on Secret Keeping, and having never met another one, Kafia did not know that the desire to know another's secret had a strange effect on the Keeper. This desire acted as a corrosive, allowing all the other secrets to slowly seep out.

Encoda looked bewildered. His mission was turning into a disaster and now he had a mad woman who had possibly saved his life jabbering next to him.

"What were you doing down there anyway? I could have you arrested for trespassing."

Kafia knew that he would not; she could talk and she suspected he was virtually trespassing himself.

"I heard a cry and a crash, I came to help you. What were you looking at? You were falling in, so I grabbed you."

"Hmm," Encoda grunted, it was a good answer.

"How about another bag of money?" he gestured at the one she had tucked in her waist band. "Twice the size of the first," he added.

Kafia was a product, if not biologically, of Henny and Donny Skinner and she had learnt well the ways of the wily. She also knew Encoda had a secret and for the first time in her life, she was curious to hear it. Apart from his lack of gratitude and powers of bribery, in spite of his lack of manners and, in part due to his brooding good looks and position of power, she was in awe of him.

"I can help you."

Encoda allowed a laugh of derision to hit her.

"Pah! And why, in the Sun's name, do you suppose I need your help?"

"With your secret..." she ventured in a whisper, "And besides, something just tried to eat you. I helped you then."

"And I thank you for that young woman, but I need no help from a common fool."

Furious, Kafia looked into his eyes.

"Fine, I'll take your money, common I may be, your Majesty; a fool I am NOT."

She scrambled up and ran down the narrow path with a lump in her throat, not caring that she scraped her shoulder on the flinty palace wall. Encoda remained slouched, preparing to return to the castle. He tried to move but his knee sent jolts of pain through him and his bruised hand and forearm refused to obey his commands. His horse had wandered off and the light was fading fast.

He needed help.

"Arghh!" he swore in a way a prince shouldn't. "WAIT!"

Silence.

"Young woman, come back!"

Kafia stopped, she was almost too far to hear him.

"Young woman, come back!"

She waited.

"Can you hear me? Please wait a moment...!" He was more polite this time.

She pictured him abandoned at the wall. The lump dissolved into her stomach which twitched and tingled. She smiled. She turned. She waited. She walked back, slowly, although each heartbeat urged her to run.

"I need your help."

"Hmmm, I thought so."

"Fetch my horse."

"Amity Mistletoe has a chest of gold buried in her garden." Kafia clapped her hands on her mouth again, aghast.

"What is your name wench?"

"Kafia."

"Ah yes, Kafia," he was calmer now.

"Please will you fetch my horse and help me up?"

He spoke as if she were a small child. Kafia sighed and clicked gently into the bushes. She spied a white horse's flank and heard his bridle clanking, she cooed towards the steed and led him back to the prince. She hooked her wiry arm under his good one and hoicked him up. He winced and with one good arm and one good leg managed to straighten himself up into the saddle, sweating with pain. Encoda had had time to form a plan and he now spoke to her in low decisive tones.

Kafia was to become his personal maid. The next morning she was to visit the palace for an official interview and would be hired immediately. Encoda's injuries were sustained by a fall from a bucking horse. This would leave the problem of the Back Door being unmanned. Encoda would sign the papers discharging Donny and a new guard would be appointed. Kafia would concoct a story to appease Henny, who would ultimately be relieved of her fraudulent income, and handsomely replaced by the legitimate one of Kafia's new engagement at the palace.

At daybreak the following morning a fresh, dewy faced Kafia announced herself at the Palace Workers Office. She was dressed in her best dress with her dark, washed hair tied in a ribboned ponytail.

Prince Encoda sat on his throne-like chair and gruffly ordered her in. As he looked up he saw her standing neatly just in front of the door and he felt something that was new to him and, for a moment, knew not what to say.

Chapter 8

THE LOST MAN IN BLULUPIA

Mallory slept and the little blue honeyfish worked their way through his stomach. Here they were drained of meat, sucked of goodness; the tough bits were crunched and squeezed until the essence of honeyfish nourished and healed his adventurous body. Then all that was left was a bundle of incandescent blue time which fidgeted and flitted and curled and swirled and pushed and poked until it worked its way into Mallory's chest. As Mallory breathed in deeply, snoring in his slumber the electric blue time caught the stream of real time and...

Mallory was surrounded. All he could see were spears tipped with green fire as three flaming torches wafted in his face. He blinked in the light and raised his hand. All at once voices screamed in fear, bodies receded and he was left alone in the chilly darkness. He realised his greed had propelled him further into time than necessary and now he was alone in the night with a bunch of marauding spear-holders screeching at him. He felt the sweat dry cold on his face and knew he was no longer in the humid jungle, and although Surge Season was unravelling its days into the balmy Sun Season, here, in the Shadowlands, it was always dank and cold.

The dark forest which covered the north rump of Mount Or, where the light of the Sun rarely reached beyond the peak gave a glimpse of how the Shadowlands would look. At the base of the mount the River Lichen curled back around from Lake Lantaba where it painfully forced its way through granite rocks and the dark forests. Here the cold whistled in from the Ice Mountains to the west while Mount Or obscured the Sun from offering much warmth. Few were game enough to live in this inhospitable northern land except a people who adapted to its conditions and were scattered among the wooded regions.

The marauding spear-holders were from the village of Blulupia. Their village sat near the River Lichen, a little way downstream from where the water filters through a mile of granite. This granite had imparted a magical element to the water which is only manifest if drank directly from the river. Many an adventurer and opportunist had ventured into the Shadowlands to try to bottle the famed and enchanted water for the masses. For when one drank directly from the river a sprite appeared who was only visible and audible to that person. These beings were very wise and could be of great benefit to the individual, *if* they ask the right questions. Not one of the adventurers had ever made it back to the other side of the mountain alive – or at least unscathed.

The granite gave this gift at a cost. When the water flowed into the land to quench the plants, they grew thin, tall and almost black. Only the inhabitants were able to digest the crops grown here and even then it turned their skin a blue grey colour with their lips and fingernails a deeper shade of blue. Hence Shadowlands remained without colour except blue and black and their various shades. The water also enchanted the plants so that each bore its own small being. The people had come to believe that homage must always be paid to the sprites and so they constantly mumbled prayers and gratitude. Over eons of reciting blessings the people eventually evolved an extra-sensory form of communication with each other so as to keep up the flow of prayer. Hence, in this strange pocket of Goaero, in a cold dark land of few resources, whispering blessings and blue skin, visitors were rare.

But the Blulupians' life was cast by the further shadow of a myth:

THE MYTH OF THE BLULUPIANS

The tear of a princess began it all. It dropped from her bedchamber window in the palace and fell for ten miles until it landed on a granite rock. The tear was full of loss and yearning and hatred and so it burned a hole in the rock. One day the rock came loose. It fell down the mountainside for ten more miles and landed in a river. The rock was so infused with loss and yearning and hatred that it stubbornly dammed the flow – all except one little trickle of water which leaked through the tear's hole. Drip by drip the water leaked out for a hundred years making a pool of loss and yearning and hatred. The river never again flowed but the pool had become deep and the bottom began to stir and churn until it formed a whirlpool. No animal or insect dared approach the water, the water that smelt of loss and yearning and hatred. One day a traveller passed by the pool. He was so hot and thirsty he jumped in the crystal, cool water. The vortex was hungry and sucked the man down to another place. Myth has it that when the 'Lost Man' returns the poisonous waters of loss and yearning and hatred will flow again and the peace of the land will be lost forever. However, if the Lost Man is destroyed at sundown without having uttered a word the curse will lift and light will come into the land.

Mallory had guessed he was in the Shadowlands by the green flames (the enchanted water of the River Lichen caused all matter to burn with an emerald fire). But he had not heard about the myth. He also did not know that he had a snow-white streak from his forehead to his nape; white eyebrows and a swollen nose from the bee sting. Along with the fact that he had appeared from nowhere next to a small new spring of amber water, led the Blulupians to believe the Lost Man had returned and the end was nigh.

Mallory looked at the compass but it was dark and could not read the hands. Until this point Mallory had not had time to contemplate his quest. He realised then he knew very little about the king and his brother and wondered why Encoda had sent him and not gone himself. He remembered the youth of golden hair and could not imagine finding him here in this blue, cold land. He wondered if his friends in the army had noticed he was gone, he wondered as he did every night in bed what his mother was doing. He went on to ponder how long he would be out here in these strange lands and this was followed by a pang of homesickness for his bunk in the barracks, his companions and the familiar smell of Mrs Buttle's tortoise soup.

James Ardent Mallory was lonely. He had wrapped this cold bubble of loneliness in his heart by joining the army but now the bubble was revealed and it engulfed *him*, he now sat firmly inside looking out. He was still staring at the compass when he snapped himself back to his problem. He switched wrist and immediately the face glowed and the hands bristled and jumped together. The dark disorientated him, he was in danger but he knew there was only one place to go – the place his heart desired. He turned around and followed the direction of the hands. His foot, however, did not land on solid ground. All of a sudden he heard the brittle cracking of branches, and leaves whipped his face. He landed heavily on soft earth, his winded breath whisked around his chest before he breathed in again and he wondered why he had not been aware of his impending fall. Like anyone so deep in thought as to not smell a pot of milk boiling over, Mallory was feeling so sorry for himself he just hadn't sensed it.

Once again he checked all his moving parts for injury and once again he seemed to be intact. He had, it seemed, fallen down a deep narrow hole. The walls of his trap were interlaced with fine blue roots, which stood out in the creeping dawn light. Once his thumping heart began to calm down, Mallory's sharp ears began to hear faint whispers. He noticed that the blue roots shimmered and as the Sun's rays broke open a new day he saw that small ethereal beings sat cradled in many of the roots.

"Strange looking specimen!" he heard.

"Yesssss, striped and short," lisped another.

"Simply spectacular!" one sang.

The hushed conversation carried on in this way.

"Hello!" Mallory butted in, "I can hear you," he added.

The elementals silenced themselves.

"He can hear us," stated one.

"Yes, he certainly seems to," seconded another.

"Where am I?" Mallory asked.

"In the Shadowlands."

"And who are you?" he asked

"We are the Whispering Wisps," one answered.

"Roots and Bulbs," another added.

"Why am I here?" asked Mallory

"We could ask you the same."

"My quest to find the key to the king's voice has bought me here!" It sounded rather pompous out loud.

A collective "Ahhh" was produced by the Wisps followed by a clamouring of chatter. Suddenly one of the Wisps broke away and hovered over Mallory's shoulder. He concisely relayed the myth of the Lost Man in his ear and Mallory now understood that the Blulupians had mistaken him for the returning Lost Man. He was trapped and in danger of being killed by sundown that day. The Wisp promised to help Mallory and with that, the entire assembly dissolved into the roots.

Mallory sat in the gently dawning light in disbelief but before he could think of a plan he felt the tread of footsteps vibrate in the ground above him. The end of a rope flew over the lip of the hole and landed at his feet. An agile woman shinned down.

"May they be blessed in the radiance of Umala," she murmured and pointed at Mallory to climb up.

As he hauled himself up he heard her chant:

"I honour the ground as thy food, the air as thy bed."

As Mallory climbed out of the hole, a misty cold light settled on the Blulupians waiting for him. Each murmured blessings and praises. Mallory took in a chilly breath and opened his mouth to speak. Instantly a large man stepped forward and placed a spear upon Mallory's lips. It was clear the Wisps were correct; if the Lost Man utters one word then the prophecy is fulfilled, the river of loss and yearning and hatred will flow again and peace will no longer reign. The woman tied Mallory's hands tightly behind his back, wrapped a cloth around his mouth and roughly pushed him forward. Even though it was cold enough to make Mallory shiver, it was the Blulupians that sent a chill through his body. Their skin was a bruised bluish tinge and the cold damp morning air did not affect these thick-skinned people, mostly bare-chested and dressed in mere scraps of animal hide. By the time they reached the village the Sun was a quarter full and Mallory's feast of honeyfish was wearing off heralding the noise of fresh grumbles boiling in his belly.

Chapter 9

ABALIN

afia did not see Encoda again for seven days. She spent this time being trained by staff in the ways of palace life. It took all this time to negotiate the numerous passages, rooms, halls and staircases. Many looked the same and she was continuously lost...and then there were the servants' quarters. Her days were certainly much more interesting than those spent at the Back Door. Now at night she fell exhausted in her small bed and snored inelegantly until daybreak when she would rush past her slouched mother snuffling in her armchair by the dying embers of the fire. Kafia itched to see Encoda again; a small hollow in her belly ached and allowed her little food; by night she dreamt of vanishing into the black of the prince's eye. She put it all down to nerves.

After a week inside the palace walls Kafia was deemed apt and able. She was allotted a small room deep in the palace's lower floors. She shared it with Petunia and her cat Oswald. Petunia was of similar years to Kafia. She was unlike the flower of her name; more like a tomato; round and ruddy. Petunia was one of the baking maids and spent her days kneading and sliding bread in and out of the searing ovens. Kafia was comforted by Petunia's yeasty aroma and was content with a mostly silent friendship. Fittingly, Oswald was a small furry secret. Petunia had found the kitten outside the kitchen and had smuggled him to her room under the folds of her floury apron. By day he slept in a tight ball, at nightfall Petunia would open the door a crack and wedge it ajar. Oswald would wander the palace until he heard the whisperings of departing dreams and flee back to the warm hollow left by Petunia's head.

Kafia was accustomed to information finding her so she asked few questions about Prince Encoda and King Bravindo (whom she rarely glimpsed). She was rewarded with snippets of gossip but she was not so interested in the complicated inner culture of the palace world. Then one morning as she was pressing the king's underwear she was given word by a footman that she was required to attend to Prince Encoda. Her heart and stomach leapt and a cold shiver went through her, despite burning her thumb on the iron. She straightened her skirts and retied her hair, quietly berating herself for her nerves. All of a sudden ironing did not seem so bad.

She entered Encoda's large room and stood close to the calming oak door, observing the prince's head bowed at his desk. He stopped wielding his pen on her entrance and willed himself to look at her. He was not at all pleased with the uncomfortable sensations this girl induced in him and it had taken seven whole days for him to summon her for he was unwilling to suffer this ague again. However, now she was at his door and he slowly raised his head, and looking just slightly past her left shoulder, brusquely beckoned her over.

"How are your injuries, my Lord?" she ventured.

She had completely forgotten palace etiquette and had spoken first but Encoda was surprised to find himself glad of a question to answer.

"Fine, fine," he said shaking the offending arm at her before adding "Thank you."

Inadvertently he looked at her face, as one of royal blood does when thanking someone and once again, the lead weight dropped from his heart to his groin creating a horribly pleasurable pain in both.

Over the previous days Encoda had been deep in thought. He had already surmised that if the king's voice was restored there would never be a chance of becoming king himself. He knew the extent of Bravindo's popularity and speculated if he could somehow undermine it, he could gain some favour and offer himself as the rightful heir to the throne. Kafia was to launch this part of his plan. He patted the small leather footstool where he usually rested his feet. She sat and looked up into his face and for a moment he was lost in her deep brown eyes. He found himself again, cleared his throat and revealed his fabricated fable.

"Kafia, I must tell you a secret."

(She was used to this kind of opener, but her heart flipped a somersault, here was the one she had been waiting for.)

"*Alby Blanket has nits.*" Kafia gulped and looked nervously at the prince. "Sorry," she added.

He looked a little dismayed but continued.

"However, this is no longer to remain unknown."

(Her heart sank. He obviously did not realise she was a Secret Keeper.)

"*Martha Mistletoe cut off her cat's tail.*" She wondered if she still was a Secret Keeper. She shook her head and looked down. The prince sighed and continued once again.

"This secret has been locked in our family history. This is what I saw the day you helped me in the Vault."

He began the story:

In the ancient land my ancestors fell like leaves off the great Tree of Light. This tree was cultivated in the soil of Sun Sand and distilled Moon Shine. Every leaf was attached to a pearl-like berry and as each landed, a man or woman rose. They swallowed their pearl berry which remained lodged at the base of the spine and to this day each one of us can feel it there. The pearl berry holds the wisdom of all that is past.

(Kafia stifled a closed-lip yawn, she knew all this and many tales began with the retelling of the Ancient Myth of Goaero.)

You may also know, Kafia...

(She felt he had read her mind and blushed slightly, but managed to keep her mouth closed.)

...that occasionally a joined leaf fell from the Tree of Light with a <u>pair</u> of pearl berries and those who swallowed them became Quills. On reaching adulthood their great wings unfurled and as they ascended their wing tips carried up Sun Sand to offer to our creator the Sun Goddess. This made her happy and the Quills became Keepers of Sun Sand. The Quills ability to be airborne required them to live at altitude and so they populated the mountaintops. Mount Or is the oldest site of Quill civilisation until the king of Goaero claimed it as his throne. There was bloodshed for the territory, many battles were fought and on Goaeron's victory of the Mount it was decreed that no Quill would ever reign.

Over time the Goaerons populated the land and the Quills the skies and the mountains. The Quills lived gently, lightly on the earth and needed little since the Eternal Mists of Life nourished them. But Goaerons needed fire and food and made life unbearable for the Quills. Soon the Quills left.

But, let me tell you the secret that nobody yet knows...

Here in this very palace on Mount Or lived Prince Abalin. Abalin, meaning 'the king who held the Sun in his eyes', had pale blue eyes which held white pupils. This was a good omen and he was set to become a magnificent king. At that time the Quills still circled the peak of Mount Or and one day a young female called Quera dropped into the garden where the prince was studying. He ran to her and called his maid for help for she was injured. The palace physician healed her broken wing and she stayed a few days whilst she recovered. After that Quera often secretly visited Abalin and they became great friends and as they grew into young adults their friendship changed and they realised a tender love for one another.

After a few years the prince came of age and was crowned King Abalin. His duties kept him busy within the palace walls and he had no time for Quera. At first he missed her and yearned for his secret lover, but his fervour waned to frustration which morphed into guilt and slipped into shame. He banished her from his mind and grasped hold of his kingly duties with passion. Eventually, the old king and queen pronounced the marriage of their son to a fine woman called Mina. Abalin rarely thought of Quera again, except on his wedding night when he dreamt she was standing before him. Her stomach protruded into the shape of a large smooth egg. Her eyes shone at him and a large crack split at her belly button and ran up to her chin. Her serene expression turned to one of agony and betrayal. He awoke sweating and shaken.

Quera had in fact given birth to their son, a beautiful robust child with white pupils and pale blue irises; in every way his father and in no way his mother, for the child was born with no wing buds. This had never been seen in Quilldom and the elders knew immediately of her transgression. Her punishment was brutal; her furious father sliced off her wings and banished her and the boy to Goaero. Quera survived long enough to settle in a remote village, secure a small hut and find work as an oyster-shucker. She never healed from the pain of her exile, her wounds festered until she died. The boy, called Abalinque, grew into a young man. He lived in the village and fished for oysters whose rare pearls he frequently found. He kept his mother alive in his memory and although the pearls made him wealthy he cared not for them because he knew he carried the mark of a Quill; a protuberance of two little Pearls of Wisdom at the base of his spine, where a Goaeron only had one. He would always be different.

Kafia was entranced, mesmerised by Encoda's telling of this exotic tale.

King Abalin and his queen tried for many years to produce an heir to the throne. Queen Mina was strong and willing but Moon tides came and went and no gurgling babies graced the palace. The old king and queen became fretful and so called a meeting of the Council. It was agreed the old king would consult The Crypt of Manola. The group of wise ones trailed down to The Crypt in silence. No one had visited the grotto in many years and the rare occasion was given due ceremony. The old queen wept quietly for she knew this was a sacrificial visit. The lamps were lit and the group stood in a semi-circle around the old king facing them. He looked each one in the eye and embraced his son. He turned and no sooner had the old man glanced into the right socket when he was pulled toward it, his feet sliding across the floor before they lifted off it and he was gone – leaving one sentence reverberating around the room like a bad smell.

"The heir to the throne is a Quill..."

Queen Mina slapped her husband across the face and stormed out of The Crypt, his mother slapped his other cheek and the six Wise Ones held their eyes downcast, shaking their heads in grief and horror.

A grand funeral was held for the old king; a procession that wound down Mount Or through Carbinia and into outlying villages gathering sorrowful citizens. The bodiless coffin was set onto a canal boat on the Brook River to be returned to the Sands of the Sun. Abalin rode beside the canal boat downstream and did not return for many years for he was deep in shame. The only heir to the throne he had managed to produce was that of a secret forbidden tryst with a Quill.

Queen Mina had not been selected for a royal life for nothing. She was a strong, intelligent and able woman who took charge of the reign of Goaero. With the help of her Mother-In-Law she ruled the land with love and equality. Never had the Sun shone so brightly, never had She shed so many tears of joy, ensuring rich and plentiful crops for all Goaerons. It was an idyllic period although many wondered what had become of their king and who the heir to the throne would be.

The many adventures of King Abalin would fill a story man's bag. He was gone for ten years or more, even he lost count of how much time had passed. His aim was to find the heir to the throne and atone for his neglect towards Quera. Abalin journeyed around the planet and discovered places larger and stranger than Goaero. After much searching he came to know that no Quills lived beyond Goaero and he came home by sea. As he entered the magical horizontal waterfall of Anishka – the Vandret Falls – he arrived at the only sea village that is a safe portal to the ocean. Here the oyster catchers made their living. Abalin was tired, he was tired of journeying, tired of loneliness, tired of guilt and shame. He could not return home and he had not the spirit to continue. He moored his boat on the quay and dismissed his men. The next morning a fishing boat returned from its work and tied up alongside the king. The captain tossed a greeting to the king and at once Abalin recognised a pair of eyes which held the Sun, his own son. Abalinque knew too, with an unusual queasiness, that his father stood before him. The king wept for that day and seven more. He slept at the resting place of Quera and told her about his searching, his sacrifices and his insights. The quiet Abalinque sat close by and listened to every story, every whisper of sorrow, every lament and request for forgiveness. It was only after seven days of mourning that the king turned to his son.

'My son Abalinque, whose eyes burn like your father, your father who has done your mother a great wrong, your father who has never known you, your father who stands here before you, I now ask you for forgiveness. And if you can grant me

that, you are a greater man than I am. This greatness will stand you in good stead for you have a weighty task ahead; as my son, my only son, you are heir to the throne.'

Abalinque was uneasy. He had no desire to leave this village, his home. It was like a warm coat and although at first it did not belong to him, it fitted him well and he liked it. He did not want to take it off, leave it behind revealing his naked self. He was not ready for leadership, he was not ready for kinship with the man who ruined his sweet mother. But finally the villagers, his friends, who were his only family, started to look at him differently, started to treat him like an outsider and avoid him. He knew it was time to leave, to face the cold.

Abalin and Abalinque, father and son, king and prince set off across Goaero to Mount Or and the city of Carbinia.

"The evening is drawing in Kafia and I must cut this story short..."

In time the prince became King Abalinque. He married and bore a daughter who became queen and from then on a long succession of strong women ruled over Goaero. But do not forget that Abalinque was half Quill and bore the mark of the Double Pearl of Wisdom at the bottom of his spine. Abalinque's parentage was a closely guarded secret and those present in the Crypt that day had all passed away. The daughters never bore the mark of a Quill, for it was only the second born male who would carry the double pearl, leaving Abalinque the only monarch who ever bore evidence of Quill blood."

Kafia was wide eyed.

"Until now," Encoda continued.

Her eyes became even wider.

"Your King, our King Bravindo, has the mark of a Quill. Our dear mother first gave birth in her early confinement to a sleeping boy who never woke. He was the first-born son, Bravindo the second born, and heir to the throne. So, there you have it Kafia. He should not, cannot, remain king of our great nation. As my brother's loyal servant I cannot publicly reveal such scandal. It must come from elsewhere..."

He looked deeply at Kafia and she stared blankly at him.

"And it will be you who leaks the secret."

Kafia was dumbstruck. She swallowed drily; neither the outcome of the story nor her role in it going down nicely.

"Of course it is I, who does not carry the mark of a Quill, that will carry the burden most heavily, I who will be forced to take the crown and...reluctantly...become King of Goaero."

Kafia thought he sounded more rejoicing than reluctant but it would not be such a bad thing for Encoda to be king, not such a bad thing for her at all.

At last she was dismissed and returned to her quarters with more than a raised eyebrow among the staff; she had been with the prince all day.

But a more pressing problem consumed Kafia. She was a Secret Keeper and it was therefore impossible for her to divulge any secret and therefore unable to do as her master bid.

THE WISPS

The procession in which Mallory was held came to a halt in the centre of the village. The houses were built from black wood and formed rough circles fanning out which gave the place a charred look and an impenetrable feel. If that was not spooky enough, the Blulupians constantly murmured prayer-like mantras with rolling eyes. Every now and then one would look directly at another after which a smile or a nod would occur with no interruption to the stream of sighed blessings. They led Mallory to a rough black pole surrounded by sticks and branches and tied him there, he nervously noted the ashes under his feet. The Wisps had not mentioned how The Lost Man would be dealt with and he feared that this crowd would err toward the sacrificial. Then in unison the Blulupians quickly disappeared into doors and down alleyways leaving whispered prayers hanging in the air. It was suddenly very quiet.

Mallory tried unsuccessfully to loosen the rope around his wrist. He tried to wiggle the pole, it was solid. He tried to use his mind but that was stuck fast too, for fear had taken hold.

He knew the Blulupians intended to kill him, he was unable to utter a word and unable to move. He was unarmed, unaided and unprepared. He was cold and hungry. He would fail his king, his country, his friends. He was without family or lover, he had no children or pets. He was useless, hopeless, homeless and ridiculous. His heart was seized with terror but, still, he did not want to die. His only hope was the Wisps' promise but even they now seemed like a dream.

Mallory watched the day ebb and flow as the obscured Sun threw fuzzy shadows of him moving around the pole. He had not seen a Blulupian all day bar the one set to guard him. The man's incantations grew more fervent each time Mallory glanced at him. Mallory continued to twist his wrists to free himself but his shoulders throbbed from being pinned back and his fingers were numb. As the cold terror of dying turned to resigned numbness, just as the last few snippets of sunlight streaked the sky, the Blulupians reappeared.

The resolution of an apocalyptic myth is an auspicious occasion and the Blulupians were swathed in splendour; each one stood before him in stunning finery. This mono-colour people had managed to create cloth of every shade of blue. A small child wore a tunic of such pure sky blue that Mallory swore he could see clouds floating in it. Another woman wore a gown to the ground which was thinly striped in every blue imaginable, mixing shimmering sapphire with lavender, electric cobalt and midnight blue. A man wore a cape made up of patchwork scales of every blue of the ocean and as the cape blew in the night air Mallory saw fish swimming there. A beauty glowed from them, their finery lifting their bruised skin colour to a shining gleam. The most wondrous thing of all though was their silence. Mallory's attention was unwillingly drawn toward a priest, the elder of the village. The people all stood in a semi-circle and he stepped from their midst toward him. His robe hung to the ground along with deep sleeves. The fabric was an ebony blue, while grey-blue hair hung down his back in three thin plaits. He raised his hands and as he brought them down the Blulupians sang a prayer. The harmonies made Mallory's head swim and once more he began to struggle. Panic swept over him as numerous men stepped forward amidst the exultant chorus. They were passed torches which glowed blue-green and they blew fire from their mouths. The congregation sang more loudly, the women swayed and closed their eyes, ready to embrace blessed lives after the demise of The Lost Man.

The priest until now had had his back to Mallory and at the crescendo of the song he turned. The reflection of green fire burned in his eyes and Mallory realised he was surrounded by a circle of fire-wielding Blulupians. As the psalm reached fever pitch the torch bearers stepped closer and closer. The priest lowered his arms, the singing ceased and all that could be heard was the hiss of flame and the breathlessness of the people.

"FIRE," the priest yowled.

The torch bearers lowered the torches, Mallory tried to cry out of his soggy gag and writhed with his last ounce of will when suddenly, out of nowhere a cloud of Wisps wafted around him.

Mallory's vision was obscured but he heard the sharp inward gasp of the Blulupians

"HALT!" the priest raised his hands.

The Wisps whispered unintelligibly but the Blulupians listened intently, mouths agape. The Wisps could not free Mallory physically but their influence on all plant matter weakened the twine and Mallory yanked himself free. The Wisps willed him to walk and, as one, they crept away from the stunned audience. As they guided him to the River Lichen they told him of a raft that would float him to safety. They wished him good fortune and dissolved into the night. Mallory thanked the empty darkness and blindly stepped on to a wobbling platform in front of him. The reeds before him parted magically, rustling against wooden edges. He felt a push and the raft left the bank and drifted into a current which tugged the boat downstream at a steady pace. Where black night met black water Mallory sat; adrift, night blind and lost. But he was alive and he gave thanks. He felt for the edge of the craft and slipped his fingers into the arctic water. He scooped up handfuls, washed his head, and drank, grateful for its cold trickle into his hot throat. He lay down on his back and stared into the starless sky.

The Sun's warm rays flooded his closed eyes with red. He blinked them open and scanned the arc of sky above him. A still branch collided with the blank sky and he realised he was no longer

moving. As his ears awoke, the gentle sound of trickling water filled them, interrupted only by delicate birdsong. Mallory was as stiff as the raft. His arms and shoulders ached, his muscles screamed as he moved them slowly but as the Sun warmed him he guessed he was no longer in the Shadowlands.

"That is correct, young James!" a voice broke the tranquil air. "Safely on the edge of the Naharancan Plains."

Mallory whipped himself up to sitting. There on the end of the raft sat a small fellow. Probably as high as Mallory's knee, dressed in blue overalls, a red shirt and heavy black boots. His blond hair sat up in bed-head spikes and he was tucking into some fruit left by the Wisps.

"Who are you?" Mallory asked.

"You can call me Jim," the fellow replied.

"Do I know you?" Mallory asked slowly, for the fellow seemed strangely familiar.

"Well, you do and you don't," he riddled in response.

Mallory eyed him suspiciously and grabbed a piece of fruit. He slobbered it down greedily (his stomach poorly neglected).

"How did you get here?" Mallory asked with a mouthful, blue juice dribbling down his chin.

"Widge you," Jim replied.

"You've been on the raft with me all along?" Mallory spluttered.

"In a manner of speaking," Jim un-answered.

"Where are you headed?" Mallory asked with exasperation.

"Ah! That'll be in the same direction as you."

"But I don't know that yet!" Mallory said with a shrug. It was only then Mallory looked at his wrist; the compass was gone.

"NO!" Mallory dropped his head in his hands, and then he frantically searched the raft.

"My compass, where is it? It's gone!" Then his narrowed eyes landed on Jim. "YOU! Have you got it? Hand it over, you miserable, thieving little..." Mallory leapt at Jim, causing the raft to slant dangerously.

"Steady on now James! To be sure, I ain't got it!" Jim leapt ashore and backed away from the furious, advancing Mallory. "It fell off...at the stake...when the Wisps helped you. I...I...I can't even read the thing!"

Mallory, now on steady ground, threw himself down and thumped the earth, swearing like only a soldier can and berating himself for his stupidity and bad fortune.

"Now, now, calm down, James! It's all gonna be alright, we got each other now, you see."

Mallory lifted his head and looked at Jim. "Who exactly are you?"

Jim winked. "It's like this; 'When you sip a nip from the River

Lic, an angel doth appear', and here I am!"

"Oh I see," said Mallory, not seeing.

"I'm your own personal 'angel' if you like, confidante, sounding-board, playmate, friend – call me what you will! It's you and me now, pal!"

"Oh I see," said Mallory, struggling to make sense of Jim but felt strangely comforted.

Tired of questioning, Mallory and Jim finished off the largely indigestible fruit, splashed some of the icy water on to their heads and set off.

Chapter 11

THE BLUE SCARF

Kafia did not sleep for three nights. As soon as she dozed off, she dreamed she was falling out of the sky and just as she was about to hit the ground a pair of wings would scoop her up and deliver back to reality – awake and gulping for air. She had not seen Prince Encoda since the day he told her the country's darkest secret and was glad of the reprieve. She felt the situation closing in like a dark blanket around her, the stuffy air in the walls of the palace suffocating her. On the fourth day she returned home. The mountain air was fresh; she sucked it in, embracing the sharpness in her chest. She stepped firmly on the solid ground enjoying the ache in her calves as she trekked down the steep road leading to the white rooftops of Carbinia. As she walked, deep in thought with her dilemma, she heard the drumming beat of hooves behind her. So fast were they that she barely had time to move aside, the kicked-up dust completely concealed the riding man but she could tell he was gentry, the fine horse well groomed, the cloak made of good thick wool. The image sowed a seed, an idea came to her, a story revealed itself and she rushed onward.

When she arrived home Henny made a great fuss of her; feeding her with sweet cakes and mulled wine. Kafia was also surprisingly glad to see her mother. It was comforting that some things stayed the same; anchoring. Henny sank down into her well-fitting armchair and grilled Kafia on the juicy gossip of palace life and couldn't help but confide in Kafia the happenings on the street. When Henny had evacuated all she knew, Kafia chose her moment.

"Ma, there is something I need to tell you...about the king himself."

Henny's eyebrows lifted and she wiggled her apple shaped backside further into her seat and leaned forward in anticipation.

Henny had sat and listened to Kafia between breakfast and lunch. Normally a glut of titbits would have passed her lips during this period but today she held her lips apart, jaw slack and breast heaving in shocked exaltedness. She asked Kafia to clarify one or two points and then rose quickly to relay the whole story (with her own embellishments) to Mrs Busslethorpe next door. Kafia sat back in her chair and smiled with relief and satisfaction.

This is the story Kafia told:

THE BLUE SCARF

It all began with a blue silk scarf. The scarf was hooked upon a bramble (the rough diamond of the weed world) and found by a young farmhand called Brodin. It was a warm day, full of the promise of the Sun Season; one of those days that calls memories of childhood and freedom. He could smell the new green life ready to burst forth and he could feel the power of manhood ready to propel him forward through life; a life that belonged to him, carved by him. He had been sent by the farmer to check the soil for planting. Brodin was a sensitive boy who could feel when the earth was ready. He would feel for its heat, he would sniff the musky fertile aroma and squeeze the umber soil. In this way he would test the outer perimeters of the farmer's land and then the centre. He had done this every morning for the last seven days. Today he deemed the earth perfect for seed. He just needed to complete his cycle with the middle field when he noticed the turquoise scarf ruffling in the breeze – as if it were waving for him. He was puzzled; the startling blue scarf had not been there the day before. It was unmistakably the scarf of some fine lady (for it was not the colour for a man, and a countrywoman would never have access to such exquisite cloth). He rode his horse to the bush and allowed its sheerness to ripple through his sensitive fingers like milk. He shivered. He gently unhooked it and held a corner to his face, then to his lips, drinking the satin texture. Its smell spiralled into his head, singing sweet notes behind his eyes and down his throat until its music sank into his body and explored every part of him.

Brodin forgot all about his job, he forgot about the farmer and his men waiting eagerly for his return. He needed to find the owner of the scarf, to return it safely. He deduced she must be only a day's ride away. The intoxicating scent gave his bones a yearning ache so he tied the scarf around his horse's neck, so his horse, as sensitive as he, could track the lost owner.

They cantered along for half a day until they were well out of his farmer's land. Brodin recognised the ancient path that was made long before the farmers manipulated the land to make food. The tracks were once used by traders who snacked on sunflower seeds en route, dropping seeds that would germinate. The landowners would always leave a few plants mid-crop in honour of the Sun Goddess who fed the crops with nourishing sunlight. He followed the narrow track which meandered through fields and over streams and often petered out altogether. Brodin could keep on the track by the occasional sunflowers that rose, like a beacon in the distance and the fresh tracks of hoof prints and wheels. He rode straight-backed with eyes scanning ahead. In the late afternoon he caught whiffs of aniseed which made his toes tingle and he dug his heels in to gather speed.

By nightfall they entered a wood. Brodin could hear the faint jingling of bells and voices. As they headed deeper into the thickening trees he heard the strings of a lyre, a drumming rhythm, clapping and laughing. He slid off the horse and tied her to a branch; sliding his hand across her mane for thanks, smoothly taking the scarf with him. He crept towards a circle of wagons which stood sentry to the throng within. Spying through the spokes of a wheel, he could see a large fire blazing at the centre of the camp and people darting this way and that. He slid through two of the caravans brightly painted with pictures that told tales, and stood at the edge of the activity.

Many sat in small groups, eating from wooden bowls, talking and joking. Some carried plates to a water trough, others sat and gazed at the crackling fire, some drank swigs from a shared bottle and some played games on the ground. But the group that captured Brodin's attention were dancing. Three musicians gleefully played while three women whirled and stamped wearing bells in their hair and zills on their fingers. Their hair shone in the firelight backdrop and their skin glistened with exertion. A small audience watched clapping and tapping, entranced. One dancer, with a jet-black mane of hair to her waist and long slender arms that reached high above her head which were thrown back to form a perfect arc from her chin to her gaping belly button, wore a loose white skirt and a bright blue silk blouse. She arched over backwards and flipped her nimble slippered feet over her head, landing with a jump which spun into a pirouetting frenzy of arms and hair and audience rapture.

The music stopped and the three women collapsed into a bow at vigorous applause. Brodin's chest rose and fell, rose and fell. The woman in blue skipped toward the water trough and Brodin slipped to the shadowed side of it. She lowered her hands and head and splashed her face with the cool water. As she lifted her head, droplets ran down her oiled skin and her eyes met those of Brodin. He held out her scarf and she *took the end of it and pulled him toward her until they were together and she spun around and around wrapping them together in the fine silk scarf, nose to nose, breast to breast in a slow sensuous dance.*

Brodin never returned to face the farmer's wrath, or see his little sister grow into a young woman, or celebrate her wedding, or welcome his nephew and nieces into life. He never returned to see his broken-hearted mother die, or to crumble the sweet earth of his homeland, for Brodin was entranced and in love and became a gypsy like his blue silken wife who bore him many jet-black haired children. And although they travelled over all of Goaero they never passed through the same village twice for in every place a maiden would leave a bright silk scarf.

Kafia paused. Henny looked confused. Kafia told her the final part of the tale:

"It has been ten nights since King Bravindo took his horse for a ride in the country; he was last seen galloping through the fields with a blue silk scarf tied around his stallion's neck."

Kafia stayed at home for two more days to ensure her mother had spread the word sufficiently before returning, with more than a little trepidation, to the palace, only to find that the king really did appear to be missing.

"The king has run away with the gypsies!" Henny was never one to mince words.

The tremor of rumour soon spread through Carbinia, then down the mountain to Shrove and Calder. In the foothills, Yendys and Blem heard the news. On Lake Lantaba, the towns of Guilder and Threp whispered to Windar and Arrebnac, then the villages of Over Bury, Under Bury and Middle Bury spread the word onto Ratchet, Sibberan and Pincton and into every corner of Pashanka, then onto the river ways which slowly and surely trickled the tale of the missing king all over Goaero. And the story gained momentum until every missing son, brother or husband was blamed on these thieving, shameless gypsies. Begrudged Goaerons began to seethe, first their menfolk and now the king! This had to stop; small groups began to migrate to the village of Brodin (such is the life of a distorted rumour). The tiny village swelled until a camp erupted on the outskirts to accommodate the vigilantes. This unorganised mass grew, disrupting village life with rising emotions and draining of food until an old man of Brodin called the strangers together and spoke:

"My friends, we have welcomed you to our humble village and we feel your wrath. But the gypsies are not here. Our great king is missing, along with your sons, your brothers, your menfolk. You must find them. I urge you to elect a leader and fulfil your quest!"

The old man's word roused the crowd and they cheered.

"Who is to be your leader?" he asked.

The crowd shifted silently.

"Anyone?"

They looked around at each other, searching for another to be found.

"I will!" A voice piped up and a young woman stepped up to the old man and faced the crowd. They stared back at her. The old man cared not one jot for the calibre of their leader and gently asked her:

"What is your name, dear?"

"Breeda," she sang out in a clear strong voice.

"My name is Breeda."

Breeda was not afraid. If she doubted for a moment that she should be standing on this small platform, facing a hundred strangers, she would not be Breeda Bolt. And if she had not been Breeda Bolt she would not have lost her twin brother, Beau, who never returned home one day last Sap Season after a trip to a neighbouring village. Sap Season is the quietest season between Sun and Sorry seasons where people often travel, for the harvest is done and the sting has gone from the rays of the Sun. Surge Season follows Sorry Season where sowing takes place and Goaero wakes up and the Sun prepares for her visit to her beloved child.

Beau was a friendly, outgoing boy. He always itched to see what was beyond the hill, on the other side of a wall or through a keyhole and he often roped Breeda into his escapades. But not this one. She had decided to stay at home for a boy in her own village had caught her eye. But once Beau was declared missing, she turned her back on the boy and wept and wept and wished she had gone with her brother.

Even though she often bickered with Beau, even though he teased her and pushed her around, even though he blamed her and put her in trouble, she felt hurt and deserted. At night she tortured herself with varying scenarios, she blamed herself for his disappearance, she relived arguments and sour words, and she berated herself for her mean thoughts and cruel intentions until daybreak when she would comfort her bereft mother and tend to her ill-tempered father.

When the rumour cart reached their village, all three jumped on board without hesitation, claiming the story as true and explaining their loss. The initial flood of relief brought the three close again and they could talk about Beau without any undercurrents of blame. This union sowed a seed of indignation, it grew into a desire for retribution, and at the end of its gestation Breeda the leader was born. She promised her parents she would find Beau and bring him home. She set out to Brodin, which was the only place she could think of to go.

Breeda was one of the first to arrive, and many had the same intention. Breeda told her story to every newcomer and listened to their own in return. Eventually, she had everyman's story firmly implanted in her psyche; a story of shocking loss, bewilderment and regret, a story of broken families, broken lives and broken hearts. A story that was not yet finished, that they had yet to weave, a story that needed a happy ending.

And so, when the time came to step up, she told it just right.

"Friends, let me tell you a story:

THE STORY OF THE WINDMILL

There was once a miller who lived high on a hill. A hundred fathers before him had milled the corn in his windmill and the mill became as sure as the very ground beneath his feet, and the wind blew. Every day the villagers came to buy the flour to bake their bread to feed their family and the flour became as sure as the very air they breathed, and the wind blew. Every month the traders came to buy the flour to sell to the people to bake their bread to feed their family and the miller became as sure as the very Sun in the sky, and the wind blew. Every day the miller rose to collect the corn to feed the mill to grind the flour that would bake the bread to feed the people, and the wind became as sure as night follows day, and the wind blew. One day the miller got up and the wind did not blow. Not a breath filled the spaces around his windmill, not a grain of corn was reduced to a pile of white gold dust and the miller and the villagers and the traders were paralysed by fear, as if the wind alone had bid them life.

Now the mice in the mill were always hungry because the corn moved so fast through the mill and the miller was so skilled at his work that nary an ear was ever left for them to eat. On this day they peeked out and, slowly but surely, gained courage to go into the mill in broad daylight. They could not believe their luck; bags of corn lying still for them to eat. They nibbled, and nuzzled and guzzled and gorged themselves on the corn and by sundown all the mice in the land congregated at the mill and rejoiced. They gave thanks to the wind for going away and danced in delight until a baby breath breeze ruffled their fur. Then a gentle gust caused the windmill to creak ever so slightly. But the miller heard and ran to the door and felt the brush of a draft tickle his cheek and he looked to the sky and gave thanks. With that the puff turned into a gust and the windmill's arms moved and the villagers heard the windmill moan and they looked to the sky and gave thanks. Then gust followed gust and word followed word until the traders heard the windmill was working and they looked to the sky and gave thanks. The wind was back and the miller fed the mill and the flour fed the villagers and the traders fed the people and never again did they feel sure of the windmill or the flour or the miller and definitely not the wind, and they always gave thanks for the wind and the windmill and the miller and the flour and the bread that kept them fed.

"Friends, we may be but mice, but together we can be great, together we can make the wind blow our lost ones home, together we are as strong as the wind and we can move mountains! Let us find our strength in each other and give thanks to the Sun that we are here, together!"

That day she stood in front of a hundred abandoned souls and when she finished they raised their arms and cheered until the dogs barked, the cows bellowed and the birds all took flight in alarm. Breeda the leader rallied the crowd into action. Within four days they had built wagons, stored food and rolled off towards Carbinia to find the trail of the king. They took the old tracks that ran more directly towards Mount Or. By night, they set up camp and entertained themselves in front of a large fire, playing games in the dirt, gazing into the flames or dancing wildly to lyres by the firelight.

THE NAHARANCAN PLAINS

To the east of Mount Or the yellow earth is dusty and dry. Low trees drop deep roots and find their way to a lake, which old folks say mysteriously appeared out of a weeping pebble. No one has ever been able to reach the bottom, which renders people suspicious and vertiginous. However, where there is water there is life and people set up home on its banks. The lake was set in the Naharancan Plains which contained many pockets of precious gems. The town and lake of Casino were home to a ragtag bunch known as the Grozlers.

"Nice hair, by the way."

"Huh?"

"The stripe, very mysterious, stylish."

"Oh?"

"Matching eyebrows, to boot, unusual touch, works well!" Jim complimented.

They had been walking through a flat, dry sandy land. Small bristly bushes dotted the yellow earth which clunked unresistingly beneath their feet.

Gongalong trees seemed to grow conveniently along the way, affording them resting places. These trees were much revered in Goaero – the Tree of Light was a type of Gongalong tree. They are fickle trees; no one has ever been able to cultivate one. They grow where they grow, the seeds infertile unless sown where it is meant to be sown. The phrase 'as stubborn as a Gongalong' is oft used, and even one or two children are christened with the name after a lengthy and arduous birth. Other than these, they had no track to follow, but picked their way through rocks and rubble heading east.

"So, where are you from?" Mallory asked, his companion's sudden appearance continuing to baffle him.

"Same place as you."

"But how did you get here?"

"Well, you know, James, it takes a special person and a little bit of magic – and 'ta da', here we are!"

Mallory was getting tired of the answers that required more questions.

"Are you here to help or hinder?"

"That depends on you, James!"

"Argh, do you ever answer a question straight?"

"That depends on the question, and on the answer needed."

Mallory looked down on Jim and snarled at him.

"Look, a Gongalong tree, let's rest here." Jim hastily ran ahead to the tree.

Under the canopy of the Gongalong tree the Sun's heat is filtered, caught in the grey-green leaves which still glow after nightfall. The Gongalong bears fruit but not from its branches. One has to dig down to the roots to harvest this nourishing little nut of nature. Mallory disliked this activity, it reminded him of his failed truffle hunting days. But a man needs sustenance, especially on a long journey and the Naharancan Plains were not offering much else. So Mallory found himself on his knees at the foot of a Gongalong tree scraping ochre earth with his fingernails while Jim watched offering 'helpful' advice.

"To the right, I tink, aye, a bit more right, no, no, back a bit... there! Now dig, my man!"

Mallory curled his top lip up on one side, sighed, and scraped at the desiccated ground. A small pile of dust accumulated by his knees.

"Deeper, deeper, get in there!" shouted Jim. Grimacing, Mallory chipped away.

"There must be an easier way," he groaned.

"Aye; the hungry way," Jim countered.

Mallory took up a stone and hacked away at the ground. Jim disappeared around the trunk hopping from foot to foot and readying to unbutton his fly.

"Gotta go," he quipped.

Mallory looked at him mildly disgusted and carried on digging.

After a while, and no nearer the root nuts, Mallory wondered where Jim had gone. He dropped the rock from his cramped fingers and rounded the trunk. There was Jim, casually leaning against the tree, throwing Gongalong nuts into his mouth.

"Where in earth did you find those?" Mallory gawked.

"They were right there, inside the tree," he said, pointing over his shoulder to a hollow in the base of the trunk.

"Why didn't you tell me?" Mallory threw his arms up in exasperation.

"You didn't ask!"

Mallory stooped and poked his head just inside the triangular opening of the tree. The interior of the trunk seemed much bigger than the outside. Mallory removed his head and reached in his arm, grabbing a handful of nuts. Neither he nor Jim noticed a wet pointed purple nose and a large pair of round eyes staring at them out of a dark nook inside the trunk.

When they were full they got on their way.

"Where are we going anyway?" asked Jim.

"To find the key to the king's voice."

"And where's that?"

"Not where, who, I need to find the golden haired youth with a key." Mallory explained as they trekked onward with purpose. Since the cuff had been lost Mallory had felt lost too. He was not only directionless but he felt his connection with Prince Encoda and the king was gone. He felt like a small man adrift in a big strange world, which was why Jim's line of questioning bothered him.

After a while, Jim spoke again:

"And where will you be looking for this lad, James?"

"This way, we'll try at the next town." said Mallory, pointing into the distance and setting his jaw.

"What if it's not?" insisted Jim.

"Not what?"

"The right town, the right way."

"Then it's the wrong way."

"Then what?" inquired Jim.

Mallory stopped, looked down at his companion and raising

his voice with irritation, snapped.

"I don't know. I don't know where I am going, or what is there, I don't know if I will get there or when. When I am there, I won't know if it is the right place. I just don't know, alright?"

"Alright!" said Jim. "But..."

"DON'T KNOW!" shouted Mallory and they walked on in silence until the sky closed her eye and darkness fell. Ahead the faint glow of a Gongalong tree called them to rest. Exhausted, they leant against the soft bark and fell asleep.

"Well, what do you know!" exclaimed Jim. Mallory opened his crusty eyes and winced at Jim who was standing not far from their resting spot.

"What is it?" he croaked.

"If it's not the same tree we ate at yesterday, my name's not Jim!" he declared.

Mallory crawled around and looked in disbelief. He poked his head inside the Gongalong and sure enough, there sat the very same pile of nuts as yesterday. He groaned.

"You mean we went in a circle?" Mallory berated himself mercilessly, thumping his head on the trunk.

With stomachs aching for breakfast, they ate more nuts and set off.

"Do you think it might be that way?" asked Jim, pointing in one direction.

"No."

"Only we went this way yesterday."

"Yes."

"And...are we heading for the same place again?"

"Yes."

"Are you sure it is the right way?"

Mallory did not even reply but frowned and continued east.

By nightfall the glow of a Gongalong tree led them to camp for the night. In the morning Jim made the same discovery. Mallory's shoulders slumped down a little further into his frame. They ate some more nuts – which seemed more of a chore than a meal – and set off. All day Jim offered the same line of questioning until Mallory was so unsure of himself he doubted if he really was on a quest for the king. Once again the familiar glow met them at the day's end and he already knew they were back where they had begun.

By the fifth day Mallory was teetering on the edge of insanity. He had now tried travelling south and north but each one led them back to the same place. His hair struck out in every direction where he had scratched in bemusement, torn at it in frustration and wrapped his arms around it trying not to cry. As they left the tree, Jim piped up:

"Now, are ye sure this is the right way?"

And Mallory exploded.

"No Jim, I am not sure. I am not sure of anything. I am not sure what I am doing here, or why, or who I am, or you. I am sure of only one thing Jim. I am a failure!"

Jim looked at Mallory with pride. "That's the spirit, my boy!"

Mallory looked puzzled.

"Who are you, Jim?"

"Well, ye'll have to work that one out yerself, my boy, but ask me another."

"Which way do I go?" ventured Mallory.

"The hungry way, I believe," said Jim.

Mallory thought about that. "The nuts?"

"Aye, I believe they are known as the 'Seeds of Doubt' in some regions."

"Well...you...could...have...MENTIONED THAT!"

"Ye didn't ask."

The next morning Mallory and Jim ate no nuts and headed east again. At nightfall a faint glow lay ahead. They arrived, fell asleep under the blue-green canopy and woke under the protection of a different Gongalong tree.

"You know, James, I seem to recall that if you dig for your own nuts you suffer no ill effects." He handed Mallory a stone and so he hacked away at the unyielding sand, which finally revealed its cache. They ate fresh nuts and set off.

Over the next three days they trekked over the plains and by the last evening Mallory could not stomach another Gongalong nut. He feared he was stuck in this purgatorial desert for eternity but by Sun-out that evening a different kind of light awaited them; the multi-dotted Milky Way of civilisation. Mallory and Jim had reached the town of Casino.

CASINO

At night central Casino pumps and thumps. Lights blaze in windows, music is played loudly, shouts of exultation and despair shoot out into the streets. In this part of town the action never wanes; the air is thick with wheeling and dealing, the scrape of coins sliding across the tables for Bloodstone. Cracked faces emerge from all-night gaming sessions and all-day dealing before they take their weather-beaten bodies home to sleep, only to disappear into the desert again the next morning.

Outside the town centre dwellings spiral out endlessly but it is not such a lively place. Here the miners known as Grozlers live, or rather subsist, for they spend little time here. It is the domain of the women; alone with their children and grinding domesticity – and the waiting. Waiting for the return of the man, waiting for the strike of Bloodstone, waiting for the strike of death, waiting. Life in Casino is a superstitious one. Any slip of a word or deed could afflict a man with misfortune or many years of barren mining. For example, a woman may not wear red or yellow, she may not let her fire go out or slay a bird, she must never say her husband's name in vain, nor whistle while he is away. Life is dull so sport is made of spotting misdemeanours; women watch each other slyly, ready to report any transgression. Yet, a false friendliness is shared, for a woman would not want an enemy in this place. Many a fabrication has caused much sorrow and bitterness.

The men go away for many days at a time; it may take him seven days to reach his pit. The first settlers who had closer pits had larger houses and as more hopefuls arrived, the homes expanded outwards and the pits got further away. Through sheer luck and dogged manipulation some miners became rich. Sick of the noisy stinking town centre – a pit in itself – they moved to the shores of Lake Casino and built bigger houses. Those who lived on the lake had considerable wealth which meant considerable power and so became the chieftains of Casino and ran the town.

The saying in Casino went thus; the Naharancan Plains holds riches and ruins; a man who enters may find one or both, but will never find neither. Many a man has been tempted and temptation fogs logic, so they continue to arrive, set up house, trek out into the Plains and cradle hope just as their wife might cradle his newborn child back in the grey quarters of Casino. And although life here is harsh and dull, a woman would be loath to swap, for life in the inhospitable Plains is bleak and unforgiving. As Mallory found out, the Plains are vast and lifeless. A man must carry food and water to survive, he must carry tools to dig and carry steely determination buoyed by hope. When he arrives at his pitch he must set up camp. He is already a lucky man if he has a Gongalong or Nappali tree nearby, but many do not.

Mallory and Jim found the main road into town. They had stepped in with a group of men who sang triumphantly. Mallory hoisted Jim onto his shoulders. Jim could see a man at the centre carrying a large sack on his back. It looked bulging and heavy. Men came up to him; shook his hand, clapped his back, gave him a wink and a nod. Women watched from doorways stony faced. Small children crowded around him and he handed crumbs of stone to them. They ran away yelling with excitement and comparing sizes. Only Mallory's sharp eyes noticed an odd shape protruding from the left breast of the man. Eventually they arrived in the town centre. A hefty man stood in front of a doorway of a brick building. His big square head sat directly on his vast shoulders which led down to log-like arms which were folded across his chest. The crowd stopped in unison and the miner stepped up to the big man.

"You bled a vein there, Ernie boy?" the large man chewed out from the corner of his mouth.

"'Ad a good day, Mr Froggit," Ernie agreed.

"Makin' a deposit?"

"Reckon," Ernie replied.

They turned to go into the building and Mallory could hear Mr Froggit:

"Ya know the terms; ya three biggest stones is my fee for keepin' it for ya; I'll take ten stones per withdrawal, then I'll need another ten for insurance; five if ya wanna withdraw the lot..."

Mallory turned to the man standing next to him.

"What's that all about?"

"A bag of Bloodstones needs protection in this town," the man answered. Mallory still looked perplexed.

"You can't make a haul like that; someone's fit to steal it or murder for it. That's where Froggit comes in. No one dares rob 'im, nasty piece o' work, and he takes his cut of it. His building 'ere is the only brick one in town – impenetrable. Thing is, it costs more to get ya stones out than the worth of 'em, better than being murdered for it though, 'Froggit or floggit' we say around 'ere." The man shook his head and shuffled off bleary eyed.

Mallory slid Jim off his shoulders.

"So James, shall we find some h'accommodation in this fine town?"

Mallory nodded and they walked to an inn on the other side of the square.

When Mallory and Jim had secured a room they went to eat dinner in the front room of the inn. Mallory surveyed the scene. He noticed a room at the back which held a circle of men around a table. They had clenched knuckles, set jaws, sweat stained faces, and placed bets feverishly, the candle flames swaying this way and that as indiscriminately as luck. Mallory turned his attention back to the front room and took a seat next to an old fellow who was ensconced by the fireplace. His shoulders hung vertically from his sinewy neck. Skirting a skinny rib cage, his arms bent at bony elbows which led to long tapered fingers and cradled a tin mug of murky liquid. His jutting jaw matched his eyeballs which also bulged out of his head.

"Evening!" said Mallory.

"Evenin' to you," the man replied. Mallory introduced himself and Jim, which seemed to puzzle the man.

"New to these parts?" the man, called Dunkin, asked.

"Yes, today."

"Hopin' to strike it rich, eh?"

"Sort of. Tell me, what is a Bloodstone, what does it look like?"

Dunkin snorted. "Now that's the question!" he exclaimed. "Anyhows, you're asking the right person!"

"Oh, good!"

"I mined a pit 'ere for many a year, but luck ain't me middle name. Near broke my back digging that 'ole. Turns out what I'm best at is sortin'. You sees these eyes o' mine? Well, they can spot a Bloodstone in a pile of rubble. I can pick a Glitch, rumble a Rubian, I could even tell you its Sun thread in the dark."

Mallory was lost.

"Ah! I remember, you ain't seen one afore. 'Ere." Dunkin plunged his endless fingers into his pocket and pulled out a pea-sized stone. He placed it in Mallory's hand. Mallory had never seen such a stunning jewel (although he had seen very few of any kind of jewel). It was shaped like a dodecahedron. Its facets shone a deep lustrous red and when he looked closely, gold flecks shimmered inside.

"Wawhh!" Mallory exclaimed in awe.

"Now you see how this is shaped...if it had only eight faces it's called a Rubian, very rare, only seen a handful in my lifetime, they're bigguns too. A Glitch, now, that's a stone that looks perfect, all the faces are identical, no chips but they cracked, see, only need to look at it in the wrong way an' it'll crumble to dust." He slid his fingers together in the air. "Needs an expert, like me, to spot 'em."

"Why are they called Bloodstones?"

"Well, some says 'cos of the blood spilt trying to dig 'em out, but I prefer to think o' it like this:

THE STORY OF TARP

At the beginning of time, not long after the first few leaves fell from the Tree of Light, a brave Goaeron called Tarp set forth to explore the land. Tarp wandered through every part of Goaero. Occasionally Quills would see him and spread word of his discoveries. It was Tarp that gave name to much of Goaero. Now, Tarp came from an unusual family. He had a mother who could not see, a father who could not hear and a sister whose voice was stole away at birth. He was ashamed of that family, all with summin' missin'. He felt guilty 'cos he was so perfect. He vowed he would find a cure for their ills.

When he discovered the Vandret Falls he found oysters as big as your 'ed. They grew so big being awashed back and forth by the pure river water and the rich livin' water o' the sea. When he uncovered a pearl it filled 'is entire palm and in its shimmering lustre he saw 'imself pearly faced and pure. He felt for sure that this pearl could restore the sight of anyone and so he took it home for 'is mother. But, alas, she did not get to see 'er 'andsome son and he set off again downcast but determined.

This time he ventured 'ere, to the Naharancan Plains. He trekked for many days and many Moons until 'is shoes were tattered and he had to trudge barefoot through this soulless desert. But still he walked, until 'is feet bled. After gettin' nowhere, he sat down and wept tears of red from the desert earth and streams of blood flowed from 'is feet into the soil.

When he was spent he wiped 'is eyes and a lake spread out afore 'im. This changed 'is mood and he dove into the glistenin' water. He shot down, down into the depths where the rusty water turned black and found a red jewel as big as 'is fist. He swam to the surface and when he looked at that stone, he felt the golden veins pumping through it and he swore it had the power to make any man 'ear the blood coursing through 'im. He called it a Bloodstone. He rushed back home and presented the stone to 'is poor deaf father but the man would never 'ear the resonant voice of 'is son tell the tales of 'is adventures.

Tarp set off distraught but dogged and once again he headed for undiscovered Goaero. 'Ere he encountered the glittering sands of Shapeshifter Territory, although he named it Sitarland. For Tarp, this was paradise and he stayed for many years. He wed a shy dark skinned girl called Elice. One day he was diving for fish. He took a breath so deep he looked like a blowfish which made Elice laugh. He leapt off the boat and clutched at handfuls of water, kicking 'is strong legs smoothly. He went deeper than ever before and through the ringin' in 'is ears, he heard his name being called. 'Is eye caught the sight of a white flash. 'Is 'ed and chest pounded but he dug deep and snatched up a stone. He flapped 'imself deliriously to the surface where hands hauled 'im onto the raft. He lay there panting, dragging in mouthfuls of air, speechless. He lifted the stone up and smeared away its sandy skin to reveal a perfect Sand Diamond. He kissed it for he knew it would unlock 'is sister's voice. He told Elice he loved 'er and left that day.

When he got home 'is sister alone greeted 'im at the door and broke down in silent tears. Over the years both their mother and father had died. In deep grief he let the Sand Diamond drop into 'is sister's hand. She marvelled at its magnificence, rubbed it on her cheek, and set it beside the Bloodstone and the Pearl of Anishka. She fingered the three, opened her mouth and said

'I would give my voice, my sight and my sounds to be so beautiful.'

She gasped and Tarp looked out of his window of sorrow and smiled.

Mallory stared wide eyed at Dunkin.

"Where can I dig for Bloodstone?"

"Are you sure that's what you wanna do, my boy? You know, many a tale ends in this town."

But Mallory knew; he didn't see how finding a golden haired youth was ever going to be possible, but now he had discovered the key to unlocking the king's voice himself; a Pearl of Anishka, a Bloodstone and a Sand Diamond, surely that was easier than finding one boy in the whole of Goaero? And if he found the boy on his travels, well, all well and good. He nodded enthusiastically to Dunkin who resigned himself to directing Mallory to the Pit Office. In his excited haste, Mallory had not noticed the absence of Jim who seemed to have mysteriously vanished.

Chapter 14

THE KING IS MISSING

Since his meeting with Kafia, Encoda had waited and waited. He had expected little on the first day. He swallowed his impatience on the second day. On the third day he expected the return of Kafia (although he had neglected to stipulate this and had no idea she had not even left yet) and became anxious to see her. He wanted her to tell him with those plush lips, adoring brown eyes and elegant little hands how their plan had worked so perfectly. On the fourth day he sent out one of his aides to garner the whispers among the people. He often fished for information this way. But his aide took longer than usual to return. Scenarios ran over and over in Encoda's head as to what was happening. On the fifth day he sent out another aide to find Kafia. And so it was on the sixth day they all converged in Encoda's chambers.

The first aide came rushing through the door, bowing low in etiquette but also to regain his breath.

"Sire, it's the blue scarf!" he panted.

"I beg your pardon?"

"The blue scarf, Sire, the king has been enchanted."

"No, no, not enchanted, you fool."

"Well, he is missing Sire, the king has vanished."

"For heaven's sake man, what are you blathering about?"

The second aide then rushed in, tripping over the carpet in his haste and offering an unbalanced bow.

"The king is missing, Sire." he blurted.

Kafia stood anxiously outside the door. She bit her lip and sweat prickled her neck. She knew she was one short step from banishment to Shapeshifter Territory but she was also very impressed at her mother's ability to spread a rumour. She heard Encoda's voice get louder and more perplexed as the aides relayed Kafia's story, until he boomed:

"WHERE IS SHE?"

The aides looked puzzled, the prince should surely be asking 'where is *he*'? Just at that moment a crowd of Advisors shuffled past her like a single beetle. They fell through Encoda's door and bowed and bumped backsides before rising up.

"The king is missing," they cried in unison.

Encoda's anger was about to shatter the windows, his beetroot cheeks stood in contrast to his white clenched knuckles.

"His bed has not been slept in."

"He is not in the chapel."

"Or in his offices."

"He has sent home his maid."

"We have searched the palace."

Kafia thought she was hearing things...where was the king? The king *is* missing? A wave of pins and needles passed through her.

"Then I must find him!" Encoda shouted furiously and strode from his chambers, surrounded by his advisors. He caught sight of Kafia who was flattened against the wall, desperately invoking the power of invisibility. She opened her eyes and saw Encoda frozen before her.

"The king is missing," she stated in a small but sure voice. He looked her in the eye, searching for a clue but saw nothing in her steady gaze.

"I'll talk to you later," he grunted and marched off.

Kafia watched the party disappear round the corner and sank to the floor letting out a long puff of air.

"*Cora Burbury fell in love with a sheep,*" she mumbled with relief and picked herself up.

Kafia went to her room. Petunia filled her in on the last few days.

"And no one knows where he is?" asked Kafia chewing her nails.

"No, he left secretly, you know how nobody pays him much attention. He's just always...there."

"Well, he's not now," she murmured in bafflement.

Kafia was thinking hard. Her situation had not become any easier but she now had some time and she knew she must use it wisely. At first she considered disappearing, but she would miss all the action and she craved to be in the prince's arms...no, confidences. She blushed at her initial thought. She decided she would be better off in the heart of it but she needed to be one step ahead. She marched up to the royal family's floors and located Encoda in the congress rooms. She had her broom and was ready to sweep but put her ear to the door instead.

"Who exactly saw the blue scarf?" Encoda emphasized every syllable. His aides and Advisors murmured nervously with no answers.

"Find out and bring them to me." he yelled and brought his fist crashing down on his desk.

Kafia knew what she was to do. She sent an anonymous note to one of the Advisors, letting them know that Kafia Skinner had been heard to admit it was she who spied King Bravindo taking off with the blue scarf. Within the day she was frog-marched to Encoda who slammed the door behind them, having sent away all the other staff.

"YOU, young lady," he yelled "have a lot of explaining to do."

He felt his fury drain away at the sight of her until the end of his demand was as soft as a lullaby. Kafia's heart galloped as she looked at her handsome prince. His green eyes flashed at her, then avoided her. Enthralled by his power and her own, she was not sure if her dry throat would spit out any words. He indicated for her to sit.

"I saw him. I was taking my mother out to the country so I could tell her, you know, the story about the king being a Quill."

"Shhh!" he hushed her.

"But on the way I saw this noble man galloping on a fine steed with a blue scarf tied to its bridle."

She thought about the horse galloping past her on her way to Carbinia and felt comforted that she wasn't entirely lying.

"Did you see his face?"

"No, Sire."

"Then how in the Sun's name did you know it was he?"

"It was his breeches, Sire."

"His what?"

"His breeches. You see I'd ironed them. I knew his were the ones with the purple stripe and, er, and bit of a scorch mark by the right knee." She cleared her throat and risked a glance at Encoda's face.

"So let me get this straight. You recognised the king's trousers?"

"Yes, Sire."

"And why did you not report to me immediately?"

"Because I followed him."

"With your mother?"

"No, I sent her back home; most disgruntled she was. I, er, borrowed a horse and set off after him...to see where he was going."

"And where was he going?"

"To the gypsies."

"He found them?"

"Yes"

"And what happened?"

"*Henry Blanket stole Imelda Limp's donkey,*" she replied.

"I beg your pardon?" the prince was utterly baffled.

"I am sorry, Sire," Kafia stammered.

"Well, WHAT HAPPENED?" Encoda's fury was rising once more.

"He danced, Sire. He danced with a beautiful girl. She

wrapped herself around him and gave him tender kisses here and here and then down..."

"ENOUGH." Encoda barked and tugged at his collar. He had heard enough to warrant an immediate intervention, no gypsy heir would steal the crown from under his nose.

That evening they prepared themselves for a journey. Kafia was to take him to the gypsies and if she hadn't already been flying by the hem of her skirts, she was now.

Chapter 15

BLOODSTONE

Mallory was overjoyed to have a set mission. His hunch was that if he collected these three precious rocks; a Bloodstone, a Pearl of Anishka and a Sand Diamond, they would restore the King's voice. His army life had consisted of fulfilling orders and after groping around for a lead for so long, he felt a surge of energy and confidence, he would be back at the barracks in no time.

The next morning he marched into the Pit Office. A small bald man sat at a large table. He was hunched over a page and scribbled with a scratchy inked quill. A crooked pile of yellowing paper was stacked perilously close to the corner. The man did not look up; Mallory waited a few moments before coughing. Still the man scratched furiously without acknowledging Mallory. He coughed again; the man raised his finger in the air impatiently. Mallory stepped closer and the finger shot up again. The man placed the written page on the pile, but instead of attending to Mallory, he took another sheet and started again.

"Excuse me?" Mallory said.

"Get in line," came the reply.

"What line?"

"THE line," came the response.

"I'd like a pitch."

"Join the queue, please," said the man officiously.

"What queue?"

"THE queue."

"There is no queue; I am the only one here!" Mallory was feeling tetchy now.

The finger pointed to a door on one side of the room. Mallory went across and opened it. It led back outside into a yard. At least a hundred men sat in a rough spiral around the walls and into the middle where a group stood jostling in the tight space remaining. Mallory's shoulders drooped and he made his way to the end of the line.

"Behind me, mister," grunted a man, "welcome to the Pit Stop."

Already Mallory was dismayed by the word 'stop'.

"How long have you been here?"

"Well, my missus has been in five times with bread and cheese."

"Oh."

The door Mallory came through opened a crack. Suddenly the men started to stand up and shuffle around.

"NEXT..."

Mallory recognised the nasal voice of the bald man. A fellow slipped through the door turning to give a triumphant wave and the queued assembly cheered and clapped.

"Second time round you kinda get used to it!" drawled the man.

"Second time round?" asked Mallory gravely.

"Yeah, you gotta apply first, then you come back for 'proval. Third time's at the Licence Office, he's a bit quicker there, they say."

"And this is the only way to get a pitch?"

The man nodded. The door opened again, everyone looked up with expectancy but it was just another man, squeezing through to join the queue. He didn't have time for this, he only needed one stone.

"How do I get out of here?" asked Mallory.

The man hoisted his eyebrows and nodded over to another door in the wall. Mallory picked his way across the mass of bodies and let himself into the street outside. He had an idea and set off to find Ernie, the successful miner from the previous day.

After Mallory had gone, the new man to the Pit Stop struck up conversation.

"Ear bout the king?" he said to the drawler.

"What's 'at?"

"Missing, they say. Run off with the gypsies."

As it happened Ernie was in the back room of the inn. Mallory stepped into the fetid atmosphere of the den and took a deep breath. He still had the pea-sized stone from Dunkin and slammed it down on the table. The five men around the table burst out laughing, one flicked the pebble back to Mallory dismissing him with a wave of his gnarled hand. Mallory thought for a moment.

"Alright," he said, "if I can predict who will win the next round, you let me in on the game."

The men looked at each other and nodded, relieved at an added dimension to the pressures of the game. Without missing a beat Mallory pointed at one of the men.

"You!"

The long-haired man looked pleased and they began to play. The game was more intense, the long-haired man first relaxing smugly until the others played aggressively so he picked up his game. Discs, coins and Bloodstone flew across the table in a flurry until the long-haired man won and scooped the pile of winnings into his lap. Mallory was asked to repeat his trick, again a heightened game ensued and Mallory's prediction was correct. From now on Mallory took a coin off each man and continuously pointed out the winner. Finally they consented for him to sit and play. All day and all night they gambled, slowly the players began to slip away, too tired, too broke or too drunk to continue. Finally it was down to Mallory and Ernie. Mallory had gathered an impressive pile of coins, stacked around his chair legs and a mountain shimmering in front of him on the table. Gambling was a game that his soldier friends had long since given up with Mallory since he seemed to predict every move and he himself found it dull. He was too honest to make a living out of cheating, even though he was not strictly cheating. Nevertheless, every time he played he felt like a crook. He was glad the long evening was over and he was finally alone with Ernie.

"It's all yours for the Rubian," he offered Ernie.

Ernie's head shot up and looked directly at Mallory, suspicion holding up his expression. He narrowed his eyes and moved closer to Mallory until his beery breath bathed Mallory's face.

"How'd you know?" he said hoarsely.

"I guessed," Mallory whispered back. "Is it a deal?"

"Did Froggit send you?" hissed Ernie.

"No, I, I'm on king's business," Mallory claimed officially. Ernie pulled his head back, doubly suspicious.

"Look, Ernie, I am in his Majesty's army, Lion's Head Regiment, despatched by Prince Encoda. My mission is top secret but I will confer with you. I have been issued orders to secure a Rubian. I would not want Mr Froggit to know about this exchange and I would also suggest to you that this pile of coin here is much more valuable to you than the stone."

Ernie eyed the heap of different sized coins, he stood up, dug his hands down into his trousers and retrieved a plum sized jewel from a region Mallory declined to dwell on. Mallory smiled his thanks and pushed the pile of coins to Ernie. He wrapped the Bloodstone in a handkerchief and placed it inside his breast pocket next to a small bottle of agitated sand.

Mallory was heavy with fatigue, he sedately took the stairs to his room while his heart leapt somersaults in excitement. He was surprised and happy to find Jim lying comfortably on the bed.

"Where have you been?" gushed Mallory.

"Oh, I'm not too good around a crowd," said Jim.

Mallory told Jim about his day and Jim nodded wisely.

"So now I need to find a Sand Diamond and Pearl of Anishka, but I have no idea where to find them."

"What we need is a map, James."

"A map?"

"You know; a where's where of Goaero."

"There are no maps of Goaero, everyone knows that."

"Do they now?"

"Jim?"

"Aye."

"Where can I find a map?"

With that Jim rolled over and began to snore and Mallory could not help but join in.

QUELTA

Mallory and Jim left Casino. After stocking up on supplies with some of the coins Mallory had kept from Ernie, they walked out on the road that had led them in, until it split into a fork. An old man sat begging where the roads separated. His eyes were like milky glass marbles but he could hear them and held out his wooden bowl as they approached. Mallory dropped in a coin.

"Old man, can you tell me which road leads to Anishka?" Once again Mallory silently lamented the lost compass.

The old man held up his bowl and Mallory tossed in another coin. The old man fingered the coin and then raised his raggedy arm and, with a crooked finger, pointed north. Mallory thanked him and took the indicated road. Once again they found themselves in the leaching expanse of desert. However, this time they were on a track and one or two Grozler settlements along the way gave them some comfort. On the fifth day the air began to cool and the desert colours changed to dull browns and grey. The track petered out and once again they picked their way through shale and ever expanding rocks. By the sixth day it was too cold to sleep at night so they inched onward in the dark helped by Mallory's senses and rested by day in the weak sunlight. On the seventh day the ground turned into a grey white ice; they had reached the glacier.

"Well, if my bones ain't deceiving me, this is Great Aunt Lek." said Jim.

"Who?" asked Mallory through chattering teeth.

"The River Lek, sister of Lichen."

"But where is Anishka?" asked Mallory.

Jim shrugged.

"Let's cross it. Maybe there is a town farther on," suggested Mallory.

"We'll perish out there!" Jim shrank away.

"We'll perish here too, onward, I say." Mallory stated with a conviction which sounded more convincing out loud than in his head.

Jim shrugged again and sighed.

Sliding perilously they set foot on the ice. They made slow progress. The ice stretched out in front and either side, and as they slipped down a slope, the dry land behind them was extinguished from view too. They crunched through slush and skated ungainly across icy blue glass. They fell over and over until every part of them was tender and their wet clothes hung on grimly. Soon Mallory's lips turned as white as his eyebrows and icicles hung from his nose. No conversation was possible with frozen solid jaws. Only the Sun gave them any sense of direction but as She fluttered her eye shut, Mallory and Jim were plunged into pitch-black whiteness. The river creaked and cracked below, threatening to swallow them up.

What Mallory, and almost certainly most Goaerons, didn't know about was the one other small region of Goaero, the unknown, untouched, impenetrable land, lodged between the Shadowlands and the Naharancan Plains called Quelta. The River Lichen ran through the Shadowlands for a quarter of her length before she split in two. The Lichen continued directly north while her sister, River Lek, flowed east before curling round to head north again. Where the rivers parted company a change came over them, for locked in grief at their separation they froze, almost solid, forming two glacial snakes which moved imperceptibly, creaking and groaning like two old ladies. Eventually they are reunited, having crept painfully, ice-flow by ice-flow around Quelta. The two harridans cast barren banks, a hostile swath of black rubble and little life, which spread deep towards the Ice Mountains sitting in between. But when reunited at the ocean's mouth, with melted hearts, they wailed and danced blowing fountains of misty rainbows into the air.

Mallory sank to his knees with his arms clutched feebly around him.

"James, James, stand up man. Don't give up now!" Jim slapped Mallory's blue cheeks. But Mallory slumped forward onto the ice unable to move, or hear Jim's cries.

"James, wake up, WAKE UP!"

"I am Que. I am a Quill."

Mallory opened his eyes for a brief moment for his face stung like lemon juice in a thousand cuts.

"Where am I?" he whispered.

"In Quelta."

"What? Where's Anishka?"

"Rest now, I shall tell you who we are:

THE STORY OF THE QUILLS

Quills came into being alongside Goaerons, we too are Goaeron, we fell from the same tree, on the same day. We built our houses side by side, our children played together. But it was soon revealed that Quills were not like Goaerons. Our wings began to grow and we came to know the joy of the sky. The Quills and Goaerons began to drift apart; Quills preferred the thinner air of the mountain tops, the Goaerons had strong limbs for the land; we sustained ourselves on the Eternal Mists of Life, the Goaerons on the fruit of the fields;

we were invigorated by stretching our wings and soaring above on pure light; the Goaerons loved horseback and the pounding beat on solid ground. Many Quills migrated to the mountains. Mount Or is the finest mountain of the land. It towers above all that is Goaero and its vista spreads ever further. The Cascades gave us water, the heat thrown up from the jungle a thermal playground.

Both peoples multiplied but Quills give birth after a long gestation and take much time between children and many do not survive. Goaerons were blessed with robust procreation and bore many healthy children. In time the Goaerons needed a ruler and many battles were fought before a king became triumphant. King Ginta needed a palace; a residence so large that no one would dare refute his rule, a castle so beautiful that all would respect his reign and a fortress where he could survey all his sovereignty. He claimed Mount Or and brutally displaced the Quills who had lived lightly on the peak.

It is here our story takes a path into darkness. Quill felt forsaken by the Sun, She who created all beings equal had shown favour to the wingless ones. Our high priest was furious. Before they left Mount Or he entered the temple and dashed the urn of Sun Sand to the ground. The plume of flame desiccated the temple and surrounding settlement. The Quills fled in disgrace to the sound of King Ginta's laughter ringing in their ears. The fire cleared the ground for his colossal palace. Mount Or is still our spiritual home and many Quills are drawn to her even though it is now forbidden to return.

It is in these Ice Mountains of Quelta that the Quills now make their home. They are called so for the ice that encircles them. They are not as high or grand as Mount Or but the peaks are plentiful in number and gifts, and the Quills are safe, undisturbed and unknown. As the Quills disappeared from Goaeron life many stories were told. It seemed the Quills were blessed by the Sun Goddess; closer to her with the freedom to fly, they became divine oracles for they saw far and wide. Then they desecrated Her, destroyed a part of Her and were banished. A sighting became rare, for we only occasionally leave the safety of Quilldom.

Quills live lightly on this earth, our footsteps are gentle, our appetite is moderate, our number is few and our respect for Sun's earth is paramount. But we are not perfect. Our children are fragile, our limbs are feeble, fury and unforgiving are our failings.

I am Que, descended from the family of Quera, bred from rejection, spawned from a disgraced family, a family outside its people. We are the only Quill to leave these mountains, as we are outside the law of Quilldom. And so if a Quill is ever sighted soaring across the blue lit sky it will be me or my two brothers whose breadth of wing carries us as far as the wind. Just like the beautiful Quera we have an itch beneath our wings. We alone know the whole of Goaero; the appetite of the Beach Eater; the wanderings of men; the meanderings of rivers. Back home we chart our knowledge; my father, my brothers and I; an island on an island. We are the Map

Keepers; we alone know the whole of Goaero."

Mallory drifted off to sleep dreaming of Mount Or and billowing white feather pillows to the gentle voice of Que.

The next day Mallory awoke to voices around him.

"So that was what kept him alive?"

"Yes, it was next to his heart."

"Where did he get it from?"

"Who knows, but he is a lucky man."

"Who is he anyway? Where did he come from?"

"He asked where Anishka is."

"I think the Sun Goddess sent him to us."

Eyebrows raised all around; the simple, maybe truest words, from a babe's mouth.

"You may be right Quty, you may be right!" the father ruffled his boy's hair.

"Sh! He's coming to; he may be feeling strong enough to talk."

Mallory sat up and the peering faces stepped back.

"James Ardent Mallory, king's army, Regiment of the Lion's Head."

The family introduced themselves. The father Querand shook Mallory's hand, mother Quella nodded to him, while of their sons, Que waved, Quarm shook his hand, as did Quirl and little Quty hid behind his grandfather's legs.

"How did I get here?" asked Mallory.

"No man has ever crossed the glacier. You were lucky I was flying back over, I noticed you just before Sun out and brought you back here, our home," Que explained.

"Thank you."

"Well, it was not I that saved your life, Mr Mallory. You had a small bottle at your breast. You would have perished immediately without the Sun Sand to keep you warm, to give you life. Please, tell us from where it came."

So Mallory recounted his journey.

It turned out the Sun Sand had kept Mallory alive by the breadth of a feather. He was much weaker than first thought and the thin mountain air slowed his recuperation. He stayed with Que and his family for ten days. The Quills treated him with utmost respect and reverence; a Goaeron in Quelta carrying Sun Sand on a mission from the royal palace was the stuff of legend. It could be a pivotal turning point for the family, of the entire Quill's future, of Goaeron future, and the family quivered in its radiance. The family was close and affectionate. There was much back slapping and wing flapping and they treated Mallory like one of their own. Mallory revelled in their midst, tasting belonging again with an added dash of the exotic.

Once again Jim had mysteriously disappeared. Mallory had tried asking Que about him, his mini companion but Que had just shaken his head in bewilderment, assuming some form of hallucination had overcome him. Sometimes Mallory would hear echoes of Jim's words rumble around his head and although this was a comfort he still worried for his well being and whereabouts.

Que, Quarm and Quirt honoured him by sharing their many years knowledge of map keeping. Drawn with intricate fine lines by quills off their own backs, the maps were swirling strokes of contours, rivers, roads and lakes. Mallory never tired of poring over this hidden beauty of his country. Seen from such a vantage it revealed secrets and patterns; a code which could only be deciphered by taking the long view.

By layering wafer thin pages over and over the Quills showed Mallory the destruction of the Beach Eater. Up to this point the Beach Eater had been a mere shadow for Mallory, a happening far away that had no effect on him. He was shocked at its advent; great chunks of coastline vanishing. It was the Quill's greatest concern. And Mallory wondered if anyone else was concerned, if the palace had any knowledge, if anything was being done.

But it was Anishka that always drew his eye. He studied routes and memorised landmarks. As his strength returned, his zeal did too and he knew he could delay no longer. The evening before he was due to leave, the Quills prepared a feast. The dinner was a merry affair, a celebration, and Mallory, so touched by his friends, declared a moment of silence.

"Friends, you plucked me from the icy grip of sister Lek and you breathed warmth back into my veins. You cradled me in the nest of your family, you shared with me your humour, you honoured me with your map work, and you have loved me as one of you own. For that I offer you my love, my loyalty and...this."

Mallory placed the bottle of Sun Sand on the table. The family all looked at it in awe and delight, an array of possibility playing in their eyes. Que rose and embraced Mallory, then all followed suit until Querand was left.

"Mallory, you have restored our faith in groundhogs! You are welcome to our home any time and we will watch out for you on our travels. Mallory, we wish you success on your mission and hope that this will help."

He handed Mallory a rolled parchment, a perfect copy of the most recent map. It was only when Mallory opened it later in Goaero that he saw Anishka embellished with jewels and stars and a small sketch of Mallory holding aloft a Pearl of Anishka.

Chapter 17

ENCODA AND BREEDA

Prince Encoda and Kafia had been riding along all morning, both deep in thought. The prince brooded over his brother and the crown slipping away through his fingers. Kafia wondered where in Goaero they would find an imaginary band of gypsies. They stopped for lunch which neither was inclined to eat and sat in silence.

Kafia watched Encoda. Out of the palace he seemed to carry less stature; his thick head of hair seemed less glossy and more greasy. He belched after taking a swig of water and had an irritating habit of clicking his neck. By evening he held just a few remnants of regality for Kafia which were then shattered after he rudely took all the bread and the choicest meat. He then proceeded to relieve himself noisily in the bushes nearby and snored and farted throughout the night. Kafia also came to realise he was not only a poor conversationalist but he had a one-track mind – his desire to be king which, in her opinion, he was poorly equipped for such a role. Not once had he pondered on the safety or happiness of his brother. He threw not one pebble of concern towards Kafia. It was at the moment when she wished a gypsy would come and enchant him away from her that they saw a caravan of wagons coming towards them. Encoda drew up his horse.

"In the name of the Sun, is that...?"

"The gypsies?" Kafia finished the question.

"Quick, behind these trees!" ordered Encoda and he yanked at Kafia's reins, pulling them out of sight.

Breeda sat on a white mare ahead of the wagon trail. She sat tall in the saddle and looked straight ahead. She was a fine horsewoman and a great leader. The party trusted her implicitly and she never wavered in her quest. She rode past Encoda and Kafia as they watched from behind layers of foliage. When the last wagon was a good way ahead Encoda ordered Kafia out of their hiding place.

"Are these the gypsies you followed? I saw no sign of my brother."

Kafia thought quickly.

"Yes sire, I believe so."

"Well, either they are or they are not."

"*Veronica Blanket told lies – all the time,*" answered Kafia.

The prince was learning to ignore these strange outbursts.

"Very well, we shall follow them," he stated.

Encoda was tiring of Kafia. She was sullen and uninspiring. He felt he had nothing in common with her. Apart from the fact she kept talking nonsense – which infuriated him no end – he didn't trust her. He felt she was somehow to blame for the whole debacle. Besides, she had not one snippet of horse skills, slouching in the saddle like a sloven. He tutted out loud. Kafia raised her eyebrows and sighed. She was beginning to think this was more torturous than being banished to Shapeshifter Territory.

At last they heard the noises of a camp; horses whinnied for joy of food, cooking pots clattered, voices chattered and a smell of cooking wafted over to Kafia and Encoda. They held back behind a ridge and waited for nightfall.

In darkness they approached. Breeda was standing in the centre of the camp, lit from behind by the crackling camp fire, her trousered legs splayed, hands on her hips. She threw her head back and let out a burst of laughter. The two men walked away chuckling at the shared joke. Then, serious again as a woman approached her. Breeda put a slender arm around the woman's shoulder and nodded in sympathy. Then she looked squarely at the woman, a hand planted firmly on each shoulder and seemed to be making a promise. They hugged and the woman left. Breeda walked around the camp munching on an offered apple, listening to folk and giving advice. Then she wandered close to where Encoda and Kafia lay hidden. She sat on a wooden crate and a young man came up to her. They were close enough to hear the conversation:

"I understand," Breeda said after the man had spoken. She went on:

"Do you know the Story of the Forest?

There was once a forest which sat resplendently in a fine land. All who entered one of its many portals gave a prayer of thanks, for it led to many great places. A city flanked one side, a paradise the other and on the third edge sat a vast ocean. The forest was fearsome and many got lost in its midst. No man would dare fell a tree for great misfortune would befall him and his kin.

Little by little the city grew and began to encroach on the forest. Still no tree was axed but the roads and houses were built under the canopy which choked and trampled the intricate lifelines of the forest. This was only part of the forest's ailments, for on the side of paradise a swath of coarse ivy insidiously crawled through, sucking the earth dry of water and nourishment. On the third side the salty seas were seeping in, crystallising every leaf into a white and brittle tableau.

For a long time a young man had been lost in the forest. He had long since given up any hope of finding his way out. He built a hut and got used to the forest and even had moments of happiness. But one day the seething city, the strangling ivy and the scorching salt all arrived on his doorstep. It was the dead of night after the pine green daylight turned a dense and earthy dark brown, when the man opened his door and stood in the threshold casting a light on the world. He knew in that moment two things; that he was no longer lost and that he needed to save his forest."

While Kafia was enchanted by the story, Encoda felt prickles along his spine. He felt the hair on his neck and arms stand up and a flood of emotion made his heart throb. His throat constricted with a sob, desperate to break free.

They could not see the expression on the young man's face but Breeda stood and squeezed his arm, smiled warmly at him and walked back into the midst of the camp.

In the silence Kafia heard Encoda's laboured breathing, he lay on his stomach very still for a long time. Sensing a shift in him, she dared not speak and so enjoyed the peaceful moment. She knew she was somehow off the hook. At last he turned to her and said, kindly,

"You go back to the horses, I will stay and keep watch."

The next morning when Kafia awoke, Encoda was not back. She considered leaving but she had his horse and she owed, she thought almost fondly, a goodbye. She led the horses back to Breeda's camp. Encoda was not in the hiding place.

Then she caught sight of him with Breeda, Kafia hung back to watch. It was clear that this was no interrogation. Obviously the king was not there and Encoda did not seem to care. Nor did he seem to mind that they were not the enchanting gypsies of Kafia's story; but Encoda was enchanted. Kafia had never seen him so engrossed in conversation, so animated and – she could barely believe it – smiling. She tied the horses to a tree and slipped into the camp. As she drew near Encoda noticed her and waved her over.

"Ah Kafia, you brought my horse, thank you. I shall be escorting, er, joining Breeda and her companions in the search for my brother. You are welcome to continue with us or do as you please."

"Thank you, Sire. I think I shall return to my family in Carbinia. I am at your service." She gave a polite bow and left as quickly as possible.

Now with a fine horse and a taste of adventurous freedom, the last place Kafia wished to be was back home in the stifling company of her family. She guessed that Breeda and her misguided bunch were not going to find King Bravindo and so, with a sense of responsibility, for she still thought she might have somehow caused his disappearance, she decided it would be up to her to discover his whereabouts.

While Breeda and Encoda were making their way back to Carbinia to pick up the trail of the king, Kafia felt compelled to head south. She had only ever glimpsed King Bravindo. In fact he would probably have been able to hitch a wagon ride anywhere in Goaero without being recognised. Kafia figured he would not be grappling with the wild regions west, north or east. She guessed he was somewhere deep in Pashanka.

Kafia would never know if it was intuition, the Sun Goddess or her secret desire since childhood to visit the Tree of Light, but she headed for the main thoroughfare which split Pashanka lengthways and had led many a foot to Spode, the sacred place of The Tree of Light. Spode was a small village which sat snugly at the base of three great mountains in the Mortlock Range that skirted the south coast of Goaero.

There were a number of travellers on the road. It was a busy stretch, with farmers and traders peddling their wares from town to village and up to the sprawl of Carbinia. Encoda had also despatched small groups of soldiers to search for Bravindo who brought out townsfolk and called on countrymen for information. In addition, there was a holiday in the coming weeks: Mid Sun Day, the height of the Sun Season when Goaerons honoured their Goddess. On the most celebrated day of the year Holy Men would always make the pilgrimage to Spode. Kafia joined the flow, each on their own mission but a thread of common ground charging the way with excitement and energy.

Chapter 18

PASHANKA

For the second time in his adventure Mallory took to the air; first when he had leapt from the height of Mount Or and glided through the air on man-made wings and now he flew under, or rather over, the wings of a Quill. He was nervous at first but he gripped his arms around Que's neck and was astounded at the stretch and strength of his wings. As they gained height Mallory sensed the ease in which Que sat in the air; a lightness, as if ropes had been severed and set him free. The air cooled as they flew over the blue white of the River Lek. Mallory shivered for he could see now the futility of his attempted passage across the ice, her frozen girth stretching interminably from black bank to black bank. Then the breeze in his face warmed as they swept across the Naharancan Plains. Mount Or towered to their right and in the distance to the left he could see Lake Casino and the town's roofs. After a day's flight they landed and set up camp for the night. A Gongalong tree gave them shelter. They woke before the Sun the following morning, and as She yawned awake and gradually shone Her light on Goaero, Mallory and Que took off in the fresh morning mists. As the dreamy eyed light of the Sun caught the land Mallory was in awe of its beauty.

When he had struggled on foot through her craggy lines he had seen every pore, every flaw, each misplaced hair and rough wart. But from here, he saw her as a whole and he understood how each minute feature told her story; a story one could only know in pieces, a story that spirals, curls and jumps but that are all part of the same. He caught sight of a small village, a village which had become a thread of the tale; its inhabitants, people just like his mother, his father, his friends, the Quills, the Blulupians, weaving the tales of their lives. His saw his own thread of blue and silver getting caught in the weave of others pulling and winding but from up here he felt free. He understood the Quills; their wisdom and sorrow, for only they knew the beauty of the place called home. And with this understanding Mallory wept at his knowing and for those without, and Que, sensing Mallory's epiphany, smiled with compassion and love.

By the end of the second day Que swept down and landed on the edge of a small wood. He hurried under its canopy for cover, for there was now a greater amount of villages within the borders of Pashanka. After they had set up camp and eaten, Que described the way to the River Pashanka; a walk through woodland and pasture. On the river Mallory would find a small boat hidden in the rushes. This boat would take him downstream until, at last, he would reach Anishka at the mouth of the river.

As Mallory lay on the soft ground of the copse he had a feeling of homecoming, of returning to a familiar dream. His body recognised the soft fertile soil of Pashanka, he knew this earth which held the treasure of truffles from his childhood.

The next day was a day of rest for Que before he returned to Quelta. Mallory was reluctant to say goodbye so stayed with his friend for the day. They spent their last night speaking words which rested in each other's hearts and wove themselves into a friendship that would last over distance and time. The next morning the men hugged and separated.

"Don't forget!" said Que.

"As if!" replied Mallory.

Mallory hiked his way to the riverbank and looked out for the Quill feather that marked the spot where the boat was moored. As he drew within the forest of tall reeds, Mallory noticed a long boat wedged in front of him. It was solid with room to stretch out for sleeping and watertight storage space under the seats. Mallory smiled; it was not the boat that caused his lips to curl upward but his old friend Jim, sitting on the prow of the boat waving jauntily.

"James! What a mornin'! A fine day for a punt down the river. A bit like ol' times, eh?"

"And a good morning to you, Jim! Long time no see. What you been up to?"

Mallory could not contain his delight and relief at seeing the rascal again and slapped him on his back.

"Ah, you know, hanging around, waiting for the boat to come in!"

"Shall we?"

"We shall, to be sure."

And they pushed off into the flat open river which flowed languidly through Pashanka; the life and soul of Goaero. For a while Mallory enjoyed the poetry of the river; its tinkling song accompanied by birds and bees, the sweeping architecture of weeping willows and the maze of roots that held the river in place. Mallory waved at Pashankans (who were not blue, or hardened hole-diggers or graced with wings). He breathed in the sultry air and let the oars lie in the hull of the boat; Mallory gauged the speed sufficient without added exertion and even Jim ceased his chatter and gazed dreamily ahead. As dusk washed over the day they pulled into the bank and ate some provisions Que had left in the lockers. The pair slept like kittens in a hammock slung between two branches.

By now the Sun Season was in its first days. Warm morning breezes quickly blew away the chill night air. They set off again after a leisurely breakfast. At midday Mallory suggested pulling up for some food. Jim agreed and they moored next to a couple of old men fishing.

"Afternoon!" greeted Mallory as he leapt to the ground.

"Aye, 'tis," came the reply.

"Caught anything?"

"Nah, not much adrift today."

"Could you tell me the nearest town to here?"

"Aye..." The old man rested his rod on his knee.

"'Bout half a day's sail downstream, on t'other side, you'll come to Biron."

"Thank you, sir, may many fine fishes follow."

The man nodded. Mallory hopped back into the boat and, forgetting lunch, pushed off.

"What's the hurry now, James? It's a beautiful day."

"Yes, and what better excuse for a holiday. Jim, my village is about a day's walk west of Biron. I thought this stretch of the river felt familiar. My father used to sell truffles here."

"And...?"

"And, I'm going home, to visit my mother, Jim."

Jim said nothing, raised an eyebrow and faced fore.

Sure enough, by late afternoon houses came into view, dogs barked as they floated by, horses drank from the water and children splashed in the shallows. Biron was a small town, but busy enough. The Pashanka River provided a good flow of traffic, and although the town was situated on the fringes of Pashanka, traders still came to sell their goods and buy Pashankan plums which thrived in the region. The cool night air and the red minerals of the Naharancan Plains on the other side of the river produced large sweet plums. And, unlike Mallory, those who noses greeted the aromas of the air, could inhale the tart spicy plum scent that wafted from the distillery in the town centre.

Mallory moored up and jumped onto the bank. He paid the boat keeper to watch his boat and strode into town.

Mallory had visited Biron once with his father as a young boy. The trip on their rickety horse and cart had been a hard one, leaving behind the softness of his mother for the hardness of man and road. The town had left a deep impression on him, so far removed was it from his rural home. The images etched into his memories began to uncoil and spring into his mind. He passed rows of buildings crammed together with the upper floors leaning perilously out above the streets below. Young Mallory had been afraid they were about to topple down on top of him. His father had cuffed him on the ear for walking in the middle of the road and getting in the way of carts and traders. He passed an inn, The Plum Tin it said on the hanging sign. Mallory recalled secretly following his father in there, after he had supposedly gone to sleep in the cart's tray under a scratchy sack; the truffle crumbs itching his skin and inviting rats to nibble at the corners. Unable to sleep Mallory had sneaked into the inn. Ruddy cheeked men lined up along the bar, laughing loudly, talking and jeering. His father sat at a table tossing back small cups of ruby juice, one for him, then one for the woman who sat firmly upon his knee. Mallory remembered the uneasy feeling he had, the irregularity of the vision. His father leered at the woman and whispered something in her ear. At that terrible moment his eyes fell on Mallory. The glowering look gave away no hint of emotion, Mallory backed away and fled outside to the cart.

Mallory did not see his father until lunchtime the next day. He had loitered around waiting for the longest time before he went to look for him. The inn door was locked so Mallory had kicked a stone along and kept in sight of the cart. The stone tumbled away down an alley and Mallory followed it. The pebble stopped at a brown pile of raggedy material and Mallory bent down to pick it up. Suddenly the rags came to life and an ancient looking man grabbed Mallory's wrist. Mallory jumped in fright and tried to pull away but the grip was as tight as an unripe plum around its stone. A head emerged from the mass, his pockmarked skin revolted Mallory but the face peered closer to reveal yellow sharp teeth. He spoke.

"Death will meet you five times..." A wet cough escaped from his mouth and Mallory managed to pull away, racing out onto the main street, not hearing the voice continue:

"And you will invite him to stay but twice."

Mallory sprinted back to the cart repulsed and shaking to see his father standing in the back of the cart yelling out his name in fury.

"You sneaky little rat, get here now, I ought to whip your pathetic hide. Where 'av you been?" he thundered.

Mallory cowered into the cart, his father whipped the horse mercilessly until they were clear of the town and into the country. His father stank of spirits, sweetly nauseating and he began to nod off at the reigns. Every now and then a rock in the road would cause his head to bob up and cursing he would whip the poor nag's battered rump. Mallory kept watch until they came to the crossroads. The horse continued to go straight but Mallory knew that their village was left. He sat beside his father and gently took the reins, pulling the cart to the left. Mallory remembered feeling a sense of purpose in that moment, a proud sense of power and control. He also remembered wishing his father dead and gone as he sat within the fug of his drunkenness.

Mallory had not thought about these things for years – that life was a different life. He stepped into the alleyway as he had all those years before and looked for a pile of raggedy old cloth, but all he could see were the sticky barrels of spent plum rum and the litter of broken wood and chicken bones that usually inhabit those places. Jim called him from the street.

"James, come here now, I don't like the look of that hole."

So Mallory turned back and met the noisy daylight once again.

"Death will meet you five times..." Mallory repeated the words he had heard all those years ago.

"Well, four times now, James, I reckon ol' Death came to us on River Lek, we'd of been Death's guest that night if it weren't for the Sun Sand."

They carried on but Mallory was tired of walking. His solid army boots were wearing thin, he felt a heaviness settle. He secured a pony to take them to Cortly; the place where he was born. Again the blood-warm breeze and singing birds cast a soporific mood over Mallory who recounted his childhood step by step back to his birthplace. Tunes that his mother sang floated into his head and he hummed in swaying time to his horse's gait. She had had a beautiful voice. She would sing stories that would loop and lull as if the notes were part of the tale. She would sing while foraging for truffles as if singing would bring them into being. She sung as she carried the sacks made of special grasses that carried the truffles to market and she would sing Mallory to sleep even when he was no longer a small child. To Mallory she was the antithesis of his father.

It was then Mallory remembered that trip again, he realised it had been the turning point of his relationship with his father, the axle his life had spun on. Prior to the trip his father had been gruff and strict, but had never laid a finger on Mallory, but it was on waking from his snore laden slumber that he had snatched the reigns from his son's hands and struck him forcefully across the side of his head. So unexpected was it that Mallory fell right off the cart and had to run, limping to catch up, scrambling onto the tray. Mallory traced the resulting scar on his knee, he fingered the welt that ran behind his ear, the roughly stitched gash on his shoulder and felt his nose that was slightly leaning to one side; all inflicted from that day on, by his father.

But it was only now, as a grown man that he realised his father had hated truffling, that he had loved the trips to town but hated the return, that he wanted out, that he wanted his son to take it away from him, that he had sired a son that would do just the opposite, that he had hated his senseless un-smelling son who had delivered him his dreams and then taken them away; his only son.

As Mallory got closer to his village a sense of dread rose up in him, a sense of how much his father resented him. The tunes of his mother petered out and the balmy air began to lay heavy on him. Up a hill they rode and as the path curled around its summit there it lay; a small collection of cottages, gathered together like a group of gossiping women, in the valley. A mixture of familiarity and fear washed over him like an icy wave and it was only his steed that saw its chance of hay, water and rest that propelled him forward.

Not much had changed in Cortly; there were a few more houses, expanding the village's waistline along the valley floor but by now dusk was falling and Mallory was tired, he did not have the energy to look around. He dismounted outside his parent's house, he watched the window's flickering light and felt suspended in time. In a daze his feet walked him up the path in between flowers and grasses, he knocked on the door, a shuffle, a small "oh" of surprise, the door swung open. The woman looked at him as one looks at a stranger at your door in the evening.

"Ma?" asked Mallory, his voice sifting through the gravel in his throat.

"Acorn? Oh my....!" She threw her arms around his neck and sobbed into his shoulder.

Chapter 19

CORTLY

As Kafia travelled further away from Prince Encoda her spirits lifted. For the first time in her life she was free; no family, no royal power, no job, only the secrets remained and even they were leaking fast. The Sun beat down on her face, the throng on the road was boisterous and convivial; breaking out into song, racing their horses and entertaining each other. Some locals would catch up with the Holy Men to take advice, discuss the future of their children or receive a blessing. Some travelled onward swiftly, others stopped frequently to rest, and so there was an ever changing panorama of people for Kafia to watch. She would get to know some from their snippets of chat, she would guess the stories of others. There were many villages on the way but fewer towns. Often these settlements had one or no inns, or they were full, so she would camp next to her horse with fellow travellers. One day the road took them along the ridge of a line of hills and she could make out a small village on the valley floor. The day was too young and the descent too steep for many but Kafia desired a bed and a wash so she peeled off the main route and headed down.

The narrow track was well trod and wound down the hillside through low oak trees and large boulders. She arrived at the village. A warm fug of spicy air hovered over the cluster of houses at its centre, a few newer dwellings were scattered further along the edge of the old riverbed. The dried bed of rocks provided a playground for children. She was pleased to find an inn, it was humble but empty. She was directed to her room and flopped onto the mattress in delight. She washed with soap in the outhouse and pumped fresh clean water over her skin and rinsed out her dusty clothes.

Kafia emerged from her room fresh and renewed but her hunger was ruining her mood. In the village she found a bakery, and then took a path that led away from the buildings. She reached a plateau a short way up the hillside and chose a smooth round boulder to sit against. She curled her back over the warm rock devouring her pastries and watching the gentle rhythm of the village folk.

As peace washed over her she began to ponder on the recent happenings of her life. She felt as if she was a stalk of corn that just missed the scythe on each pass. First she had managed to be party to Encoda's secret, then asked to reveal it, then her story about the missing king coming true. Slowly she picked apart the threads, seeing if they were all joined and how she could make it into something beautiful.

Voices interrupted her reverie and she noticed a couple below her walking. The young man was short and broad of shoulder with a shaggy head of bi-coloured hair. The woman was much older, slight and frail and he tenderly propped her up with a supporting arm. At first Kafia could not make out the words until they came closer. Suddenly the man dropped to his knees.

"Here, here Ma, and over here. I'll mark the spot."

"How can you know, son?"

"I, I don't know, I just feel it. They are here too, pass me that stone."

"But even I cannot smell them so early in the season, and your nose is..."

"It's like I've got different ways of smelling now, Ma, I just know where they are. Let's walk on, I'll mark the spots."

They meandered away again. Kafia watched. The woman turned to her son and laid her hands on his cheeks, then hugged him hard. Kafia could see the man's face, saw his eyes glistening and watched him press his face into his mother's shoulder. She swallowed the bulge constricting her throat and knocked a stray tear off her cheek. Something about this man fascinated Kafia. She did not want to lose sight of him just yet so she gently stood up and trod softly behind them. Presently the pair sat down and the old woman unwrapped a parcel of food, offering some to her son. After a while of chewing in silence, she lifted her chin and spoke softly to the man.

"Acorn? You remember that story I used to tell you?"

"You told me so many, Ma."

He smiled at her with a twinkle in his eye.

"Don't chaff me!" she clipped his ear gently. "You know the one. About the rabbit, it was your favourite, I can't imagine 'ow many times I told it."

"And you never told it the same way twice, that's why I loved it so. How'd it start...?"

"THE RABBIT AND THE WOLF

There was once a rabbit called Lionel because from the moment he was an itty-bitty rabbit he wanted to be a lion.

"Go on," Mallory urged.

Ma shifted her old bones to be as comfortable as they could and began:

There was once a rabbit called Lionel because from the moment he was an itty-bitty rabbit he wanted to be a lion. His Ma 'ad no idea 'ow he knew bout lions, for as you know, there are no longer such beasts in Goaero, only in fairy tales. And his Ma 'ad no time to tell 'im fairy tales on account of his seventy-six brothers and sisters. Lionel 'imself was not sure why he wanted to be a lion, but he knew it felt good when he roared at the top of his voice, and how powerful he felt when he leapt from rock to rock – and how happy he felt when he purred from the bottom of his belly. And presently Lionel began to look a bit like a lion with thick strong whiskers and a lustrous mane of golden fur around 'is neck. As Lionel grew up 'is Ma and Pa got fed up of his prowling and preening and sent 'im out into the world. But Lionel wasn't afraid because he felt the fearlessness of a lion beat in his heart even though from the outside he just looked like a strange little rabbit.

One day when Lionel was practising 'is roar, a wolf bounded up to him and stopped, his black pointed nose one whisker away from Lionel's twitching one and stared intently at Lionel's soft blue eyes with his own yellow gleaming ones. He snarled back his lips to reveal a handsome row of pure white shining fangs which dwarfed even Lionel's front chewing ones, and said:

"Oh do stop that racket, I am trying to dig a burrow back here!"

And being lion-hearted Lionel, he felt not a quiver of fear and replied in a rather superior way:

"Dig a burrow with those great paws? You will start a landslide, my dear wolf!"

The wolf looked at Lionel and, blinking back tears, put his tail between his legs and howled:

"Ohhhhh! I will never be a rabbit. I am too big and too fierce and not at all fluffy. You are the first rabbit to ever talk to me,

how will I ever become a rabbit?"

Lionel nodded in sympathy for he knew what it was to be a lion in rabbits' clothing, although he was a little puzzled as to why a wolf wanted to be a rabbit, of all things. But he wished to be helpful so he spoke again:

"Av you tried wiggling your nose around and about like this?"

And Lionel's nose darted and quivered and danced around his face like a spinning top. The wolf examined Lionel's nose and tried but his whole head jolted from side to side and up and down until a long drip emerged from it and the wolf sneezed loudly and Lionel thought he looked more like a frog trying to catch flies, and smiled into his paws. The wolf sat on 'is tail and licked 'imself despondently.

"Mmmm," said Lionel, seeing 'is problem.

"Av you tried flicking your ears this a' way and that a' way, like this?"

And Lionel flipped one long silky ear back while the other went forward and finished with one bent over at a jaunty angle.

The wolf watched and nodded. He screwed his face up and wiggled 'is flat brow up and down, but 'is stiff sharp ears only moved slightly outward and always together. Lionel thought he looked more like a cow chewing a porcupine and stifled a laugh. The wolf dropped 'is haunches and sighed deeply.

"Mmmm," said Lionel, seeing 'is problem.

"Av you tried jumping up and flicking your tail from side to side, like this?"

And Lionel hopped this a' way and that a' way around the wolf. The wolf watched closely and tried the same but he just kicked his back legs out and Lionel thought he looked more like a donkey trying to do a backward somersault. Lionel let out a snort of laughter.

"Like this, like this!" sang Lionel hopping about again, and immensely enjoying 'imself as a rabbit, when:

SNAP!

The wolf opened his impressive jaws and ate Lionel in one bite.

Mallory gasped.

"Oh Ma! That's not how the story ended."

"No, but like you said, it never comes out the same way twice."

Mallory looked dismayed.

"Aw, Acorn, think about it though," she said gently.

"Lionel would never 'ave found 'appiness in trying to be a lion, and besides, he spent 'is last few moments bounding in joy as a rabbit should. And that lion heart of 'is went into the wolf who, from that day on, knew not if he was wolf or rabbit or lion and he wandered the land alone and in confusion for the rest of 'is sorry days."

Kafia sat and thought about the tale. She wondered if she was trying to be someone other than a Secret Keeper and if she ever would...

Before she knew it, the wind picked up and brought her out of her thoughts. She saw that the man and his mother had gone and so gathered herself up to return to the inn.

The man's image stayed with Kafia; vainly she looked out for him for the rest of the day. That night she slept deeply and dallied around the village the next morning, hoping to see him. Finally, she left the gentle place and led her horse up the hill sighing. Eventually she reached the road again and mounted. She set off, putting the village and man in a pocket in her heart and set her mind once again on the road ahead.

Chapter 20

ANISHKA

"He is dead."

"I am sorry, James."

"I wished it once, you know. Now he is."

"Aye."

"She thought me dead too."

"And you are alive."

"She...half mad with grief, half mad with loneliness."

"You brought her peace."

"I hope. She had a cradle. She said a baby was to come."

"Maybe it will."

Mallory raised an eyebrow at Jim and snorted.

"Her wild predictions are yet to reveal themselves."

"Aye...not yet anyway."

Mallory raised an eyebrow again.

"Come on, let's move along faster. I am on a quest for the king, this truffle air makes me drowsy."

Mallory had spent ten days in Cortly with his mother and had completely forgotten about his quest. The days rolled by like waves of hypnotism as his mother relayed the story of his dying father and Mallory told his mother about his life. It was on the last day that Mallory had finally got to the part where he had been summoned by the prince that he remembered, as if the story was unfolding afresh. Before he left he promised her he would visit again and often and he left her sobbing into her apron.

In two days they were back on the river paddling along with the current. Whenever they stopped to eat or rest Mallory would take out his map and study it intently. It gave him a renewed sense of purpose, the firm lines leading him to where he wanted to go, there was no room for doubt and with the Bloodstone nestled safely in his pocket, Mallory felt the thrill of confidence ripple through him as he had on the first day in the jungle. He breathed in a deep breath of satisfaction.

"Que told me to pull up here," he pointed to a spot down river on the map. "Any further and we may get caught up in Vandret Falls and swept out to Shapeshifter Territory."

The following day they turned a sharp bend in the river. Immediately the landscape changed. The lush oaks and willows petered out and low shrub-like trees with wiggling branches and pale, almost violet, bark spread across the flat land. The country around Anishka was no less colourful than upstream but it held an iridescent quality.

"We'll leave the boat here," said Mallory. "This is the salt line, the outer reaches of Vandret Falls; our feeble raft would get swept through the rapids. Jim, my friend, we are back on our good old two feet."

The map showed the town to the west of the river mouth which opened out into a large almost circular bay. Mallory and Jim struck directly towards the road into Anishka which ran a short way from the river's bank. The Zoto trees grew together thickly and their long branches tangled with their neighbour's creating a fuzzy thicket overhead under which Mallory barely scraped. Clearings would occasionally open up before them which housed strange haphazardly scattered columns.

The bases of the columns were large oval stones, about the size of a big head. Five or six decreasing oval stones were stacked on top. The stones were coloured a deep purple-black which glittered like granite. Mallory had never seen such a structure and could not work out whether it was a living animal or dead mineral. When he tapped on one it sounded hollow yet when he tried to lift it, it was as solid as the root of a Gongalong tree. As he studied the crust it looked moist and glistening, yet to touch it was as dry as the Naharancan Plains. The sparkling specks leapt out at the eye yet seemed to be set in an inky sky of stars. Their mystery unsettled Mallory but he and Jim pushed on towards Anishka.

It was midday when they broke out of the bush onto the road. Anishka was a busy port, the only safe harbour and least dangerous Portal to sea. It was rich in pearl and fish; the salty delicacies the sailors caught were highly sought after in Goaero. Immediately they passed traders travelling to and from Anishka. They could see the rear of a wagon a little way down the road.

"I suppose you'll be disappearing again soon?" Mallory said

"Aye, you know I have an aversion to folk."

"Where do you go, Jim?"

"Oh, here and there, round and about." He riddled.

"You're a hard man to pin down."

"Aye, that'll be 'cos I t'aint a man."

"Mmmmm," pondered Mallory.

The wagon ahead had paused; a man was adjusting the horse's bridle.

"Good day, kind Sir." Mallory greeted him. "Would you see to giving me a lift into town?"

The man looked at him blankly.

"I'll pay you for your trouble," Mallory added.

"No need. I'd be glad of the company. Spin me a yarn and I'll be a happy man."

They sat side by side and the man flicked the reigns. The horse jerked before settling into a steady rhythm.

"Mallory; James, Regiment of the Lion's Head, pleased to meet you."

"Carl Corner, likewise."

Corner waited expectantly. Mallory took his cue, closed his eyes until it was there, and begun.

THE STORY OF DRAGONFLY

There was once a fountain shaped like a bell and from it ran a river. Many people came to the fountain to listen to the magical sounds of the water drops and watch crystal dragonflies emerge from the spume. One day a mother was so mesmerized that her baby fell out of her arms and into the water and quickly swirled away down the river. The mother tore at her hair, screamed in agony, and wept bitter tears into the fountain so that the delicate chimes turned to deep tolls of doom. The melancholic music drove all the people away except for the mother who followed the river to search for her child. Soon the river split into two and she begged the Sun to cleave her also in two. The Sun Goddess was sympathetic to the poor woman and acquiesced. So on one stream She sent the woman's body floating on the water and on the other the woman's spirit - one with eyes but no soul; the other with soul but no eyes.

Now the baby who had been in his mother's arms had been trying to catch the dragonflies and as he fell he caught one in each hand. The child, so pure and light in spirit was no effort for the dragonflies to keep him aloft and they winged him away into the spray. The child dipped and soared in delight until the fountain music changed and made him cry. He remembered his mother's face but when he went to look for her, she was gone.

The child became a young man and because he always had a crystal dragonfly in each of his two pockets, he was known as Dragonfly. For many years he searched for his long lost mother. One day he was fishing at the river and he caught a fish that was so beautiful and so easy to net that he almost went home there and then. But then he saw a forlorn woman looking at him from the opposite bank. Dragonfly waded through the water and looked at the woman's vacant expression.

"Do I know you?" she asked.

"Yes you do," he said and took her hand and led her to his house. They ate the fish he had caught, and then the woman suddenly regained life and she threw her arms around the boy, sobbing with joy. For the spirit of the mother had entered

the fish that Dragonfly had caught that day and the woman had eaten it. Once again mother and child were whole and they lived happily ever after.

Corner remained silent for a long time after Mallory had uttered the last word. They sat and reflected in the comforting click of the horse's footsteps. Eventually Corner turned to Mallory and with watery eyes thanked him hoarsely. Mallory just smiled back and they jiggled along in silence until nightfall.

As day dawned the following morning, Mallory knew that they were on the outskirts of Anishka. He could hear voices and barking dogs, his skin felt the prickle of salty air and strangers. He sat up and saw Corner doing the same.

"Good morning!" hailed Mallory.

"Likewise" replied Corner.

"Mr Corner, I'm guessing you know your way around this town...could you tell me where I might find a pearl?"

Corner burst out laughing.

"Everywhere and nowhere, Mr Mallory."

Mallory sighed inwardly; he could see that this was not going to be straightforward.

"Well...where would one begin Mr Corner?"

"At the docks, follow this road through town til you reach the water."

"Are you going that way?"

"No Mr Mallory I'm not, I'm going to visit my mother. Good luck to you Sir, it's been a pleasure."

"Likewise!" grinned Mallory. They shook hands and Mallory headed off into a stirring town.

The breath of the early Sun Season wafted a shimmering breeze over the town. The road was cobblestoned with glistening violet pebbles whose rounded shapes echoed the curved houses on either side. The thatched roofs swelled over the walls generously, which housed nests of pink tinged seabirds. The air had a metallic grainy taste on the back of Mallory's throat. He began to realise that instead of waking, the town was busying itself with a surge of returning fishermen who were walking back in through front doors instead of out. The air was filled with strange accents and the thud and clatter of netted shellfish on doorsteps. As he got deeper into town more bodies came his way and he was swept along into the flow which led him into a marketplace. Men and women were clamouring, waving money in the air and throwing bags of fish and produce around. Suddenly a table turned over behind him and an avalanche of black shiny shells covered Mallory's feet. A fight had broken out the other side of the upturned table between two men. Mallory crunched his feet out of the shells but slid on the shellfish until he lost balance and fell.

Suddenly the two men were on top of him thrusting punches and clutching at each other's throats and hair. Mallory felt a sharp pain in his leg as a foot kicked him and sharp shells cut into his back under the weight of the two grappling men. Mallory's extra sense suddenly kicked in.

"One of you will DIE!" Mallory's shout and strange accent cut through the men's fury and they stopped.

"One of you will die if you don't stop this now," Mallory said sombrely.

One of the men opened his palm and a knife which was poised at his opponent's stomach, fell to the ground. "Horse-licking weakling!" he growled. The men looked at each other and backed away. Mallory winced as he stood, his leg oozed blood through the rip in his trousers. A young woman helped him up.

"Here let me help you. I'll take a look at that."

He allowed her to lead him from the resuming market to a small shop in the main street. Inside the shop, the walls were lined with shelves that followed the rounded contours of the walls. Herbs and tinctures filled the shelves along with dried fish and unidentifiable insects.

"Are you a healer?" he asked.

"My name is Samia, I am a herbalist," she replied. "Sit here, show me your wound."

Mallory peeled up his trouser leg removing a painful strip of congealed blood. Samia washed the wound and smeared on a ground root. The pain receded and his skin felt numb.

"What is your name and where are you from?" she asked.

The directness of the question took Mallory aback, no one apart from Que and his family had ever shown interest in him.

"James Ardent Mallory. I have travelled..." He was not sure if he could or should tell her his entire itinerary, "...from Carbinia."

"And what are you hoping to find in Anishka, James Ardent Mallory?"

Mallory was unsure of her tone and questioning.

"Ur, a pearl."

"Ah, you seek wisdom and mystery!"

Mallory was beginning to wonder if they were speaking the same language.

"Do you know how I could find one?" he ventured.

"The docks. He who searches must start at the docks."

"Well, thank you for your help," he said and rose to leave.

"Anytime, James Ardent Mallory, anytime."

Mallory hurried out of the shop into the shimmering mid-morning air, he continued down to the docks against the stream of people heading into town. As he got closer, the streets opened up and as he passed the last building a wide expanse of deep purple water lay before him. It rippled and whooshed onto the silver dotted sand and caused rainbow prisms to arc through the light mist. Mallory stared in wonder. He had never seen the sea, such a vastness of water, he had not even contemplated its splendour. He could see the coast curl around and small boats dotted the surface. Where the land ceased the water turned black and a cloud rose above it before the gap joined onto the land on the other side and started its sweep around to his right. On this side, close by, a wooden jetty stretched out. Dozens of stout vessels were tied to either side; they floated like reclining ladies after a hard day's work. He could see men sloshing down the decks with brooms. Mallory glanced again towards the black water which seemed to undulate like a snakes head, in and out of the bay.

"There lies the Vandret Falls," a voice drifted over Mallory's shoulder. Mallory started and turned.

"And beyond the sea..." Mallory mused, captivated by the thought of an even greater volume of water.

"Aye. Jethro Subani. I came to thank you."

Mallory recognised the man as the fighter who narrowly escaped a knife in his stomach.

"Oh, it's you, I, er, you are welcome. I'm Mallory."

Mallory offered his hand. The tall man had bleached white hair and fair skin. His white stubble gave him a salt encrusted air. He took Mallory's hand in both his and shook it sincerely.

"I'd like to repay you," said Jethro.

"I would like to go out to sea to find a pearl," stated Mallory.

Jethro smiled. "I can take you out to sea..."

Mallory nodded, trying not to look too excited and remain business-like.

"Meet me here at high Moon, my ship is Sea Hawk. Go and get some rest, it is a long night's work."

Chapter 21

ARFAN

Kafia had continued to enjoy observing her fellow travellers. She would have been happy to remain detached but gradually as her presence became familiar, the travellers sensed her secret-keeping and one by one moved in to unburden their innermost revelations. Secrets by definition are happenings that one does not want to be made public and Kafia began to feel tainted by them. The gruesome, the dirty, the dishonest deeds jangled inside her. Ever since her desire to know Encoda's secret, the old ones had welled up and popped out almost every time she opened her mouth. She felt every sorry secret smouldering away and it was making her sick.

In a few days she would reach the town of Arfan which sat at the foot of the Mortlock mountain range. She had heard stories about Arfan; mystical tales of witches and magic. She decided she would stay there for a few days to try to find a cure for her ills. After two days the flat block of mountains that had lain far off in the distance suddenly appeared to grow. They loomed ahead of her swathed in a pink shroud of mist which took the cruel edge off the jagged rocks that sat on top. Already the roadsides were dotted with houses, and lanes leading off to the outer suburbs of Arfan.

The town was a stopping place before or after one had tackled the mountains. Kafia followed the street as it led into the busy centre. Groups of Goaerons pooled in the squares, six of which circled a large space right in the middle of town. Inside the circular plaza sat a huge building. It was the largest building – other than the palace – Kafia had ever seen; its grandeur thrilled and unsettled her. The high walls shimmered and rose to form three tall spires that disappeared into the clouds. Mirrored tiles dispersed the Sun's light which gave Kafia a chilling shiver. The gift of the Sun was always welcomed in Goaero, not reflected, as this roof seemed to do. Kafia circled the building. It seemed there was no entrance yet she noticed one or two people somehow emerging. Unnerved she walked away down a street that led to Fargo Square. Here a market was in full swing. Old women shouted out, listing herbs and tinctures, men sat behind stalls selling dried fruits, fish and brightly coloured liquids. Unable to identify much there, Kafia took a busy road leading out which led to another hive of activity. Gruin Square hosted musicians, poets and bards. Each filled a different spot and yelled for attention. Words and notes seemed to float in the air, rhyming or clashing, creating weird rhythms which snapped at your ankles. The din made her feel light-headed so she tripped through and out the other side. Here she came into a narrow street, the buildings leaning in towards each other which led to the third square. Carillon Square was a haven of peace in comparison. It held a pond in its midst and the surrounding houses bowed towards it, leaving the air dark and dank. Unsettled by its eerie quiet

Kafia hurried out the other side to the fourth, Begly Square. This was awash with dusty pilgrims and road-weary traders. All the doors were opening and closing as people left or arrived. Kafia noticed a few familiar faces and guessed it was here she would find accommodation.

Kafia selected a likely looking inn, walked up to a wide door and walked through. A large room held a crowd of people. Many had bags on their backs and staffs at the ready. A squat middle-aged lady bustled up to her.

"Looking for a bed m'dear?" she asked.

Kafia nodded.

"Orright, high, low or middlin'?"

"What do you mean?"

"Ah! First time here, is it my lovely? Follow me!"

The lady led Kafia along a corridor and opened one of the doors along it. Inside was a large dormitory. The room housed about twenty beds. Some sat squarely on the floor but above them, two tiers of beds floated in the air.

"Oh!" exclaimed Kafia "How?"

"Magic of course! Now, bottom's five pieces, middlin's ten and top's fifteen."

"Oh, um..."

"Safest and most comfy at the top, plus more private."

"Well, top then please. But how do I...?" Kafia indicated at the height of the levitating bed.

"Use the ladder, dear," answered the woman.

"What ladder?"

With that, the woman bent down and lifted Kafia's foot onto an invisible rung. Kafia cautiously climbed up thin air until she reached the floating mattress. She flung her bag onto the bed and felt her way down, feeling dizzy and weak.

"You look a bit peaky, lass. Go on to Fillery Square and get yourself a feed."

"*Harvey James talks to plants. George Little wears a codpiece – all the time.*" It was getting worse.

The landlady gave Kafia a queer look and hurried away. Kafia shouted out her thanks feeling quite embarrassed and followed the directions. The fifth square was filled with eating houses and food stalls. Kafia sat, ate and drank until she felt a little better.

Fatigue took over her. She made her way back to the inn, successfully climbed the non-existent ladder and slept soundly until the morning.

That morning Kafia set out determined to find a cure. She found the innkeeper and asked her where she might find balms for certain ailments.

"That'll be Herkon Square, the next one after Fillery," she announced before bowling off to business.

And so Kafia came to visit the sixth and final square of Arfan. The houses lining the square were decorated with strange emblems; feathers, ribbons and other paraphernalia all shaped into a three-pointed star. The plaza itself was crammed with small tables, chairs and stalls under umbrellas. Strange looking characters manned each spot. Most were old women, some younger and a few men. Townspeople and visitors strode around asking questions of the stallholders, others sat, already engrossed in conversation. Kafia realised she was in the Square of Witches. This was a general description of those who worked here. Some did indeed weave magic spells and spun curses, but others saw into possible futures, some conversed with the past or the Sun herself. There were healers, sealers, feelers and others who just gave good advice or lent open ears.

Kafia wandered around, unsure where to start.

"*Rory Jump killed a man,*" she murmured to no one in particular.

She was worried she was doing the right thing, worried she could not change her fate, worried she would be eating secrets forever more until she grew fat with other peoples' trickery and subterfuge. Maybe she *was* a lion in rabbits' clothes, or maybe she was just a rabbit, her thoughts were getting blurred.

"Veronica Blanket and Jeffery Biggle eloped to Casino," popped out unexpectedly.

And then she wondered if the secrets were eating her, gnawing from the inside out until there was nothing left but a sheer shell, a ghost.

"Mr and Mrs Smith never were married," she mumbled.

She wanted to know what would happen to the secrets once out, who looked after them, if they would return to the source to wreak havoc, or got into the wrong hands.

"Jeffery Biggle gambled – all the time," sobbed out.

The questions and secrets riddled her as she tried to pick her way methodically through the rows of witches. But a flash of colour would catch her eye, then her ear would cup a phrase and she would veer off in another direction until she had lost all bearings. She spun around, looking for a clue to her whereabouts, trying to fix on a landmark but faces kept whizzing past her, voices called out, hands yanked, colours swirled like kaleidoscope, bodies pushed, bells rang, shrieks, ribbons, flashes, lights whirred. She panicked, unable to fix on any still thing, the market was a blur, she spun around and around, unable to stop or think or cry or...and then one face shone out, motionless. She stumbled toward the face, the only thing she could focus on. The face's arms caught Kafia.

"Sit, sit child."

Kafia lowered herself unsteadily on a small wooden milking stool and collapsed her head into her hands. When the dizziness ceased she looked up at the woman.

"Pearl Blanket (Alby, Veronica and Henry's mother) drank grog – all the time," Kafia wept.

"My name is Marika. Here, take some water."

"Thank you. I am Kafia."

Marika had an open face, her eyes looked directly at Kafia, she was still and loose. She did not talk but quietly engaged with Kafia. Kafia felt the woman to be an open space waiting to be filled. She felt something within her tug, felt a bubble shift upwards until almost gagging with it Kafia opened her mouth and spoke.

"Gideon Boot lied to his brother about the money...that is not the first, they are escaping...*Jimmy Jank cheated on his girlfriend*...I don't know why...*Bill Crinkle stole a horse from Bru Linkin*...I don't want anymore. Please...*Jarrad Poppin cries himself to sleep every night*...please...*Marsha Crump likes girls and not boys*...make them stop!"

Marika smiled and tutted shaking her head. "You are not the first Kafia. I have been haranguing the council to round up the Secret-Keepers for many a season now. They need some guidance, you see. It's a hard road we find ourselves on, my dear. You are lucky you've made it here. Many don't," she tutted, "many don't."

"You can help me?" Kafia brightened.

"Hmmm, well, we can shift things, shall we say."

"Can you shift these secrets?" Kafia asked, her eyes wide with hope.

"I will have to consult first. There is usually something we can do. Why don't you tell me how you came to be here, Kafia."

It was a relief for Kafia to spill her story, for her to be the one to talk for once. Kafia told Marika how she worked at the palace and that Prince Encoda had entrusted her with a secret, how she had made up a new story, that had strangely come true and how now the king really was missing and that she felt responsible for finding him. When she finished Marika nodded.

"I need to consult the council. Meet me at the southern entrance to the Zarbor at high Moon."

PART TWO

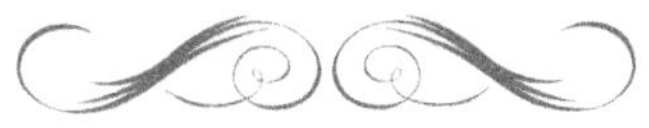

THE BOY

At dusk in a small alcove a boy willed himself to sleep. He was not sure if the alcove would still be there in the morning. Only yesterday had he seen his shack disappear into a puddle of crabs and cold water. He had been lucky then, as he had been fishing further up the beach. He had noticed the purple horizon roll towards him and felt its icy chill as it prepared to feast on his home. He had swept up his basket and his piece of cloth; a raggedy, faded red tablecloth that morphed into a backpack, a towel, a sheet, a sarong and ultimately his comforter. Then he ran, chased by the violet frozen fingers of the Beach Eater into the bush to the waterfall where he collapsed for the night. Normally this place would have given him no concern; it was some way inland and he had never seen another dweller here. But the Beach Eater had been hungry of late and this was the seventh time in one season he had fled from its clutches. He had not seen his only friend, Mutilin, the sea turtle, since that first attack and missed him sorely. Before the Beach Eater, Mutilin used to give him rides to the salt flat lakes and occasionally out to sea where the boy would dive for sea lupins and Sand Diamonds. He would peel the lupins and eat them with coconut juice and play pick-up with the Sand Diamonds. Then he made them into a necklace to keep them on him at all times – five round clear balls flecked with gold and, unusually, pierced through with a hole. He would finger them around his neck as he drifted off to sleep at night. He dreamt, as always of Guffer. In his dreams, Guffer had Sand Diamonds for eyes and they would blink to life. The old man smiled fondly at the boy, cracking his face as he wept sand from the sparkling eyes. Then Guffer would collapse like a sand castle, reaching toward the boy, dissolving into the beach. The boy would awake to the faint call of his own name, which would then escape him. Every night the dream was becoming briefer and the boy would wake in a panic, holding his hand toward the disappearing image, unable to remember his name.

Many years ago, around twelve or thirteen, Guffer had been despatched with the newborn child to the edge of Goaero; Shapeshifter Territory. Guffer had already been in his late seventies but he was in good health and pure of heart. He loved the boy and raised him well. It was about a year ago, as he was approaching the end of his boyhood that Guffer failed to wake up from his sleep. Guffer had always told the boy he would die one day, that *they* had planned it that way. He never told him of how they arrived at the beach or who made them come, and as a small child he did not think to ask. It was only now that he wondered who *they* were and who he was and why he was here and where else there was to be.

Guffer was wise and had seen most of what there was to see in the world. He had succeeded and erred, he had loved and hated, he had believed and rejected. The child was not raised on mother's milk but every time he looked into the old man's eyes, he drank from them, absorbing the contents of the old man's mind, so that each experience that had affected his heart, every nuance of his life nourished the boy. Guffer told many stories and taught the boy the practicalities of life; fishing, making camp, hiding and escape. Even in the Sorry season, the worst time of all, the boy managed to find an egg to eat and feathers to keep him warm.

The boy knew he lived in Shapeshifter Territory. Guffer had told him about how the land of Goaero changes and that is why it has never been mapped. Inhabitants have been known to fish off a beach only to have it disappear beneath their feet. Rivers had tendencies to hurriedly carve new paths in order to reach the beloved ocean and many a sandy swathe has sprung into verdant growth with wild flowers and trees appearing overnight. Guffer told of the many Goaerons who lived towards the centre of the country where shifts occur minutely and life is more comfortable. He said only few of the most adaptable, brave and clever people inhabited the shores.

What Guffer didn't say was that there are only two types of people who live here; those who relish living life on the edge and those who are banished, or fleeing, to the outer reaches of Goaero. And now the Beach Eater, who had arrived only two years ago, made it an even more dangerous place, where not only did the land shift shape but was being completely consumed by its ever increasing appetite.

THE BOY LEAVES

The boy awoke reaching out for the old man Guffer. He wrapped his sheet around him and allowed the tears already pooled in his eyes to fall. He unfurled himself from the hidey-hole and heard his stomach talk to him. The boy picked up his spear and inspected its point. He clambered over the rocks to the edge of the water. On his haunches he glared into the pool. He noticed his reflection distorted by the ripples; golden shining hair in sleepy tufts, skinned painted brown by the Sun, startling sky blue eyes and shoulders growing broader by the day. As he blinked at himself he wondered who it, he, was, that contorting face. Suddenly a fish darted behind the reflection's eyes and he threw the spear. And in that instant, and only for an instant, the fish had cracked a hole in the question and he knew. Then, for the first time in his life, the boy made a decision. He would leave this lost place and find himself.

After breakfast, the boy tied his cloth around himself and the spear on his back and began to climb the waterfall. Initially the climb was easy; fed, watered and fresh from sleep the boy had energy and determination. The steepness increased but still he powered on, stopping only briefly here and there. Eventually after a vertical scale he heaved himself over the edge. He was amazed to see a vast plain stretch in front of him which finished in the far distance at a sheer cliff face of cascading water. He looked more closely at the plain before him realising it must be water, though not a ripple broke its surface. It sat stubbornly unmoving, like ice, despite the great volume of water pouring into it. The boy looked back down whence he came and saw water gush reassuringly down. He turned back and poked a finger into the lake. The water absorbed his finger without a flicker of movement, he wiggled it but the liquid did not respond. He plunged in his hand and thrashed it about; nothing. And nothing, his hand had disappeared. He frantically yanked it out to see that it was whole, as before. He put both hands in and tried to clasp them together but all solidity had gone. He resurrected them into the air and sat contemplating on the boulder. Down below the familiar rainforest hummed, all he could see up here was a giant lake lipped by boulders and backed by an enormous cliff decorated with a curtain of water. He looked down once more. What empty life did that hold for him? A lonely life, nameless, and pursued by the Beach Eater. Going back, he decided was the worst choice. Normally he would have swum this lake, although even his strength may have failed over the long distance, but this, this emptiness, he knew not what he would be swimming in. Just looking into this liquid 'nothingness' made him feel vertiginous. He leapt over the mouth of the waterfall to the neighbouring rock, then again and again. He carried on this way, aiming to walk around the vast lake, until the Sun was at her brightest.

After a morning of stone stepping, the view had not changed;

he was apparently no closer to the cliff. The stones afforded no shade and they were beginning to burn his grazed feet. He was now hungry and thirsty. The still lake began to look inviting, it gave off a cool air, its silence was intoxicating. The boy's ears drummed, his feet screamed. Finally he stopped hopping and spread himself over a rock. He sunk his hands in the 'water', then submerged his head and opening his eyes...he tried to open his eyes, he opened his eyes, open eyes, open eyes, he was sure his eyes were open except for the 'nothing' he didn't see, only an irresistible white light that curled toward him, leading him into himself, turning him inside in. He panicked and had to use every muscle to pull out his head, he shook it and held up his hands. They were almost transparent and watched as they became solid again. The heavy warmth of the air on his skin was reassuring but he despaired. Nothing seemed to stretch in every direction; a blank meaningless life below, empty eternity up here, oblivion below the water. Not knowing what else to do, he took his faded red cloth and curled himself up inside it to hide. As he lay in his cocoon he wondered just how he and Guffer had arrived here in the first place and then fell into a light sleep.

He dreamt. Guffer was sitting on a flower. It was deep scarlet, its many large oval petals drooped like lolling tongues. The stalk faded from red to green and stood straight and high. The old man was cupping his mouth and yelling at the boy.

"Go back down! Go back down!"

"Go back down," the boy murmured aloud and woke himself.

He was sweating in his tent, stiff and sore. He peeked out to see the Sun was in her last quarter. The boy had resolved to go forward, he hated the idea of retreat but he had to agree that the only way onward, it seemed, was backward.

He peered over the edge of his rock and saw a tangle of roots and vines. He turned his cloth into a cloak and cautiously lowered himself over. As he got closer to the forest floor he was able to pick fruits, the juices seeping over his quivering limbs, giving him the strength to go on. Twice he lost his footing as a branch snapped and he slid down painfully. Finally, he jumped a distance twice his height and landed heavily on the friable forest floor. He slumped where he was, both triumphant and defeated, into a deep sleep.

For the first time in many moons the boy slept in a dreamless sleep; no image pestered him on waking; no ephemeral visions teased him, and he felt changed. Without forming a plan he set off, foraging on the forest berries and drinking from the myriad of streams trickling off the cliff face. He did not know what he was looking for but knew that he must stay close to the rock wall. The moon visited five times and still he trekked onward, the greenery blurring into one jaded paint stroke and the bird song into one lamenting note. He stopped only to sleep a blank sleep. Then, on the sixth day he saw it; embedded high up on the cliff face its colour rang out like a bell. The scarlet flower became the centre of his intention, without breaking his stride he leapt on to the knotty rock wall and hauled himself up. Like a red-backed spider he used one limb at a time smoothly scaling the vertical. He could smell its sticky aroma now, the scent gliding above the musty green forest smells; it urged him on. But as he came closer he lost sight; a flat piece of rock jutted out above him. He felt around for a handhold, foothold or finger hold but the surface became as smooth as an eggshell; his only way up was under the overhang. The boy held the flower's image in his mind and slowly dug his fingers around anything that would hold him and hooked his toes into anything that would fit them and, defying gravity, found the edge of the ledge. With one last burst of power, he flicked his shaking legs onto the flat and as he did so his faded red cloth loosely fluttered to the forest floor. He howled in agony, "NO" in full throttle his small shrill voice breaking into a husky roar. He beat his head on the ground and sobbed.

Sleep again washed over him, an exhausted boy who was growing into a man, with lean muscular limbs and a few small golden hairs sprouting on his slumbering chest. The Sun winked open her eyelid and the first shaft of a new day's light hit the ledge. The boy woke up puffy eyed and sore. He rolled over and there it was nodding above his head. He gazed deeply into the velvety red cup and felt the softness wash over him. He noticed that his spear was lying on the ground, its end embedded into the green veined rock face. He picked it up and moved the creepers aside to reveal the mouth of a tunnel. Amazed, he smiled and turned, made a polite nod to the flower and disappeared inside.

Chapter 24

CLARISSA CROWCRONE

The boy's early triumph of finding the tunnel soon turned to dismay. After a few steps he found himself in complete darkness. He stayed close to one wall feeling his way but often tripped on rocks and hollows and scraped his skin on the hard stone as the tunnel changed course. There was no light, not even a glimmer for his eyes to become accustomed. Then a horrific stench reached him, a gut turning reek of rotting flesh, a smell so odious to the soul that it can only be the decay of a fellow being. The boy retched and choked as he crunched over bones and sunk his feet into the fetid sludge of ribcages and skulls. He did not dare wonder what caused the death these poor souls endured for he had only one way to go – onward. After many hours the smell lifted slightly and was replaced by a teeth chattering chill. The tunnel became colder step by descending step. The boy, now without his cloth, wrapped his arms around his body and stumbled forward. No longer could he feel by the walls as the ice gripped his fingers. He sensed a sharper decline, his bare feet slipping on shard-like rubble rolling him faster down until he fell and slid on his backside and broke the ice on the surface of a pool of slush. His in-breaths were sharp and painful, he tried to stand but his head hit the roof. He felt out with his hands and feet shuffling forward in shaking jolts, his blood threatening to freeze mid-vein. Soon he had to crawl, immersing his body in the water until he could go no further – a wall abruptly blocked his way. He felt in the pitch black all over the wall, panic rising, whispering words, questions, until they became gasping screams and he scratched and punched the wall, crashed his whole body against it, willing it to move, wailing at it to give way, fighting and screaming, thrashing and bleeding, beating the water, the rock, himself with his fists in frenzied fits...

Mid-thrash he sank down and down, his untidy tangle of limbs straightened out into an invisible chute.

A watery beaded curtain softly jangled in front of him. He lay crumpled, shivering, tear stained and bleeding. He crawled through and saw an old lady stirring a large pot over a charged fire.

"Furious little thing, aren't you," she said into the pot, in a voice that did not match her years. The boy had not seen anyone in a very long time, he had never seen a woman.

"And fiery, very few have churned enough heat to melt through the bottom of that torture chamber."

The boy had almost forgotten how to talk.

"Come and sit by the fire and have some soup. Oh, look at that pool of water you brought in with you!"

She shuffled over to him and gently took his bony arm, he unfroze his muscles and allowed her to herd him to the fire. He huddled close to it. The old lady covered him with a blanket and cooed at him in her girlish voice. She held out a bowl of thick broth. He took it and drank directly from the bowl, the warmth flowing into his hands and the welcome brew defrosting his insides.

"What is your name, boy?"

He stared at his feet poking out from the blanket and then into the fire. He didn't, couldn't answer her. After some time she said:

"I shall call you...Fifery. I am Clarissa."

He wanted to stare into the fire endlessly but he felt Clarissa's eyes on him and lifted his chin.

She was old, like Guffer but with more hair, tied in a rope down her back. She had a long straight nose and square jaw with large, clear blue eyes. Her skin was papery and her large hands sat one on each splayed knee.

"Thank you," he managed huskily.

"More?" she offered.

Fifery nodded and drank again from the bowl, this time more slowly.

"Where am I?" he asked.

"In Goaero, dear boy, on the edge of the Fuschian Jungle."

"Away from the sea?" he asked hopefully.

"Away from the sea," Clarissa confirmed.

With that a surge of exhausted relief washed over him. His mouth tongued his new name, "Fifery, Fifery," before he closed his eyes.

Fifery did not know, but it was many days before he woke up. He was in a small cot with a feather mattress that had him dreaming of a cloud and he awoke to the sound of a gentle bleating outside. His fingers found the Sand Diamonds around his neck and he realised that Guffer had not featured in this sleep. He rose stiffly and noticed his wounds were bandaged and clean. Pants and shirt lay on the end of the bed. A narrow window in the room looked out on the small holding, chickens scratched peacefully and, what Fifery was later to learn, a trio of goats grazed on bushes. He dressed and ducked through the door of the room into the space where he had first met Clarissa.

Again she was cooking.

"Good morning" she sang. He ventured a smile.

"Sit, eat," she ordered brightly.

The food looked odd to Fifery. A white water and a brown ball, he recognised only the honey.

"Bread, milk and honey, dear boy," explained Clarissa, seeing him eye the food suspiciously.

"You will like it."

She handed him the bread. First he bit tentatively, then dipping it in the honey devoured it all. He sniffed the milk, took a sip, deemed it fit and drank it down.

"Tell me about yourself, Fifery."

So Fifery told Clarissa his story, about Guffer and Mutilin, the Beach Eater and his journey. Clarissa listened intently to every word. Fifery felt as if she had heard more than his mere words; she had listened to his face and hands, to the sharp intakes of breath. She had heard the echoes of his story. When he had finished, she simply said:

"Thank you, dear boy," and sat absorbing what she had heard.

Then she spoke.

"I am Clarissa Crowcrone. I have lived here in the Fuschian Jungle all my life, just as my mothers did before me. We are guardians to this threshold of Shapeshifter Territory. Very few pass back through this portal. There are three other portals; one where the River Pashanka turns into the Vandret Falls at Anishka, another at the mouth of the River Brook and the last where the two sisters meet in Quelta. There is no other way to Shapeshifter Territory, for Lake Vanish, as you discovered, flows in between. The most common route is down the River Brook which floats into a mystical waterfall that whisks rafts into its mists where the 'Judge' decides if it should land safely. The Judge hangs in the mists and turns each person around in his hands, weighing him up, searching deep into their soul. Some he will drop into the ocean, some he will eat. He is hungry though and would rather eat. This portal is one way. There is no returning up the Brook River. Those who are not so pure of nature may go via Anishka. Here skill is needed to navigate the Vandret Falls and Anishkans do not give up her secrets easily. Many have to work for the knowledge. Some try to marry for it. Either way, many a corrupt man has transformed in Anishka and lost the desire to escape to the outer reaches of Goaero. No one knows about Quelta, and even then no one would survive the crossing of the glaciers, or the terrain beside it.

"You may wonder why my portal is not part of a river like the others. There was once a river here, running right past this cave. Once upon a time the music of water accompanied Crowcrones in their work. The Wryan Waterway dried up, her story with it. Now a dry creek lies there but the portal remains. You cannot reach the Shapeshifter Territory from my kitchen, only return from it.

"A Crowcrone has a special gift; we understand the animals. I do not converse with them, they do not talk to me, but I can understand them. There are few who have this gift, we are very rare. I am descended from a Crone of Arfan. A Crowcrone can bear only one daughter. Ha! There are not many suitable sires in this part of the woods. When the Wryan flowed she brought more folk to our dwelling. My father was one of the last to explore these parts. Now men are too busy tending their fields and flocks to roam. And I am here alone, the last of my kind."

Clarissa's shoulders slumped and her thoughts drifted off as she gazed into the flames. Fifery was struck by her sorrow. He had not encountered it before. He sank to the floor at Clarissa's knees and put his head in her lap. She stroked his hair.

"I would like to understand the animals," Fifery whispered. "My friend Mutilin spoke to me, I know it, but I couldn't hear him."

With that Fifery felt exhaustion sweep through him, he closed his eyes. Clarissa gently lowered him to the rug and covered him up.

When Fifery came to again Clarissa was sitting in her chair nearby staring at him intently.

"I have been thinking, Fifery," she said as soon as he looked at her.

It took Fifery a moment to remember where he was and his new name.

"Fifery," he said again and smiled. "What have you been thinking?"

"Let me teach you!"

"Teach me?"

"Yes, teach you, animal tongue! Who else can I pass the knowledge onto? I knew you had come here for a purpose!"

Fifery tried to protest.

"You are a special and gifted young man. You, Fifery, are destined for great things, and you, Fifery, need some tools in your kit."

He could not – and dare not – argue, so sure was Clarissa. They began lessons the next morning.

Fifery was a natural learner and he absorbed the art with ease but there was so much to learn. Firstly, Fifery had to learn to listen, to hear the sounds. Secondly, he had to learn the different clicks, whistles, the separate languages and what they meant. Then there were an infinite number of insects, birds and animals who all, each and every variety, spoke a different tongue.

The days were spent out in the jungle, translating the layers of sound into meaning. When he woke in the morning to the goats' bleats he now knew they were announcing breakfast, he could hear which birds were ready to mate and which were roosting, he knew where the bees were collecting their pollen and where the monkeys played in the afternoons. When they were hungry Clarissa collected fruits and roots, showing Fifery what he could eat from the jungle. Some of the plants were similar to those on the beach but there were hundreds of new ones he had never seen before. By night they sat in front of the warm fireplace. Clarissa did most of the talking, Fifery asked many questions about the country but although Clarissa knew a little more about Goaero than he, she still lived on her own away from others and had only travelled into Pashanka once as a child. What she did know were stories. Some nights she would settle herself into her chair and arrange her face in a certain way. Her eyes would stare off into the fire, her lips would slacken and after a while she would ask Fifery an obscure question. He began to look out for this special expression and watch her in anticipation, getting himself comfortable and prepared for a journey into one of her tales.

"Do you know what a gate is saying when it creaks?"

Fifery knew an answer was not needed but he shook his head anyway.

"Well, I'll tell you about a gate I once came across. It was a peculiar gate because it wasn't attached to any walls; it stood all alone. It was made of old oak, as lined as an old man's face. The wood shone, polished by years of hands pushing it this way and back.

"On the other side of the gate I could see a field full of knee high, lush green grass. I wasn't quite sure if that was the

way but all of a sudden there seemed no other way to go. As I stepped up to it a breath of wind rippled over the grass. I lifted the latch with one hand and pushed the gate with the other. The cold, hard wood resisted me and as I heaved through the gate it creaked loudly,

'Chuuuz!'

"Well the noise went right through me and I hopped through with a fright. But what scared me more was that the field was now behind me, on the other side of the gate! I spun around and shook my head in wonder and gawked all about me 'cos I had certainly stepped over that threshold.

"Once again I felt my way was through that gate so I stepped up again. This time ready for the creak I boldly pushed the gate and stepped through.

'Chuuuuz' It screeched at me again.

"Was I standing in that fertile green field? No I was not!

"Now, I don't get cross very often but I was getting in a right old tizzy. My fists were clenched and my face turned pink and I leapt backward and forward through that creaking, screeching, rusty old gate a hundred times.

"Well, by now I didn't know which way was north, south, up or down, right or wrong. And I didn't care, 'cos all I wanted was to get into that field. I shouted as much to that darn gate. Then, this time, when I placed my hand on the wood *it was soft and warm and it swung open in blessed silence. The beautiful green field of rustling grass welcomed me and took me on my way.*

'Choooooose'

"The gate swished closed."

After some moments of quiet Clarissa looked at Fifery.

"I didn't know the way, Fifery, but the moment I chose that path the old gate made it easy for me. Always travel with purpose, my son."

Chapter 25

FIFERY IN THE JUNGLE

Fifery had learnt the art of animal language. Clarissa had also taught him the art of cooking, the art of cleaning, the art of conversation and the art of friendship. Each morning he awoke and looked forward to being with Clarissa. She told him jokes and teased him, he tried the same and failed, but his failures made them laugh anyway. Fifery became familiar with the little cave house, his cot and Clarissa's broths. He was happy. But one morning his shoulder blades began to itch and as he walked past the glass bead curtain, he felt an icy breeze which reminded him why he was here. Clarissa had given him a name but he still knew not who he was. He went to find her. Clarissa was busy packing herbs into a leather bag. The wise old Crowcrone already knew she was about to farewell her charge. The two embraced wordlessly. She pulled away moist eyed and offered him the satchel.

"You'll need these," she sniffed and she handed him the bag filled with healing herbs, dried fruits and flat bread.

They walked slowly back to the house.

"Where will you go, son?" Clarissa asked.

"The birds tell of a man. He is on a quest; he is searching for something that is lost. He may be able to help me find myself too."

Clarissa nodded. She had heard about him too.

"Clarissa, you have been my mother, I feel much sorrow saying goodbye," Fifery's expression of feelings were still a little stilted.

"And you my son," she put a hand on his head. They embraced again. This time Fifery broke away. He took her hand and placed a Sand Diamond into her palm.

"Thank you," he croaked. He picked up his spear, his satchel already slung across his chest and strode out.

Neither of them noticed a single pearl of Sun Sand drop out of its niche in the gem.

The next morning a morose Clarissa creaked her bones out of bed and padded to the kitchen to kindle the fire. She would have trodden on her in the dim morning glow if she hadn't mewed; for there on the hearth lay a baby girl. Clarissa gasped and, arms quivering with tenderness, lifted the baby to her chest and turned circles of joy around the room. With tears streaming down her face and her heart fit to escape, she managed to name her daughter:

"Miracula."

Fifery had become familiar with the secrets of the jungle. He heard her myths from the birdsong, he learnt her moods in the calls of the monkeys, he grasped her pathways in the beat of the insects' wings. He listened his way through her thicket. His route to the cave was not direct for he could not ask the way, but like a blind man, he felt his way. Each day he would climb a tree and would raise himself above the canopy. Here he felt such exhilaration, breathing in the unfiltered air, catching scents on the wind and gazing over the green carpet of treetops; it was his favourite part of the day. In the distance he could see the tumbling sheen of The Cascades dropping from the enormous mountain. He felt it pulling him and somehow knew that it was his destination.

One day he heaved himself above the stilted air of the jungle and a flash of purple smeared across a patch of green. He was so excited by the vision that he did not linger on the Cascades or suck in the light air. He raced down and sped off in the direction of the purple cloth. He knew from the animals that the man had dropped from 'a purple tree' – he was finally on the man's trail. It took a day's tussle with jungle roots and the vast leaves that would wrap around him three times, shinning up tree trunks more times than usual to check his progress until, exhausted, he collapsed on the spongy forest floor. The next morning he awoke in a purple haze for directly above him flapped the violet curtain. Fifery smiled until his dimpled cheeks almost bored into his mouth. He stared up at the sheet, eager to retrieve it but as usual he needed to quell the itch that plagued him every day on waking. He scratched his back like a wild bear on a tree trunk. Relieved, he hoisted himself up to untangle the cloth. As he climbed up the tree the air became lighter, its jungle floor density being released like a trapped moth and as he climbed higher his chest opened and the ferocious itch on his back grew more desperate. Finally he could bear it no more and he spun himself to the trunk to rub it away. He was only a hand's width away from the rippling cloth but the narrow branch under his foot cracked as he scratched and he fell. The branches shook as he stumbled down trying to grab onto the tree and unable to stop, his body lurched forward and managed to grab a corner of the cloth that had dislodged and fallen through the canopy. Fifery held on with both hands, one foot resting on a thin branch and the rest of him swinging perilously in the tree tops. The parachute shifted, he heard a ripping and he fell a bit further. By now the branches were thicker, he managed to put both feet on one which held his weight and curl his arm around another. Slowly, he shuffled toward the trunk tugging the cloth behind him. With one last rip he returned to the ground triumphant, cradling a swathe of purple silk. It was frayed around the edges and ripped right through the middle but it was now the most precious thing Fifery had ever owned. He tore the cloth diagonally and folded one piece into his satchel. The other he swept around his shoulders and tied below his necklace of Sand Diamonds. The soothing silk was like a balm on his sore, red shoulder blades. And, perhaps by chance, his new cloak arrived just in time to conceal a pair of small-feathered bones that had protruded by the next morning.

From here on Fifery could track Mallory's route. He found the pool and dipped his fingers in the water, hoping for a clue, hoping he would see the man, feeling rather in awe that he was standing in the same spot as him. After lingering at the pool Fifery followed Mallory's crushed path to the cave mouth. The cave held bushes of small blue flowers; leaves and stems tumbling over itself. Many bees hummed around the petals which dripped with nectar. Fifery crouched down and crept just inside the rocky wall. He listened. The bees sang a song:

The wings of a grand bird let him drop

To drift in our world of green,

A-ho-hum, honey we come, blessings to our Queen.

The leaves did sway and he found his way

To a pool so cool and clean

A-ho-hum, honey we come, blessings to our Queen.

He clutched in his hand the magic sand

From where the blazing Sun did stream.

A-ho-hum, honey we come, blessings to our Queen.

The man, so brave, stumbled to our cave,

Casting buds of blue velveteen.

A-ho-hum, honey we come, blessings to our Queen.

Not missing a step in the deep dark he crept

And met a bear, sharp-clawed and mean.

A-ho-hum, honey we come, blessings to our Queen.

They roared, clawed and jawed, back and forth,

Such courage has never been seen.

A-ho-hum, honey we come, blessings to our Queen.

Then the blast of the Sun was used to stun

The bear into a long white dream.

A-ho-hum, honey we come, blessings to our Queen.

We led the man down into our amber town,

The victor's hunger growing keen.

A-ho-hum, honey we come, blessings to our Queen.

A-ho-hum honeyfish we come

A-ho-hum honeyfish we come

A-ho-hum honeyfish we come, blessings to our Queen.

Fifery crept further into the cave; he could see something on the floor. He reached out and put his hand on a hat, a hole singed through the brim and white ash dusted the top. But the man was nowhere to be seen.

Chapter 26

FIFERY AND MUTILIN

A-ho-hum honeyfish we come
A-ho-hum honeyfish we come
A-ho-hum honeyfish we come, blessings to our Queen.

Fifery listened to the bees' song all day but could not work out how the man had just vanished. The birds told a similar story. The trail had gone cold; the man could be anywhere. He did not feel it was necessary to seek out the bear and he was not especially fond of tunnels. He sat in the cool shade of the cave and tried to think. But Fifery could not stay still, his shoulders itched and he longed for something; a thing that vaguely reminded him of Guffer and Clarissa but he could not name it. He left the cave and moved aimlessly through the jungle. After a while he heard a faint hiss, he smelt a fresh earthy smell on the air. He followed his senses when, without warning, he broke through a thicket and found himself on the banks of a river. Across the water he could see dwellings and people moving to and from the riverbank. With a mixture of fear and fascination, he crouched down low and crept along. Even if he could have crossed the river, he had no desire to enter the throng. His chest tightened, his stomach turned and the pull of jungle solitude tugged him.

The following day he crept upstream, keeping hidden. Most stretches of the snaking flow were uninhabited; he swam in the water and meandered along, breathing in the grassy air. The river gradually widened and flattened out and Fifery took stock of his surroundings. A huge mountain rose in front of him, he realised that the gentle incline of the foothills had already slowed him down. In between him and the mountain now lay a vast lake, the source of the river. Across the river mouth he could make out the dotted marks of settlements. Where he stood the lush green bank sloped down onto a sandy beach. Fifery sunk his toes into the cool sand and remembered his life before. He stood for a long time looking into the lake's glassy surface, suspended in time, caught in a dream, laying down memory upon memory. It was the jolt of hunger that snapped him out of it. Fifery noticed a small rock a little way off shore. He thought it a good place for fishing from and tentatively put his toes into the water. He was relieved to find it just that; a moving wet liquid. He paddled out to the rock, spear at the ready. The smooth rock was warm, it had an almost leathery patina and Fifery stroked a hand across it. He sat for a while studying the underworld of the water. Then in a flash he threw his spear down. He pulled it up to find a writhing fish on the end. He slid off the rock.

"You very nearly impaled my head!"

Fifery stopped stock still, listening. He heard nothing, shook his head and carried on wading back to the shore.

"I do hope that fish is for sharing, it's way past my suppertime."

Fifery now ankle deep spun around.

"Who's there?"

"Purple suits you, my boy, very regal."

The rock wobbled and a head popped up next to it. Fifery squinted in the dying light.

"Mutilin?"

"Good evening, dear boy."

Fifery chucked the speared fish onto the sand and waded as fast as the water would let him until he splashed with his whole body to the rock. He flung his arms around the shell and laughed and wept at the same time.

"There, there, you mustn't make a turtle cry...very bad form."

Fifery asked a jumble of questions – how did you get here, what happened, why are you here? Then he tried to blurt out his passage to the jungle, Clarissa and his name.

"Steady on, dear boy, one thing at a time. Now, let's get supper on."

So they sat on the beach on the edge of Lake Lantaba in front of a small fire and shared a fish and all their tales.

Now that Fifery was able to understand Mutilin, they talked freely. Fifery spoke first and recounted his journey. He proudly told Mutilin his name and the affection he felt for Clarissa and how he heard about a man who arrived in the jungle looking for something and fought off a great bear. He told Mutilin he was sure the man could help find out who he was and where he was from. When he was done, he questioned Mutilin.

"Where did you go? I thought you'd been taken by the Beach Eater."

"I am sorry I did not say goodbye, though you would not have understood me then anyway. It was the first Beach Eater attack of the season. I was fishing for those little silver fish; the ones you say are too bony."

Fifery nodded and screwed up his nose. "They are bitter too."

"Hmm, well I like them and all was going splendidly until I felt it; hardly a shiver at first, just the faintest finger of coolness wrapped around my tail. But I did not hesitate, I could feel it the moment I took off, the icy current chasing me, grasping at my feet, then the water ahead started to turn a hazy violet so I could not see where I was going. I veered to one side toward the portal rock and just as my eyes were freezing over, the sand shifted and the portal was open. I dashed through and swam on until the water shallowed. A few tendrils of the evil purple reached into the tunnel before it was snatched out by the tide. I had no choice to continue on my migration and hope and pray my fellow turtles would get through."

"What portal is this? Clarissa Crowcrone told me of only four, at the mouths of the rivers."

"There is a fifth, close to our beach. It is but a small tunnel just big enough for the largest of sea turtles."

Fifery looked at Mutilin's broad shell and thought the tunnel would be wide enough for a man too.

"Where does it go?"

"Sea turtles are a solitary kind but we must bring young into this world. Once a year in the Surge Season, the portal opens for a few days. It takes many moons to reach the end of the tunnel for it runs right to the centre of Goaero, to here. Deep within Mount Or is a great cavern which holds a clear lake, it is quiet, warm and safe. Here we congregate to mate, relate and confabulate. The egg bearers lay the eggs in the sand close to the lake. Long after we have gone, in the middle of the Sun Season the eggs will hatch and the young turtles make their way to the ocean."

"Then why are you out here, in this lake?"

"There are three other tunnels which lead out of the mount. Here in Lake Lantaba we can fish and bask in the Sun."

"How is it you can understand me Mutilin? I was taught to understand animals but did not know they could make sense of me."

"Ah! Sea turtles are very, very wise, dear boy and very, very old. Our ancestors have been here since the Tree of Light was a tiny seedling. All knowledge is passed on. That is also why our gathering is so important and takes so long. All that has occurred, all knowledge, is shared. We have come to understand all language, even that of Goaero herself."

Mutilin shook his head in concern.

"What is it?" asked Fifery.

"Something is amiss this year, dear boy, all is not well. She laments and weeps."

Fifery put a hand to the ground and he *could* feel a sorrow there. He had noticed it before, he realised, even in Shapeshifter Territory, after the Beach Eater had attacked but he had assumed it was his own dismay. He had grown used to the heavy metallic pangs that travelled up his legs when he stood still for a while, and how he was shaken with the sobbing sensations after a night spent on the jungle floor. He had always thought they were his and it was now a small but potent relief that they belonged elsewhere.

"Why? What is happening?"

"She does not...cannot say."

They sat in silence for a while. Mutilin spoke first.

"Tell me why you seek this man."

"I, I don't know. I heard the jungle animals speak of him and thought...felt, he could help. He was so close. But he was gone from the jungle and now I have lost him."

"The lost man," Mutilin said thoughtfully. "The Lost Man." He fell silent for a moment. "It could be, must be? Yes, yes, dear boy, I think I know of this man. He went to the Shadowlands. There was talk of it. But he was not the Lost Man and he escaped."

Mutilin was not making any sense to Fifery.

"What do you mean? Do you know him? What is the Shadowlands?"

"I know of him, dear boy. Well I have heard about a man. The Blulupians believed the Lost Man had returned..."

He told Fifery the myth and what he had heard, that a man had arrived and was about to be burnt at the stake only to make a miraculous escape.

"The Shadowlands are north of Mount Or. I can take you there. The quickest route is through The Cascades, it will take too long to walk around the lake. You will find him."

"Oh Mutilin, will you come with me, will you help me find him?"

"I will come as far as I can come, that is all I can promise."

"You and me, just like old times! We can travel together, I will be alone no longer."

The old sea turtle's lined face had always looked melancholy so Fifery did not notice the sadness in Mutilin's eyes.

"You will never be alone my boy, and I will come as far as I can."

But Fifery jumped for joy and hugged the old turtles shell.

The following day they glided across the lake. Fifery would occasionally dive into the warm water to swim alongside Mutilin, or slip through holding on to his short tail. As the sun went down they camped at the lake's edge at the very foot of Mount Or. Here they could hear the rumble of the Cascades which led Fifery through wild dreams.

The next morning they woke early and had breakfast. Mutilin was quiet but warned Fifery:

"Hold on tight, dear boy, there is a mysterious force at work behind these falls, it is not at all without danger. At no time must you ever look up, even if you hear it calling your name, for if you look into the heart of the falls it takes you up and throws you down. Look straight ahead and sit still and hold on tight. It will take all my strength to pull us through. This is the mightiest force in Goaero. Be strong, my boy, and...good luck."

Mutilin's words made Fifery uneasy but there was no time to reply; Mutilin pushed them off the bank. Fifery slung his spear and bag across his back and pulled his purple cloak around him. He clenched his knees around Mutilin's shell. Mutilin took them close to the rock face; a small channel of overhang where the curtain of water did not fall. All of a sudden Fifery felt Mutilin's deceivingly strong legs pull them into the turbulent water. It bubbled up like volcanic eruptions all around as the miles of falling water crashed down. They passed through the curtain of water and Fifery swore a thousand knives were raining down on him but within a few moments it had passed. Inside, the blast of the crashing water was deafening. Fifery's head pounded and he was soaked as the water sprayed back at them from the impact. He closed his eyes and lay down flat on Mutilin. The turtle was rocking from side to side and Fifery could feel him straining to pull through the powerful current. Time seemed endless and Fifery gritted his teeth, willing it to be over.

Then, all of a sudden, the roaring ceased. The absence of noise was like music; as subtle as the sweetest cucumber and twice as refreshing. Fifery raised his head, he could still see the cascade to his left and the black shining rocks to his right but he felt as if he was inside a huge pearl. The air was iridescent and beams of light shone through the waterfall, pale rainbows arced in front of him. The air was silky, caressing his skin, and soft, sweet smells of vanilla exuded from miniature flowers embedded in the rocks. He languidly watched the dancing rainbows which slowly drifted upwards. As his eyes began to follow them, he swore he heard girlish voices calling his name. He felt his chin lifting to follow the colours and tinkle of voices. His eyes followed an emerging rainbow up, and then another until his head was tilted backwards and he felt heavy, dreamy, as if his life was being erased. Fifery began to slide into forgetfulness, a huge soft cloud which enveloped him, cushioned him into a bliss of nothingness. Suddenly Mutilin rocked steeply to one side. Fifery shrieked and slipped so his leg was trailing in the water, his cloak was dragging him down. He felt undercurrents pull at his feet and Mutilin struggled forward, shaking with exertion. Fifery's mind trickled back with the cold water, he tugged at the cloth around his neck and pulled it off. Clinging on with his fingertips, his muscles bulging out of his arms, he heaved himself away from the clutching water.

Then the roar assaulted them again, the dragging current weakened and Fifery remounted the shell. He sobbed against the brown shining patterns as his purple cloaked swirled around inside the bubble at the centre of the waterfall. Time seemed to cease as Mutilin struggled on. Fifery felt as if he had lost consciousness when he heard Mutilin calling in a muffled voice:

"Jump off, jump off!"

He looked up and saw the turtle's mouth grasping a root on the edge of the falls; he could see the shrubs on the shore ahead of him. Shakily, Fifery stood on the turtle's back and jumped onto dry land. He turned to see Mutilin let go of the stump and swirl back into the frenzy of the waterfall.

"NO, NO, NOOOOOOOO!"

Fifery threw himself on the bank, his arms stretching out over the water as Mutilin disappeared from sight, swirling in circles like a piece of loose seaweed.

Fifery cried. It was not the piercing wails of a boy but deep resonating sobs of a grown man, grinding out powerfully into the dark earth.

THE BRIDGE OF EVERAFTER AND BELLMAN

Fifery may have stayed face down forever had his shoulder blades not started to scream out for the rough bark of a tree. He was no more surprised at his emerging buds than the rest of the changes his body had been making. He wrapped an arm around and felt the bones sticking out awkwardly. He pulled the second half of the purple cloth out of his satchel and flung it across his back.

As he walked away from the roar of The Cascades loneliness seeped in to fill the void. After his brief time with Mutilin he felt more alone than ever, but he used it to propel him forward to find the thing that might fill him up. He had not walked far through the sparse wood when he came to a river crossed by a rough wooden bridge. He was grateful for the bridge as he could feel the icy air from the water creep up his leg. This river, the River Lichen was not as wide as the Brook River which Fifery had encountered in the jungle. From here he could see the other side and he was already contemplating which direction he would take. He stepped on to the bridge but instead of striding across a kind of lethargy came over him. His knee began to creep slowly up, his hand inched past his thigh, his head moved forward and down bit by bit. Frustrated he exerted his muscles to go faster but his motion remained relentlessly plodding. He managed to look up and saw birds flying normally above, flitting through the sky. The breeze moved the branches as usual but down below the water lazily swirled under the bridge as if on a leisurely stroll. Fifery considered going back but turning around at this speed was unimaginable. He edged onward. After what seemed like eons he reached the middle of the bridge, he looked ahead but his vision began to swim. He slowly turned his head from side to side but the air around him went opaque as if the colours had turned to oil leaving a smudged palette on the air. Unable to see properly he stopped moving. The air settled into an image in front of him. There floated an angelic looking woman. Her arms and legs drifted off into smoky points, her face was soft and her hair floated in curls around her head. He could almost see through her except for two studs as solid as stars in a cold night sky; her bright yellow eyes, surrounded by solid black which bore into Fifery.

Along with his legs, his tongue moved like honey in his mouth. Words from his head were lining up to be let out, except the first word could not get over the threshold. Instead the apparition spoke.

"I am the Angel of Time and you are walking upon the Bridge of Everafter. There is a condition for using this bridge. I may bestow time upon you or feast on your future." Her eyes darkened for a moment. "It is your choice."

Fifery felt frustrated.

"How?" He managed to let the word slide from his lips.

"Stay with me awhile and tell me your tale. If you refuse I shall eat your life up, if your tale does not please me you will leave here an old man and if I like it, you may proceed with time to spare."

Fifery did not know many stories, except his own, which he felt was incomplete. He had to move on but he was afraid he would not be able to please the angel. He managed to nod in the sultry air. The angel's face lit up in glee and she drifted over to him. She reached above his head and plucked an invisible string loosening his tongue and letting his lips drop open. Fifery did not know what to say but her yellow eyes were fixed upon him. He bravely tossed a few words from his mouth and hoped more would follow; and so he began:

"There walked a man. There walked a man in a strange country. No one knew his name but as he travelled he rang a bell, a large silver handbell with a polished oak handle. So he became known as Bellman. Bellman wore an orange hat with a tall feather in it. No one knew from whence he came; some say he strode out of the ocean for he wore a shell around his neck, some say he floated from the sky for he wore a feather in his hat and others believed he was born of a golden fruit. Every time Bellman came to a village he would ring his bell.

The people would come out to listen, for the one bell gave out many different chimes which formed beautiful music. Each person heard his own song which invoked in them each a unique image.

"*Thrice each year Bellman would pass through and each time his bell rang a new song, every time he left the place changed. The villagers were also somewhat altered by the bell; perhaps a man a little kinder to his wife, or a young maid a little more tender towards a boy. But it would also cause trickery. The bell turned some into thieves, even sent some demented.*

"*One day he came to a place. He stood in the middle of the village, closed his eyes and shook his bell. People came out from their houses, away from their work, slipping through doors and alleyways and stood enchanted. Suddenly, a large man called Torro came sprinting through the village square. His jaw was set and his growl turned into a roar. He pounced upon Bellman, snatched the bell and shook it with all his might.*

"*The last time Bellman had visited this village he had rung his bell as usual but Torro had been deep down in his cellar tending his beer and had not heard Bellman's song. His wife had listened with the others but the song fell uneasily on her ear. From that day onward her back was turned toward her husband. Torro, in jealous agony, thought his wife was in love with another. In feverish nights Torro tossed and turned and dreamt that Bellman had stolen his wife's heart. By the time Bellman returned, Torro was convinced of his guilt.*

"And so Torro stood shaking the bell until it released from its handle and clanked gracefully through the air liberating a few final dongs before it splashed into the village pond. The villagers gawked with open mouths. There was complete silence, and then the pond exploded into a fountain of silver water. Bellman turned to the startled Torro, put his hands together and bowed. Then, to the villagers' surprise, his orange hat and feather dropped down around him like a cloak, his nose sharpened into a beak, his legs narrowed into scaly red stalks and Bellman flew away. Torro still clutched the handle of the bell in his fist. As he looked down and unfurled his fingers, he saw instead a tiny silver key sitting in his palm and although no one could ever read what it said, there was a name inscribed along its shaft.

"The bellbird still flies over that land, his chiming song changes people a little each season and a fountain still flows in the square of the little village."

Fifery suddenly realised he had stopped speaking. Although his words had barely left his lips, he felt as if he had been asleep for a long time. As he awoke again to his predicament, he glanced at the angel. But she was gone with just a mere whisper of a tinkling laugh, disappearing with the water flowing down the river. He moved, a little stiffly at first until he walked on and stepped off the bridge. He then felt clarity return and the world around him came back into focus. He remembered Mutilin, the loss stabbed his chest again, releasing a sob, but it seemed like a lifetime ago. He set off down the path that roughly followed the curving line of the river.

FIFERY IN BLULUPIA

Mutilin's legacy to Fifery was the knowledge of the Lost Man in Blulupia. Without this Fifery would have lost the trail. Signposts were few and far between in Goaero. Not many Goaerons travelled, and locals knew their way as the birds know migration paths. Fifery followed the riverside path hoping it was the right direction. The chill air made him shudder, he wrapped the cloak around him tightly. More than ever he wanted to arrive but the path kept on winding with the river. As time wore on Fifery came more doubtful and with each step, worried he had taken the wrong way. He stopped and started to retrace his steps before spinning round again. He knew he had to put one foot in front of the other. Moving was not the problem. It was direction that puzzled him. He became frustrated and desolate, his mind playing tricks on him.

The Shadowlands began to lose what little it had of daylight. Fifery stopped and made camp. As he sat gazing into the small fire he became aware of something tickling his back. He removed his cape and stretched an arm back and round to feel the fine down of feathers which reached down to his backside. The Angel of Time must have not been entirely happy with his tale, he pondered, for she had made him a little older. But Fifery found he was thankful. The infernal itching had lessened and he stroked the feathers in wonder, first one side then the other, feeling over his shoulder and across his body trying to make out their contour and size. It occurred to him then that he should be able to move them, open them up. He closed his eyes, puffed out his cheeks and strained... nothing. He shrugged his shoulders up and down; the wings remained lifeless. Gently he pulled a tip out and around him. It created a delicious sensation of satisfaction, as if that itch, that had taunted him for so long was finally scratched just in the right spot. He pulled and pushed his wings until he fell asleep, one wing across his body like a blanket keeping the cold night air at bay.

Fifery awoke refreshed the next morning. He exercised his wings a little before shrouding them with his cape and set off along the path once more. Quickly his doubts of yesterday crowded back. Fifery ground forward relentlessly and watched the river flow gracefully beside him. He envied her intent, her surety of direction. He stopped suddenly and smiled. He remembered Clarissa and her story of the gate. She did not know if the gate took her the right way but she learnt to simply choose. He turned and looked back the way he came, then the way forward and decided to keep going along with the flow of the river. As he gratefully watched the water, a flash of amber caught his eye. He peered at the spark and saw a feather floating on the current. Although it was small, the burnt orange hue shone out and it reminded him of Bellman. He hurried along to keep up with the feather, the river took it faster, it swirled and eddied, he ran, leaping up to see over bushes between him and the water. Losing sight, he ran faster and kept his eyes on the river, faster and faster, racing with the currents, his purple cape billowing out behind him, not thinking of anything but the feather, almost flying through the air, when suddenly he was stopped and crashed right into a blue man. Fifery landed on his backside looking astonished and rubbing his head. The Blulupian also looked surprised although faintly amused too. He held his hand out to the young Quill and Fifery took it and leapt up.

"I am looking for Blulupia," Fifery stated.

"And you have found it," the man replied. "Come. I will take you to our village."

As they walked the man said "I am Coll, this is Manee and Kinto." He waved at the two men following him.

"I am Fifery."

Both parties walked in silence, both full of questions, neither knowing where to start.

"What brings you to Blulupia, Fifery?" Coll got in first.

"I am looking for the striped man."

"He has been here."

Fifery could barely contain his excitement.

"When, where did he go?" his pounding heart hardly let the

words escape.

"Many moons ago. We know not where he went but we know where he left."

"You must take me to that place!"

"Yes, lad, we will, all in good time but we have something for you, to give to him."

After some time they left the banks of the river and followed a narrow path through low dense vegetation. By and by they came to a small pool. The golden water was bubbling up at its centre.

"We will stop here a while. We have something to show you."

Fifery had noticed along the way how black the tree trunks were and now, in contrast, the trees near the pool were a deep blue-green. The flowers and leaves were brighter here, glowing with vitality.

"This is where he was. He gave birth to this spring, or the spring delivered him, we do not know. This sweet water seeps renewed life into our land. This golden drop, this holy well has brought much good fortune to our people. We thought he was an evil spirit, but he was our saviour. We tried to slay him but it is our lives that are saved."

Once again Fifery looked into a pool and felt close to Mallory, standing in his footsteps. He was in awe of Coll, a man who had actually seen him, met him.

"Come, you must be hungry. It is not far," said Coll.

When they arrived, Fifery viewed a cheerful village. Colourful plants were posted by doors, woman chatted and laughed and a peaceful air permeated the houses. Coll led him to the village centre through circular rows of dwellings. A circle of stones surrounded a wooden statue of a man.

"This is he, your man. Kinto here carved him. He is our master woodman. It was he who stood watch that day and burned the man's image into his eyes."

Fifery walked around the image, he himself trying to etch the contours into his mind.

"What is this?" Fifery asked.

"His hands are tied, as they were that day, to remind us of the freedom he gave us."

"And on his wrist?"

"Ah! That is his compass, he left it here. We did not know why until this day."

Fifery looked puzzled.

"The spears on the bracelet have pointed to the place we met you. We carried it in that direction and when the spears spun, we stopped. Every day we have waited at that place. Today you met us there."

Fifery was still confused.

"It is for you, to take to him. Come, let's eat."

They went to Coll's home where his wife reverently welcomed them. They ate a feast of sweet dishes with the village elders. Now they told Fifery the whole story of the striped man's bravery at the stake, how they mistook him as the Lost Man and his dramatic escape with the help of the Wisps, whom no one had ever seen or conversed with before.

"What are these 'Wisps'?" Fifery asked.

"That is the question we asked ourselves," Coll replied. "Here in Blulupia all living beings are gifted a sprite from the water of the river. Each plant, animal, bird and man has one that only it can see and converse with. We had never known of the underground sprites, the Wisps, until they rescued your friend from us."

"And you? Do you have these sprites?" Fifery was incredulous.

His hosts smiled and nodded, their eyes shifting to empty spaces around them. Fifery shook his head in amazement. They went on to tell him how the spring water from the pool neutralised the magical properties of River Lichen which now grew sweet and colourful plants. The women soon found they could make vibrant dyes which, when added to their spectrum of blues, produced the most startling colours in the whole of Goaero. Word and samples of the dye spread and now traders slowly began to pass through the villages of the Shadowlands. They told of how, with the curse removed, they no longer uttered blessings and prayers incessantly but could once again speak to one another and live in harmony with the spirits of their land.

Fifery was urged to stay a few days, all the villagers wanted to meet him. They told him about the many wonders of their land and made him beautiful clothes. The children were brave enough to stroke his wings and he revelled in their attention. Each day, as they stroked and played with his wings he felt a deeper sensation in them, until one day he closed his eyes and willed them to move. The children squealed in delight as they softly vibrated. By the next day, after caressing little hands had worked their magic, he could open his wings wide and he would run and sweep at the cavorting children who screamed in delight. This new found motion gave Fifery an inkling of being airborne and he resolved to try after he had left the village. Every day Fifery studied the striped man's likeness. His name was still a mystery but now that he was carrying his compass and his image he was happy.

On the evening before Fifery was to leave the village, the Blulupians conducted a serious ceremony. The high priest Jacarando handed over the cuff and incanted many blessings on Fifery. The Blulupians each dressed in their finest attire and ate and drank a feast. At daybreak Fifery bid his farewells and embraced his new friends. He removed his necklace of Sand Diamonds from his neck and placed one solemnly into Coll's hand. Kinto and Manee took Fifery to where they had found Mallory's abandoned raft at the edge of the Naharancan Plains and waved Fifery off until he was a mere dot in the sand.

Legend has it that the Sun herself shifted a little to the West that day, so that she could gaze upon her beloved Sand Diamond and the Shadowlands had a little less shadow from that day hence.

Chapter 29

FIFERY IN CASINO

Although Fifery had enjoyed the company of the Blulupians, he was yearning to be alone. He had an exciting experiment to undertake; he believed he might be able to fly.

On his first day on the Plains, Fifery awoke and stood in the warmth of the early Sun. He stretched out his wings and slowly moved them around. Already he felt lighter on his feet. Then he ran as fast as he could, shifting the feathers up and down until he was gasping for air. He collapsed on his knees, exhausted. He had not flown, but for just a few moments, his feet had left the ground. It was enough to encourage him further. Throughout the day he walked, then ran and flapped and folded. He tried every combination of wing position, he trotted, jogged and sprinted but his feet still only left the ground momentarily. That night he slept under a Gongalong tree. He was sapped of energy from wing tip to toe and fell into a deep sleep.

At first he thought he was dreaming, but as the sunlight filtered through the leaves, he realised that the chatter was coming from the real world. Inside the trunk an animal with large round eyes and a shiny purple nose, was squeaking. Fifery was unfamiliar with the dialect but he managed to pick up a few words of the rodent's diatribe.

"Tsk, tsk, tsk! Unk, teo, tee, thor, ach! Stripy beast chowing me gonga nuts! Teo leggies, teo arrms, fingies a'plenty! Dig ye owen gongas, ach! Tsk, tsk, tsk!"

Fifery could only assume his man had been right here under this tree and had eaten the creature's cache of nuts. Once again, a now familiar feeling of awe came over him. He checked the sandy earth for tracks, sure enough several trails led away from the tree. He was confused but encouraged and renewed, he jumped up and tore off to practise. After sleeping on the trials and errors of the previous day, this morning's attempts were greatly improved. He worked out the winning combination of run, flap, jump and, at last, he was airborne. Fifery laughed aloud with elation. Suddenly it felt so easy, so right and he swooped and yelled and marvelled at the changed land below.

Fifery was no stranger to footprints in the sand. He had spent his childhood with Guffer tracking animals and avoiding the marks left by other people. Here on the Naharancan Plains there was no rain, nor tide to wash them away. He chose the freshest looking imprints and flew low enough to follow them and practise flying at the same time. His sweeping wings now carried him faster than his feet and he covered greater distances. But his newborn muscles became fatigued by midday and he went on foot in the afternoon. Each day Fifery's flying improved and each day he ventured a little higher. He longed to soar high but he was anxious to keep track of the footprints.

On the third day he stopped early and decided to dedicate his afternoon to exploring the heights. He ran and left the earth, beating his wings strongly to gain speed. This time he doubled back on his path and made wide circles in the sky. As he climbed the air became clean and sharp. He inhaled deeply and felt a surge of energy power through his wings. His entire body tingled in the airstream and he quivered with exhilaration. The air was completely different up here, for although it was thin, it seemed to fill him up, like a good meal. He had never felt as strong and free, almost invincible. A fine mist covered his body which cooled him while his inhalations felt like they were stoking a fire within. Reluctantly, as the Sun began to fade, he finally began his descent but he could now see something sparkling in the distance. Dark brown buildings emerged from the yellow dust and a lake lay shining like a new coin, a little east of what he thought was a town. He suddenly realised this was where the man was heading and that by tomorrow he would reach it himself.

As he foresaw, Fifery reached Casino by nightfall and landed noiselessly at a crossroads. He folded his wings, flung his purple cape over his back, and began the walk into town. The old beggar with milky marble eyes sat at the junction holding a wooden bowl. He croaked out to Fifery as he passed.

"Hi ho, old man," responded Fifery "Is this the road to town?"

The old man nodded and held out his bowl. Fifery dug into his satchel and pulled out some dried fruit. The man sucked on it hungrily.

"What is your name, old man?"

"Call me Ree, son."

"And what is the name of this place?"

"They call it Casino, though I refers to it as summin' else! Good luck to yer, son," said old man Ree as he tore the last morsel of food with his teeth.

Fifery walked into Casino and came to the town square. Men with creased faces stumbled in and out of doors. Lanterns were being lit in the dying day and cries of triumph and dismay filled the air. Fifery had never encountered a space filled with so many people and so much activity. The peace of flying quickly faded and the jangle of noise and emotion cut through him.

Across the square a dominating brick building was surrounded by a crowd of men. They stood in front of the large door and carried spades and pickaxes.

"Froggy out, Ernie in, Froggy out, Ernie in!" they chanted.

The furore unsettled Fifery, he was afraid at the vehemence

of the voices. He noticed a place bearing the sign of a bed on the opposite side of the square and guessed he might find lodgings there. Relative peace reigned within the tavern. There were a few men talking animatedly at the bar and one old man sat by the fire. Fifery arranged accommodation and retired to the front room to eat and relax by its warmth.

"They still clamouring out there?" said the man who caressed his long fingers around his mug.

Fifery nodded.

"What's happening?" he asked.

Dunkin related Ernie's tale of new wealth and influence in the town, all thanks to a striped man who lost all his fortune to Ernie. Fifery's ears pricked.

"Striped man?"

"Yes, canny fellow they say. Ole Ernie must have been on a winning streak to take all that coin off 'im."

"And what did you say the man's name was?"

"Ah, don't think I did...er, now let me think." Dunkin took a swig of beer and stared thoughtfully into the fire. Fifery fidgeted beside him, willing him to remember. Suddenly he gasped and looked pleased, then shook his head and resumed his deliberation.

"MALLORY!" Dunkin suddenly exploded.

"Mallory," breathed Fifery, he shook his head, once again in awe and disbelief.

"Mallory...where did he go?"

"Well, he was in a hurry to leave – didn't catch where – but he was mighty taken by the Bloodstone."

Fifery did not stop to ponder what Mallory was doing; he was not used to normal civilisation, he didn't know it was unusual for one man to cover such distances or to move on so quickly.

Dunkin gave Fifery one more piece of advice:

"Well, wherever he went, there only be one road in and one road outta this town, I'd be starting there if I were you."

Fifery spent one restless silence-free night in Casino. That evening he sat alone in his room and turned the bronze compass over and over in his hands, he could not fathom the symbols on its face but felt, if he only understood its language, it would give him answers. At daybreak he thankfully left the bustle and headed for the fork in the road. As the one road forked into two, Fifery saw the old man slumped between the junction. He stopped again nearby and looked thoughtfully at the ragged heap.

"Greetings Mr Ree."

The old man raised his eyebrows. "I never seen a man leave so quick."

"I didn't find what I was looking for. Maybe you can help me, father?"

"Aye, sit a while then."

Fifery sat and shared his breakfast.

"I was a young man like you once. Aye, I had teeth and muscles and hope. I tell ye, it were a long, long time ago. You ever been to Mistletoe? Nah, no one ever heard of it. It were a tiny place, tucked into the eastern foothills of Mount Or. No' many people know of it; easy to miss on account of it being full of 'oles."

"Holes?" asked Fifery.

"Caves, ya see, it's a village of caves. That's why I'm near blind; Mistletoe folks live in darkness most times. Even harvesting and such we did at dusk."

Fifery wondered how the old man came to be here.

"That's a good question, son."

Fifery had not said a word but the old man seemed to have heard his question anyway.

"Why am I here in this eye-sizzling, sun-baked desert? That's a very good question, an' I'll tell ya.

THE STORY OF OLD MAN REE

Me Ma were a long sufferin' type, She 'ad nine o' us, aye. Me ole man choked to death after I were born so it were me oldest brother Somin who raised me. He were a sour type though, allays complainin' and chuckin' rocks about. Ma got old, sick. I 'ad to get outta there. No life for a young man. Somin told me if I left and looked for Ma Starry that she would give me vision, so I could live in the outside world forever. Aye, he were a wag old Somin! I spent years hiking all over Goaero looking for 'er, Ma Starry. Wherever I looked I found ridicule, wherever I asked I got jibes, wherever I stopped I got mockery. It were many a year afore I reached Casino. It was here that one kind fellow took pity on me, sat me down and told me that Ma Starry didn't exist. And do you know what? It was at that moment I found her, aye – Mastery! From that day on I was the master of my own destiny; I was the master of choice. And I chose to sit right 'ere. Mr Ree they call me now 'cos I'm a mystery, no one can work out why I chose this life, but I sees the faces of them coming in and of them coming out of that cursed place. I reckon you and me's the only ones found our fortune in that there town!

Old man Ree took a swig from his cask, not many stopped to talk these days, it was thirsty work.

"I think maybe you are my fortune Mr Ree...tell me, do you remember seeing a man with striped hair leave this town?"

Ree's rheumy eyes gazed ahead, he nodded slightly. "My

eyes don't allays get a fix on faces, but I got a feeling I know who you're looking for."

"You do?" Fifery panted.

"He'd be the one in a hurry. He tossed me a few coins which I can't eat. He was after Anishka, that's right. Thought I'd slow 'im down a bit so sent 'im north instead a south!" The old man cackled at his mischievousness. "I reckon he's a found it by now. You'll find 'im in Anishka. Due south, son, fly away and may you find Ma Starry yourself!" He chuckled once more.

Fifery grasped the old man's hands. "Master Ree, thank you, thank you! Farewell!"

Fifery was off but not before leaving a small parcel of food by old man Ree's side which also held a Sand Diamond. As soon as he was out of sight, he ran and swooped up into the air, exhilarated by flight and with Mr Ree's help which had gained him considerable ground on Mallory.

The next morning Mr Ree woke up later than usual. As he opened his eyes he realised that he had slept longer, not due to the full stomach thanks to Fifery's breakfast, or due to the colourful dreams of rainbow coloured Bloodstone oozing out of the ground, but because a canopy of leaves were shading the bright spears of Sun's light that normally jolted him awake.

He gasped and scrabbled up onto his elbows and stiffly onto his knees, craning his neck and sweeping his blurry eyes across the huge ceiling of leaves. He knew instantly that it was a Gongalong tree and he scurried out from its cover to see where he had been taken – for that was the only way he could have woken under a tree. But the familiar fork in the road to Casino was still there. He scratched his head and surveyed the tree, whistling through his missing teeth. Then he heard a gentle trickle. The noise reminded him that his morning ablutions were pressing and he hopped behind the tree to relieve himself. But something stopped him; for there, beyond the Gongalong tree, stood a small orchard of fruit trees. Apples, plums, oranges and pears hung plump and ripe on the branches, and in the middle, a pool with little brooks delicately burbling around the trees.

It took Mr Ree a long time to stop listening, then a long time to feel his way through the orchard, then a day or two to find the courage to pick a fruit. But gradually he got used to them and wasn't afraid that they would disappear as suddenly as they had arrived. And he began to sell the fruit off the trees to travellers, as he could not eat it all himself. And over time he made a little money and had a small house built. As he tended the orchards his old bones remembered how to move again and he became more able, and as he drank the water of the spring and washed himself in it and ate the fresh fruit his eyesight began to return. One day Ree decided he needed help and he took on a boy from town. In a few years the boy married and built a house at the place now called Reestrees and they planted more trees. Mr Ree never knew how this miracle had happened but he often thought of the young man he had spoken to that day and he never discovered the Sand Diamond buried deep in the trunk of the Gongalong tree.

PART THREE

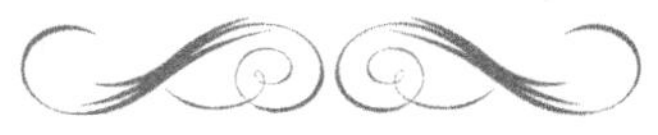

MALLORY AT SEA

Mallory spent the morning gazing out to sea and exploring the docks. The large flat boats were crammed with pulleys and joists, equipment and tools that fascinated him. His ears sorted through the unfamiliar sounds of the ocean; the clanking of halliards, the wash of the waves on the sandy gravel, the screech of seabirds, all melding with the relentless roar of the falls in the distance. He located Sea Hawk, the figure head of the ship stretched out into a curved beak, large eyes and feathers carved into the wood.

Eventually he reluctantly pulled himself away and trudged back into town to find a bed for the half night. As he walked back toward the centre, Samia appeared before him.

"Ah! We meet again." she pronounced.

Mallory smiled and nodded his head politely.

"How is your wound?" she inquired.

Mallory had forgotten all about it and said as much to Samia, thanking her for her skills.

"Do you know where I might find lodgings for the night?" he asked

"I have a spare room above my shop, you may lodge there is you wish, James Ardent Mallory. Five pieces a night is a reasonable fee."

Mallory was not entirely comfortable in this bold young lady's presence but he decided to accept her offer since he would be gone before dawn.

The room was small and stifling. The small round window set deeply within the thick walls did not open. Mallory reclined on the narrow bed and wondered what the night ahead would entail. He was nervous about setting foot on the watery expanse of sea, an unfamiliar environment. He wished he had his compass to tell him which direction to turn.

Samia knocked on his door late in the afternoon bearing a tray of fish soup, bread and a bitter tasting tea. She stayed with him while he ate.

"How long do you intend to stay James Ardent Mallory?"

"A few days perhaps, until my business here is done."

"Well, I shall take twenty pieces in advance, that should cover it," she stated.

Mallory was too polite to object, he dug into his bag and gave her the coins. Still she remained. He obligingly winced down the last dregs of tea which she then whisked away with the tray and left. He did not see the faint play of a smile around her lips.

Soon Mallory fell into a deep sleep. Swollen mouthed and sweating he writhed around the sheet, dreaming of bucking ships and bloody, salt encrusted knives.

He awoke with a start to see the moon's light fading. He leapt off the bed, foggy but furious and ran down to the docks. He just caught sight of a ship gently lifting over the waves and a flash of blonde hair; the captain steering at the wheel.

"Spitting fittocks!" Mallory swore and ran his fingers through his hair in anguish. He could hear voices on the jetty as more boats prepared for the night's fishing.

"Perhaps..." Mallory muttered.

"You looking for someone?" A gruff voice emerged from the shadows.

A man appeared after the voice. He was thick set, his square chin jutting through black stubble and clear eyes escaping from bushy eyebrows.

"I...er...missed that boat."

The man's eyes narrowed.

"What boat? That one?" he pointed at the departing vessel.

"Hah, count yerself lucky, son. You don't wanna be on that pile of planks."

"Do you know when another boat is leaving?" asked Mallory.

"Whose asking and why?" The man pulled in close to Mallory so that he could feel his breath on his face. Mallory had always been honest with his answers, often brief and edited but never false, but tonight Mallory was nudged by caution.

"I was looking for work, thought I might try my hand on a boat."

"Ever been to sea?"

"No."

"Are ya familiar with an ocean going vessel?"

"Er, no."

"Orright, are ya a quick learner?"

"Yes."

"Well, I be one man down, we'll give ya a try. I'm the captain, call me Asher."

Asher seemed to look past Mallory's shoulder but he did not miss the swift wink and the recognisable sound of a woman's skirts swishing away into the night. Mallory followed the captain to his ship. The soft quiet clanking that Mallory had experienced earlier that day was replaced by the furore of shouting and shifting. Ropes were being hurled across the deck, nets and wooden crates shuffled from dock to deck, buckets of slopping bait were being carried by wiry youths.

"Stand at the prow, look, learn, follow and don't get in the way." Asher grunted at Mallory.

The moonlight was steadily fading and Asher yelled orders at his crew until the boat drifted away from the docks. Once unleashed, a current seemed to carry the ship. Even though the sails were still folded at the foot of the masts, the vessel moved faster and faster. Mallory looked forward and just saw Jethro's ship disappear between the two headlands. The roar of the falls began to ring in Mallory's ears, he could no longer hear the shouts of the crew but just in time turned back to see what was happening. To his horror each man was clinging onto the ships stanchions, their arms wound around the ropes and feet braced on the deck.

"HOLD ON!" He could not hear but could vaguely see the closest man mouth the words, frantically screaming at him. The ship suddenly jolted and Mallory crashed to the deck. He managed to grasp one hand on the ropes between the stanchions. The ship lurched from side to side, as if it were on the end of a happy dog's tail. Mallory managed to get his other hand onto the rope and he sat face forward, unable to turn around. The noise was titanic, cold salty spray whipped Mallory's exposed face, his legs bashed onto the bow as the ship skittered over the surface of the water and then plummeted into a navy blue darkness. The song of the waterfall was suddenly muffled, the boat's motion suddenly stilled. Mallory saw nothing, he stopped breathing yet his heart pumped; he was not under water yet not in air; he was free to move yet paralysed; his mind felt clear yet he was blank.

With a thunderous crash the boat was suddenly borne into the ocean beyond. Mallory and the crew took in a collective gasp followed by a moment of silence before the hubbub of activity resumed. The men disentangled their limbs from the handrails, orders were tossed back and forth, sails were hoisted and each man took up his position. Mallory likened it to a well-drilled battalion.

"Orright, let's get that son of a bulboid!" Asher gnashed.

"That double crossing, horse-licking, lowlife, I'll have him. We'll drop our nets later to feed the mouths. I want to taste his blood on my lips tonight!"

The crew cheered and continued to spit curses on the ship ahead. Asher calculated how he would catch up with Sea Hawk. He ordered the sails be set this way and plotted his course across the rolling waves.

Horse-licking, Mallory thought to himself, *horse-licking*, he had heard the phrase not long ago. Then he remembered; the knife in the market, he had heard the insult that morning in town. It quickly dawned on Mallory that he was on board the ship of the second man in the market fight, and that the fight was not over.

THE CRONE COUNCIL

I t was mid-night and Kafia stood on the southern wall of the Zarbor, unsure of where the entrance was actually located. Marika appeared behind her.

"Kafia!"

"Oh! I wasn't sure where you went in."

"Anywhere, child, the Zarbor is all entrance. Come."

Kafia followed Marika who was dissolving into the shimmering walls of the Crones' headquarters. Cold sluiced her senses as she passed through and a mild apprehension touched her heart. Inside she stood in a vast hall, the walls formed a circle and shot up vertically seeming to never end. Kafia looked down feeling a reverse vertigo. The floor was intricately decorated in a geometric pattern; small coloured prisms were interspersed with mirrored tiles. The patterns fooled the eye into thinking the floor was ridged causing Kafia to stumble clumsily over a perfectly smooth floor. The pattern wound round and round which led to an opening in the middle, where the tiles appeared to be cascading and Kafia felt in danger of being swept down with them. But she had stopped at the edge with Marika.

"I have consulted with the Council of Crones. They are assembled in the Hollow; we shall join them now."

Kafia was shaking, the Zarbor had unnerved her but she had never in her worst nightmares thought she would come face to face with the Crone Council.

As children, Goaerons would be threatened with 'I'll send for the Crone Council!' or 'We'll see what the Crone Council will say about that!' It was almost as unbelievable as the wind changing a pulled face forever. Almost. There was a story that had been told for many years, a story that was witnessed by the grandparents of the elders of Goaero which was fresh enough to believe.

Witches had become a myth in Goaero. Magic did not occur in their lives. Goaerons knew what they could see – sun, rain, plants, animals and each other. Most people stayed within the boundaries of their town or village and only a few traders, gypsies or messengers would pass through. These travellers were outgoing types, and so usually doubled as storytellers or entertainers. They spun tales, recited poems, chronicled happenings, mixing truth with fiction and serving up exotic mingled yarns. More often than not the most humorous stories were about witches. Lanky raconteurs would lampoon as witches, casting ridiculous spells and mismatched magic. Witches had them in stitches, the gags were on the hags, crones tickled funny-bones, short witches were the butt of most jokes in Goaero – except, of course, in Arfan. At some point the Crones got wind of this. They had kept their heads down in order to enhance their potency, to take it away from everyday life. Peace reigned over the land and their skills were not needed but ridicule was a symptom of disbelief and disbelief led to dissolution. The Crones had to act. All tall tales, jokes and songs were collected and analysed, debates were held and after many seasons, they reached a resolution. It was time to put the wind back up Goaerons, give them a taste of Crone power and reinstall themselves as the fearful and potent force they were.

The Crone Council had special powers. They had a unique relationship with Goaero; they could converse with her. In the deep dark Earth Chamber hidden beneath the Hollow, information was exchanged. This information gave them power, which seemed to be a kind of magic. The knowledge of gravity allowed them to reverse it; the knowledge of pattern allowed them to rearrange it; the knowledge of weather allowed them to play with it; the knowledge of land allowed them to cross it. Most Goaerons had forgotten how the Crones had once secured the land with dangerous Portals.

The following Mid Sun Day they launched their plan. The members of the Crone Council took up their positions, dotted throughout Goaero in towns and villages and Ma Crone with her aides in Carbinia. Celebrations for the high happy season were in full swing. They had given thanks to the Sun Goddess that morning and Goaerons gathered in communal groups to sing, drink and feast. Entertainment would follow with skits and plays to a receptive audience. As usual, the parody of witches began. It was now that Ma Crone pointed her staff at the Sun. Immediately an unseasonably black cloud gathered in front of Her. Each Crone stood by with a cup of water. As the black cloud was summoned, they blew into the cup and then tossed it at the mocking minstrel. In mid-flourish each one froze wide eyed and terrified in whatever farcical position they held. The audience gasped in wonder, thinking it may be part of the act, laughing at the captured clowns in front of them. The Crone then slowly entered the stage, hobbling or floating to garner most reaction.

"Laugh will you. Take heed people of Goaero."

The audiences' titters ceased.

"Jokes and tales and songs you weaved.

The Crone can smell these words.

The odour sours, our nose aggrieved

They cut like sharpened swords.

They seepeth down into the ground

And fester long and hard

And grow into a little mound

Which rents the earth apart.

When evil spawns upon the morn

The darkness will be freed,

The beast will eat Goaerons all;

The witches you will need.

So hark your words and turn them sweet,

The Crones love a merry song;

And so will never turn their back

On a world that has gone wrong."

The Crone then pointed the cup at the inert artiste and the liquid rushed back in thus freeing the unsuspecting performer. The Mid Sun Day celebrations ceased that day all over Goaero and no one poked fun at witches or Crones ever again.

Kafia shivered and wondered what was in store for her in the Hollow. She could now see a staircase spiralling down the hole. It was made of glass, almost invisible. Marika stepped on and slowly wound her way down with Kafia close behind. As the light of the great hall diminished, the stairs became more visible against the rock wall and she began to feel a little more sure-footed. She could now feel an intense heat radiating up from below and although the icy hand of fear still clutched at her heart, her skin began to seep sweat. Then she could hear a faint chanting. The steps seemed endless; they circled and circled, the singing rang around her head in the opposite direction until she was dizzy. Suddenly, the wall ceased and the see-through staircase disappeared from view, even when her feet told her otherwise. Kafia wobbled and turned to the step behind to steady her. Down below she saw a cavernous space, lit by thousands of candles and tiled with a million differently shaped mirrored tiles. She saw images of flames, hands and hoods refracted everywhere. She closed her eyes at the disorientation and felt Marika tug at her wrist.

"Come on, nearly there."

Kafia stood and stared at her feet and put one in front of the other without glancing up until she saw herself reflected in the mirrored floor. Twenty-three Crones stood in a circle ahead of them, their mantled heads bowed and chanting in rounds. Marika led her to the circle which opened and placed her at the centre before returning to the Crones to close the gap. The chanting ceased until four lone voices finished the round.

"What is your name?" a crackling voice asked.

"Kafia Lily Skinner," she replied quietly.

"You are a Secret Keeper?"

"Yes."

"A broken one?"

"Er, yes." Kafia was terrified a secret might spill there and then.

"Our Mother Goaero will decide how to help. If you are a chosen one, she will take away your secrets but she will give in return. That is the Natural Law. Do you agree?"

"Er, yes." Kafia could not think. Her mumbled answer was not considered, nor right or wrong. It just emerged from her lips like a duckling from its shell. In that instant the floor opened up and she fell down a narrow shaft onto a soft pile of earth. She screamed and looked up to see the mirrored Hollow disappear and the chanting resume. Kafia listened, she was shaking and gulping in gasps of air, terror numbing her from her toes up. When the chanting ceased she burst into tears and dug the earth, desperate to get out.

It was dark and very warm; the earth was surprisingly comfortable, giving off a faint aroma of fertility, the nutmeg warmth of a mother's love. It calmed her. She lay down and thought. Her mind wandered through her life; backwards and forwards; brothers, sisters, Ma and Papa, friends...she fell asleep. She did not know how long she slept but on waking she panicked and wept into her skirt. When the tears ran out she started talking; firstly to herself, then praying to the Sun Goddess and finally, in a moment of revelation, she began to talk to the Mother herself, Goaero. Before long she began to spill the secrets. Tiredness washed over her again and she dozed, and then stirred to resume the reams of secrets in her heart. She was amazed at how many she had stored and recalled. At last she came to Encoda's; the secret of the past and the future, a secret that would change history and shift power, a secret she had yearned to know. She revealed then, her own secret; the story she had made up in order to keep a secret. Finally the most recent confidences of her fellow travellers fell out of her. Kafia suddenly felt hollow, purged. The pain of emptiness curled her up in a ball and dropping quiet tears, she cried herself to sleep.

Up above a satisfied Crone smiled, removed the side of her head from the hatch, straightened her robes and furtively bustled up the glass staircase.

In the hours of sleep that followed Goaero spoke, in turn, to Kafia. Few ever hear the voice of a land. It takes a Crone scores of years to receive and understand her messages. When Kafia awoke, she could barely breathe. Soft earth filled her mouth, her limbs felt encased by stiff mud but the real horror was within; she had been given one secret in return. Kafia screamed. She screamed and screamed until she was hoarse. Then she heard the chanting, words she could now recognise; a blessing on the land, a blessing on the air, a blessing on the Sun and a blessing on the sea, a line which made her gag with repulsion. The hatch door was raised and Kafia blinked in the light, a rope was lowered. Kafia held on weakly as the rope was raised magically, quickly and effortlessly. She lay bedraggled and dazzled on the cold-mirrored floor, and sobbed. The Crones stood around her in silence. Ma Crone stepped up to her and removed the hood from her head.

"Stand, child, you have survived; you are a chosen one. Stand, there is work to do."

The Crone held out her hand and Kafia managed to stand. Unbeknownst to her she had spent seven days in the pit, seven days without food, water or light. They all gravitated toward the staircase keeping Kafia in their midst with the help of Ma Crone. As the Crones began to climb the stairs, Ma Crone and Kafia lifted off the floor and singing a single note in rounds the Crone Council levitated them up the middle of the staircase. Gently they landed at the top. The crazy paved tiled floor did not disconcert Kafia this time for she passed out and woke up sometime later in a small bed in a normal looking bedroom.

Chapter 32

A Fight at Sea

The moon's light was fading, her veil was dropping and soon the black hole of night would descend before morning, when the Sun would slowly yawn awake and make the world real again. Asher skippered the ship away from the speck of Jethro and followed the coastal current which swept them into a wide arc out to sea. Mallory could feel the churning slipstream of water below the boat rumble and recoil from the waterfall. But Asher seemed to have mastered its invisible trajectory and was determined to use it to his advantage. Soon they silently glided to within sight of the starboard flank of Sea Hawk; Mallory could see the pointed beak of the figurehead sitting boldly aloft.

The moonlight had all but disappeared and Sea Hawk looked like a white shadow on the waves, noiselessly dipping nets into the depths like a ghostly puppeteer. Asher's crew were intentionally silent, hidden by the rise and fall of the waves, he took them closer and closer. Suddenly Asher lit a flare signalling the men to launch their missiles. The crew bombarded Sea Hawk; grunts of exertion preceded the thud of metal on splintering wood. Cries of surprise and horror came from the ship before they returned with flurries of arrows. Two of Asher's men fell back shrieking in pain. Mallory could hardly see what was happening but the battle's bedlam reached his ears.

It wasn't the fighting that concerned Mallory now, for he had been trained in the king's own battalion. He had practiced for combat from the age of seventeen, he had dreamed of such a moment to put his skills to good use. But, he was cautious of being used, of allowing himself to become a pawn in someone else's feud when he knew he had a higher mission to fulfil. Mallory decided to take action and he made his way to the stern to find Asher.

"Got ya!"

Hands suddenly grabbed at Mallory's arms and he was manhandled across the deck. As he stumbled over the rigging, Mallory realised that it was, in fact, weaponry and the ship was as well equipped to fight as it was to fish. Again, he felt foolish for not recognising the paraphernalia of warfare.

"Get off me!" he shouted "What in the Sun's reign is going on?"

"Aaagh, shut up, stranger."

Finally Mallory was hauled up to Asher.

"Welcome aboard the Ulven. How are you enjoying your trip?" Asher threw back his head and guffawed crudely.

"What are you doing?" asked Mallory incredulously.

"Aw, the brave Mr Mallory wants to know what I'm doing," Asher replied sarcastically.

The cannon balls had ceased.

"Take him and secure him up the mast." Asher nodded towards the top of the mast. Mallory struggled and yelled.

"You won't be rescuing anyone tonight Mr Mallory. Hah – he'll be saving you!" Asher laughed again. The men held knives to Mallory's throat and forced him to climb the mast. Towards the top they stopped and tied him onto the lookout platform. The sails flapped below him, then the boat tacked sharply and the sheets snapped taut, Ulven took off.

From here Mallory could see Sea Hawk was racing away in the distance, as a pale glimmer of light began to wash the sky into a violet haze. Despite the imminent danger, he noticed that the sky was beginning to lighten earlier; Mid Sun Day was not too far away and for some reason he felt it was a looming deadline. His fingers worked frantically at the mariner's knots that bound him, aware that he was about to be exploited, but they held fast.

Now that night was slowly fading into light Mallory could see other vessels dotted far out on the horizon. He could not imagine being so far out to sea, so unanchored from earth, released into an unfamiliar and powerful realm.

They were closing in on Jethro. He could now see Sea Hawk was slowing down as the crew hauled heavy ropes over the stern. The vast nets were dragging on the strong currents acting as a brake.

"HA! He's net bound! It's my lucky night." Asher yelled. "Oi, Subani! Where are you going? I got something for ya," and he cackled his throaty laugh.

Jethro appeared. "Stay back Asher or my crew will fire."

"I wouldn't do that – you might hit your little friend here." Asher pointed up to Mallory who shook his head in shame.

As the boats humped over a large wave, one after the other, they lost sight of each other. Only Mallory could see from his vantage point the Sea Hawk crew splice the ropes and take off along the trough of the wave, leaving an empty space in her place. Asher roared.

"After them!"

Mallory's thoughts had quickly assembled themselves. In this battle of sea dogs, he knew whose ship he would rather be aboard. Asher had held the knife in the marketplace, Asher had been pursuing Jethro across the waves and he surmised Asher had also been responsible for drugging him and consequently tricking him aboard Ulven. Mallory was now his prisoner, dangling like a piece of bait.

Mallory knew he must help Jethro. He gazed intently in the opposite direction of Sea Hawk. Asher noticed and ordered his crew to head the same way, giving Sea Hawk valuable headway.

Ulven crashed over the waves and slowly the Sun reached out to shake hands with the ocean, creating explosions of light on the crests. By now, Sea Hawk had caught the waterfall current and sped up behind Ulven. Jethro stood in the middle of his men lined up along the prow, bows and arrows poised at Asher and his crew.

"I am sick of your tyranny Asher. Let the man go and we will fight it out twixt ourselves."

"You piddly horse-licking grittock, I should 'a stabbed ya both."

Asher shouted at one of his crew.

"Fetch the ugly coward-kissing bowl of puke!"

A man scurried up the mast and deftly untied the knots with which Mallory had struggled. He shoved Mallory down before him while a man below waited. The rest of the crew stood on guard, purple faces throbbing with bloodlust, cutlasses drawn.

"It's you or him Subani," yelled Asher.

"Let him free or I will shoot you right here."

"Go on fool! Ya wouldn't dare."

An arrow shot past Asher's ear and stuck in the wooden wheelhouse. Asher let out a deep screech of contempt.

"What? A bad aim or were ya just trying to scare me?"

Mallory could see his fury rising, spit flew from the corners of his mouth; he was a man on the brink of no return. Suddenly a yell went up from the stern of Ulven.

"The Beach Eater! Return to harbour, return to harbour!"

The dots of black fishing boats began racing away from the horizon, rapidly increasing in size as they got closer. But one, then two vessels suddenly tipped and disappeared behind the skyline.

"Aaagh!" Asher groaned in un-thwarted frustration and, without hesitation, shoved Mallory overboard. Mallory screeched as the planks whizzed past him and gasped in pain at the cold water. He had swum before, in still lakes and meandering rivers but never with a salty mouthwash of undulating waves in the face of the Beach Eater. He thrashed in panic and screamed as the wooden hull of Ulven moved away.

"Take hold, QUICK!" he heard a voice. Mallory disappeared below the water, his arms desperately trying to keep a hold on the surface. His legs dragged him down further and the water stung his eyes. He tried to find the air but it was liquid all around, bubbles confusing him, the gush of water in his ears, the cold wrapping itself around him, paralysing his muscles.

"Mallory, here, here!" he heard the voice muffled from somewhere but he was tumbled again and knew not how or where to move. Then his hand broke free of the water's clutch. He kicked off his boots and followed his hand and for a brief second he felt the air on his face, he sucked in a gulp but the water broke over him again.

"...rope..." he heard again and grasped at water in vain. He swallowed seawater and began to choke, his legs refused to move now, his body ached and felt empty. The crashing waves numbed him and he started to let go. Let go of the panic, the effort, he let the water do with him as it wished. He felt like a graceful piece of weed dancing in the currents, his chest heaved still trying to breathe but he wanted it to stop now, he just wanted it all to stop, to rest...

There was a thump on his shoulder, it scratched across his face and he flicked open his eyes. His body screamed to stay still but he managed involuntarily to feel for the intrusion. His hand grasped the wiry thick rope and it instantly hoisted Mallory up, crashing him into the barnacled side of the ship. His awareness sprang awake and he held on as he was bumped up and dragged on board the ship. Hands pumped his chest and slapped his face while a flurry of movement navigated the ship along the currents. Mallory vomited and coughed. Hands slapped his back. Mallory sobbed on all fours. The crew furiously sailed their ship, their jaws set and faces serious. He looked behind them and saw the wavy sea turn dead flat, a purple shadow raced across it as fast as they were sailing, freezing the air above and consuming the world below. Mallory had never imagined anything so invisibly terrifying, remembering the Quills' stories. Suddenly hands dragged him to the stanchions and threw ropes around him securing him fast. He was too tired to object still reeling from the struggle.

"Hold on!" a man yelled at him.

Mallory braced himself against the ropes, closed his eyes and they entered the void of the waterfall. It was nothing and everything, he felt as if air pumped around his veins and that he was breathing in blood, he felt rearranged and that strangest of all, he could smell, but could not say what. Then they broke free. The crew and Captain breathed in a gulp of quiet air as the falls spat them back toward the docks.

Mallory was untied. He wobbled his way to the helm and found Jethro.

"You alright?"

"I think so. Thank you."

Jethro nodded "One good turn..."

"What happened?" asked Mallory.

"The Beach Eater," said Jethro grimly, "the Beach Eater is what happened."

"Asher is a bully and a thief. He poaches fishermen's tracts, he trawls the seabeds that are full of young fish and plunders the catches of vessels returning home. He has terrorised the fishermen for many years. One day I'd had enough. I armed my crew; we decided to retaliate. We took him by surprise so the attack was a success. I shot an arrow through his shoulder. The injury never healed properly, despite his daughter being an herbalist. He suffers great pain to this day but it just increased his hatred and fury. Now he hounds only me, for that I am grateful. But his pillaging of seabeds has driven the fishermen further out to sea and they face the evermore potent danger of the Beach Eater."

Mallory was sitting in Jethro's kitchen. They had not returned to the docks where Asher was thunderously yelling for blood. They had dropped anchor off the eastern beach and rowed ashore. Jethro lived a short way up the hill from the beach with his wife and children. His wife, Luna, was serving them a fish stew.

"What is this Beach Eater?" asked Mallory. "I have heard of it once before."

"No one knows what it is. Sometimes a whole season will pass with no attack; sometimes it visits twice a week. But there is always death. We are lucky the force of the falls protects us in the harbour."

They sat in silence for a while, Mallory could still feel the freezing chill that tugged at him in the water. Jethro wondered who had lost their lives that day and said a prayer. The day was now fully awake but Mallory and Jethro snoozed by the fire until the afternoon. Luna woke them and hustled them out the door to make room for the children and evening meal preparations.

They rowed back to Sea Hawk. Jethro gave Mallory a tour of the ship. A few of the crew lived on board and came on deck when they heard footsteps. Jethro introduced them and Mallory shook hands and thanked them for saving his life.

"Let us take the boat back the docks, it should be safe now. We can give our friend Mallory a sailing lesson on the way."

The men aye-ayed their captain and the work of crewmanship flew into action. As they sailed around the harbour Jethro and his crew shouted instructions to Mallory, threw him ropes to pull and gave him the wheel to steer the ship. He was exhilarated and excited, he had never been in control of a ship and his extra sense allowed him to naturally adjust to the wind currents. Jethro was very impressed with his protégé and they sailed in happy camaraderie to the dock. But the mood was morose on the docks, the emerging news of who had not made it back was filtering through and groans of grief rang out as friends prepared to break the news to the families. Asher had not yet left the docks and his fury had multiplied. He marched along the jetty ranting and spitting a thousand curses. Sea Hawk approached the last berth and Asher ran to meet it. The crew tried to secure and defend the boat simultaneously.

Jethro leapt onto dry land, Asher squared him off, and they circled.

"Alright, let's finish it," Jethro said.

"Be my pleasure, you scum. I'll slice you in half from the skull down, that'll shut that pretty mouth of yours up."

He lunged at Jethro with a short knife. Mallory flew off the boat and jumped between them.

"Brothers!" he called.

Asher threw his fist at Mallory with strangled grunts of anger, furious he was still alive. But Mallory caught the fist mid-air with lightning speed.

"Is this how brothers love one another?" he asked, glaring into Asher's bloodshot eyes. The eyes screwed back in contempt.

"What?" he spat.

"You are brothers, of the same blood, your father's blood."

Jethro stepped forward.

"Mallory, what are you talking about?"

Asher pulled his fist from Mallory's, wincing in pain and grasped his shoulder with the other hand.

"I'm no kin to this...this animal," said Jethro in a low voice. His eyes seemed to be searching for something, something in his memory. "No, it can't be...can't be true."

But he had remembered something that made the absurdity a possibility. Asher stood heaving his shoulders up and down. They looked at each other but Asher just grimaced, planted a globule of spit on the ground between them and fled.

Apart from the creaking of boat bones, the shrill of sea birds and the scrape of decks, silence reigned over the docks. Mallory turned to Jethro.

"Are you alright?"

Jethro ran his fingers through his coarse salted hair and nodded.

"How do you know?" he asked. "How do you know we are brothers?"

Mallory sighed. "I do not know the answer to that question. I just know, the way I know when the wind is about to change, I just feel it. It is up to you to uncover the story, and, I hope, make amends. Maybe I will come back one day and you can tell me!"

The men shook hands.

"Now I have a question for you." Jethro gestured for Mallory to continue. "Where can I find a pair of shoes and a pearl of Anishka?"

Jethro smiled.

"In the same place?"

Mallory chuckled and shrugged his shoulders.

"They grow inland, Mallory, in sparkling towers of purple eggs. Good luck, and please, come and visit us one day."

They shook hands again and Mallory turned and limped up the jetty toward town.

KAFIA THE CRONE

K afia woke up trembling; both hunger and fear were jostling for room in her fragile body. It was a new, different Kafia who emerged from sleep. Where once she was the guard of an unused back door she now held the entire land in her hands. The door clicked open gently and Marika padded into the room with a tray. She sat on the edge of Kafia's bed and placed a hand softly on her forehead.

"How are you feeling?"

Kafia thought for a moment. "Different," she replied.

"That is to be expected. Here, eat. We need you to build up your strength."

"What for?"

"Well, firstly you will be initiated into Cronehood; for all who survive the Earth Chamber become Crones."

Kafia stared into space.

"Then you will be taught Crone knowledge and how to turn the knowledge into power."

Tears rolled down Kafia's face. Marika hugged her.

"I'll leave you now, we will talk some more later. I know it is a lot to take in." She left the room.

"What have I done?" whispered Kafia. She cried into the pillow at the unfairness of it all. She wallowed in self-pity until no more tears flowed and hunger took over. She ate the cold soup and bread and felt a little better but the space inside her, where the secrets used to be, still made her feel empty. The secret of Goaero was not in this place, instead it seemed to engulf her. She felt as if she was inside of it rather than the other way around. She began to panic as she had done in the Chamber but then she remembered the soft, gentle earth holding her, supporting her. She calmed herself and pushed the secret aside, pretended that she had dreamt it and focused on her soon to be status of Crone. As the word 'power' drifted around her mind she began to feel a little thrilled. She realised her life would never be the same and that this was just what she had wanted. She had had a taste of the Crone power when she was levitated up the staircase. She wondered what magic she would learn. She imagined her mother's face when she saw her daughter turn a stone into a cake! Kafia's thoughts wandered until she dozed off.

A little later Marika re-entered the room with a fresh tray loaded with cheese and dried fruit.

"Are you feeling any better?" she asked.

"Yes, yes I am."

"Is there anything you want to ask me?"

"Yes, so many things! How long does it take to train as Crone?"

"Many seasons. I am still learning all the arts and I have been here since I was a young maiden."

Kafia's heart sank; no matter how hard she tried to ignore it, the secret would not go way; she needed to find the king, now more than ever.

"Anything else?" continued Marika.

"No, no, not now," she stumbled over the words.

"Are you sure? What is it Kafia?"

"It's nothing. What happens now?"

"We go to meet the council. Are you ready?"

"I think so."

"Good!" Marika trilled, "I shall let them know." She rushed out of the room, again leaving Kafia deep in thought.

Kafia's lodgings had been outside the Zarbor in a small wooden building at the edge of the square. All her belongings had been brought from the hostel. Kafia washed and changed and Marika led her out into the street and once again through the membranous wall of the Crones' Headquarters. This time the tiled floor appeared flat and she smoothly glided across to the stairwell. They descended to the now familiar chanting which ceased as she entered the circle of the twelve head Crones. Ma Crone peeled back the hood of her cloak.

"I am Ma crone, Head of the Crone Council. Welcome! I am the teacher of Crone Law."

One by one the Crones revealed their faces and told Kafia their names and Crone art.

Minneka; the power of Water-blasting.

Craven; the power of Beast-eavesing.

Zantra; the power of Crone-lip.

Agruella; the power of Up-downing.

Finka; the power of Land-fleeting.

Griselda; the power of Cloud-spinning.

Gentia; the power of Healing.

Crystal; the power of Earth-whispering.

Shimeny; the power of Shape-shifting.

Felicia; the power of Nosing.

Cora; the power of Patterning.

Kafia looked at each one, unable to read any of the impassive faces. Ma Crone continued.

"You will now be an Apprentice Crone. Each member of the council has a special skill to teach you. Your apprenticeship will take many moons, many seasons. One day you will become a member of the council. Marika is a senior apprentice and she will be your mentor. Know her and trust her, she will help you. You will meet many challenges and do many good works. Farola!"

All the Crones repeated "Farola!" and began to chant. Ma Crone produced a goblet and a phial of green liquid from within her cloak. She poured it into the cup and presented it to Kafia. Kafia drank the bitter herb tincture and winced. Ma Crone took back the goblet and the chanting finished.

"Repeat after me," said Ma Crone and sang the first syllable of the chant, a clear note that rang around the hall. Kafia sang, her voice was gravelly and quiet. Ma Crone sang the second note and Kafia repeated. On each note she became clearer and louder until the chant ended and Ma Crone ordered her to sing.

The chant had somehow embedded itself deep in her bones, etched there forever and she sang it perfectly. The Crones joined her and soon every voice weaved the incantation to the rafters producing a sensation so uplifting, a vibration that resonated so deeply that Kafia felt her feet were lifting off the ground. She wanted this invigoration, this belonging to last forever. Indeed it went on for most of the morning, but Kafia's brain was then nudged by an empty stomach and pins and needles in her feet. She ended the chant and gradually the rounds drew to a halt. Marika appeared and took Kafia's hand and they climbed back up the staircase and into the dazzlingly mundane street outside the Zarbor. It was then that Marika turned to Kafia with a big smile which Kafia returned and they ran back to Kafia's room laughing and skipping like excited children.

That night Kafia dreamt she saw an old man with a long beard sitting under a silver tree. He tried to speak to her, his eyes pleading but no sound came out. His feet then turned to water and in horror she watched him dissolve. A white bird skittered up through the tinkling branches and flew away.

As soon as Marika came to her room that morning Kafia urgently told her she must leave. Marika thought Kafia had become scared of her future and tried to calm her. Eventually she persuaded her to speak to Ma Crone. They went over to the Zarbor and entered on the opposite side. Here a door led through into Ma Crone's chambers, although Kafia was surprised that she was not back out on the street. Finally Kafia spilled her story. Ma Crone knew of the missing king although none of the Crone powers could find him. She nodded knowingly, seemingly unsurprised at this young lady's involvement.

"It is most unusual to leave after initiation and before training. You should know that by now you have already absorbed some Crone power. However, it is unlearnt, unpractised and unharnessed – a very dangerous state to be in. You are very vulnerable at this stage and must take great care. Go now and return as soon as the king is back at the palace."

Outside Ma Crone's door Agruella hastened away and sank down the stairs to the great hall just before Marika and Kafia emerged.

Kafia and Marika walked to the stables where Kafia had left her horse. She positioned her saddle bags on the horse's flanks and said goodbye to Marika. Neither noticed the familiar deep maroon shade of the cloak of a Crone, Agruella, on the far side of the yard talking to a young messenger boy on a horse, who held a letter close to his breast. She wafted her arms, recited a verse and spun the horse faster than an eagle north towards Carbinia. Kafia trotted off in the opposite direction and headed into the looming bulk of the Mortlock Range.

FIFERY AND MALLORY

Guffer had taught Fifery how to tell where north and south lay, so he knew he would be able to travel at nightfall by reading the stars. Until then he followed the road that Ree had indicated. The road carved its way through the golden sand, etching its weaving pattern onto the canvas of Goaero. Fifery noticed few travellers on the road. He now knew that having wings was not normal; he sensed his uniqueness which made him feel vulnerable. When he was certain he was free from being seen he soared up high into the sky until the people were mere specks on the earth. As he climbed he felt a vigorous force take the air under his wings and propel him along faster. Here the air transformed into a light mist which coated Fifery's tongue and throat. It tasted sweet and fizzed on contact and gave Fifery a delicious feeling of vitality. He laughed out loud and opened his eyes, mouth, even his nostrils wide to take in the elixir.

After a day cruising in the Eternal Mists of Life, Fifery noticed the edge of the desert as it faded into jade. He could see the dry eastern flank of Mount Or towering up in the distance and the river meandering from the east shore of Lake Lantaba. He landed on the edge of a thicket and rested feeling strangely satiated and drowsy. He fell asleep.

It was still dark when he awoke. He could tell that Mid Sun Day was approaching for already a faint glow heralded the Sun's longest day. Fifery remembered Guffer telling him about the Sun Season festivals that raged all the short night long. He loved watching the fire in the old man's eyes and the joy that evaporated his wrinkles for a moment, when he recalled the celebrations. They would then perform their own ritual and stay up all night. The approaching Mid Sun Day filled Fifery with trepidation which expanded his heart and belly. He packed up his things and crept to the edge of the thicket to read the sky. Within moments he was up and away. In the steadily increasing light he could see the moon dancing on a watery snake which soon revealed itself as the river. Along with the river came people, lots of them. Fifery felt nervous flying above so many eyes. He scanned the ground for a safe place to land but all available flats were too close to people and the area east of the river was too thickly vegetated. Fifery began to panic. He flew up to the Eternal Mists, too afraid to come down until it was dark. After such a long day of flight, he was exhausted and desperate to land. At last he dived into woodland with a small clearing. He landed clumsily through entwined branches too late to notice a group of men sitting around a fire to one side. He lay in the leafy earth. His wings were shuddering with fatigue, his chest heaved, his eyes were eager to close for a restful sleep.

"What in the Sun's name!"

"Summink fell."

"Quick, light a torch."

"Careful, might be a bear."

"Mole, ya idiot, bears don't live 'ere!"

"Bears don't never fall outa trees."

"Well, might be dangerous."

They inched closer holding the torch as far ahead as the arm reached.

"What the ...?"

"It's a bird, is it?"

"It's a bleedin' man!"

"With wings?"

"It can't be..."

"My mother-on-a-donkey!"

"Whoa boys, it's a stinking Quill, on my mother's grave, it's a Quill."

"Quick, grab it 'fore it takes off."

"Arnie, get me the ropes, quick! Juke, hold its legs, Ham, tie its legs. Cor, just wait 'til the General sees this."

The men tied Fifery roughly along his own spear.

"Stop, please, what are you doing?"

"Argh, shut up!" A boot whipped into Fifery's ribs. They dragged him off to their camp.

The men stared down at him in the light of the fire. Fifery tried to talk to them.

"Fell from the sky did you? Ha, how the high and mighty 'av fallen."

The men laughed adding jibes and insults along with the odd boot.

"Look at it all dressed up in fancy rags, think you're royalty do ya? Ere! What's that around its neck?"

"Whoa, look...at...that! That's a Sand Diamond, Sarge."

The sergeant snatched the necklace off Fifery and licked his lips. Fifery whimpered in pain, fear and exhaustion. The Sergeant kicked him again.

Fifery shivered through a mercifully short night. He was stiff, bruised and unable to move. In the morning when the camp stirred, the men talked in low voices.

"'Av ya decided, Sarge?"

"Our orders are to search Anishka for the king. We'll just take it wiv us."

"But it's a day's walk!"

"And your point, Arnie?"

"Well, it's heavy."

"Agh – you're weaker than a pot of baby pee. GET ON WITH IT!"

The men hoisted Fifery onto their shoulders, Fifery screamed and struggled.

"Shut it UP!" Sarge shouted.

Juke was happy to oblige and kneed Fifery in the back and punched his head, Fifery now hung limply, a trail of blood dripping from his nose and a piece of cloth stuffed in his mouth. The soldiers did not want to draw attention to the Quill so they covered him in an old sack and tied it around him to resemble a slain deer. The men stumbled slowly along the road, each dreaming of his stake in the Quill and how it would release them from the drudgery of army life. The heat of the Sun beat down on them accusingly; there was not a whisper of a breeze. They then saw a man coming towards them on the road. He was obviously deep in thought but as he looked up at the passing company a wave of recognition swept across each face.

"Arnie, Juke! Wha... what are you lot doing here?"

"Smouldering Sun holes, Mallory. Where 'av YOU been? Hey, you look different."

Hugs and back slaps were exchanged all around. The men dropped their bounty and sat down to eat and catch up with all their stories. It appeared that Mallory's regiment had been kept in the dark about his special mission. Most thought he had absconded, some said he got sick, others guessed he had fallen in love and disappeared. Not one had considered he had gone on a royal quest. The men looked at him in stunned silence. Mallory glazed over the details of his journey, missing out Quelta altogether and his acquisition of the Bloodstone. It was time for his comrades to tell Mallory why they were so far from home.

"Well, I'm afraid your quest is null and void, my friend," the Sergeant said smugly. "Not much use finding the king's voice if there ain't no king." The soldiers roared with laughter. They explained they were despatched to search Anishka and then Spode to try to locate the missing monarch. Mallory froze. At first confusion played his face like a guitar; a whole scale of emotion ran across his features. But Mallory realised he was being belittled.

"Then I shall return to Carbinia to receive fresh orders," he announced stoically. He wanted to change the subject.

"Been hunting?" he pointed at the large sack slung across the spear.

"Sure have," the Sergeant answered. "You know Ham here is a crack shot." He laughed weakly for Mallory knew them all to be hopeless marksmen.

"Mind if I...?"

"Oh, it's not a pretty kill...er...trying to keep the flies off..."

The Sergeant rushed over to Fifery and stomped on the cloth. Fifery was now conscious and listened to the conversation. With all his might he extended his wing so the tip escaped from a corner of the sacking and he yelled into the gag.

"What have you...?"

Mallory swooped down, pulled out his knife and cut through the cloth in one swift movement. He pulled off the sack to reveal the poor battered Quill, blinking in the bright Sun. Mallory gasped.

"Que?"

By now the five soldiers had surrounded him.

"It's ours," sneered Juke. "We found him." His nasty fists were raised.

"Untie him!" Mallory demanded.

The Sergeant jumped to Mallory and grabbed his shirt. "I ORDER you to stand down!" he snarled in his face.

"I take orders from Prince Encoda – no less," Mallory whispered loudly back into Sarge's face.

Sarge nodded at his men and they jumped on Mallory. But his extra sense predicted the strike and he threw himself at

Fifery, slicing through the ropes at his feet. Mallory rolled off and kicked up his feet which caught Ham squarely on the chin. Meanwhile, Fifery flapped his huge wings sending the rest of the men into confusion and contortions as they waved their arms around like small children batting away scary moths. Fifery's hands were still attached to his spear which he raised and charged at Juke. The blunt end struck him heavily in the stomach followed by a thwack around the side of his head. Mallory and Fifery stood side by side, pumped with adrenalin; Sarge, Arnie and Mole stood opposite pumped with fear and surprise.

"You'll be exiled for this," warned the Sergeant

"Then back away now and no more harm will be done," replied Mallory.

He raised his fist with the knife.

Mole started whimpering. "Please, don't hurt me, I done nothin' wrong!" He began to cry.

"Shut up you frog spawn...or I'll get you meself," shouted Sarge.

With that, the terrified Mole turned on his heel and ran off into the bush.

"Get after him!" Sarge shrieked at Arnie who ran with relief after Mole.

"I ain't finished with you, Mallory." The Sergeant knew he had lost this battle. He backed away and ran to bring back his two men, leaving the other two lying on the ground.

"Are you hurt? Quick, follow me!" Mallory asked as he slashed the rope from Fifery's wrists. He dived into the thicket followed by the taller Fifery who stooped down to avoid the entangled branches above.

"Mallory; James Ardent, pleased to meet you." Mallory held out his hand formally. Fifery ignored the hand and drew Mallory toward him in an embrace.

"I know who you are."

"You do?" Mallory looked confused "I thought I knew you at first but I am mistaken. Did Que send you?"

"No, no one sent me. I have been looking for you, tracking you."

"How? Why?"

"I first heard your legend in the Fuschian Jungle, I met your likeness in Blulupia and I heard your name in Casino. And here I find the man."

Mallory was dumbstruck at his listed itinerary. But he was puzzled.

"But Quelta, didn't you know I was in Quelta?"

Fifery looked blank. "I know no such place," he stated.

"But you are Quill, is that not where you are from?"

"I know not from where or who I am. That is why I searched for you."

"So where did you come from?"

After they had walked far into the Zoto trees they stopped and made camp. Fifery told Mallory of his journey, he told him about Guffer and Clarissa, his stay in Blulupia and how Mr Ree sent him in the correct direction to Anishka. Mallory shook his head in wonder. He was astounded that he had now met yet another Quill. Mallory told Fifery of the Quills and his experience in Quelta. He assured Fifery that, yes, out of all the people in Goaero he was the one who could show him the way to his people. But first he had to complete his mission – to find the key to the king's voice.

THE GUARDIAN OF THE
MORTLOCK RANGE

Kafia rode out of Arfan and eyed the mountain range before her. Their peaks did not reach the regal heights of Mount Or, but they stretched themselves east to west as far as the eye could see. They rose so abruptly out of the soft, green land of Pashanka they had a startling quality, as if they had just jumped up and shouted 'BOO!' Once the traveller was within the ranges, they had to overcome not one, but several rows, arranged like jagged teeth. This meant the traveller would spend their journey sweating uphill or picking their way through deep ravines strewn with fallen rocks in perpetual shadow. There were few settlements in the rocky terrain besides two or three small villages which raised large flocks of goats.

Kafia had to choose her route to Spode; the long dangerous track that weaved around the base of the mounts, or the more arduous but direct trail that rode the mountain ridges. Kafia was pleased to be on horseback and conscious of time slipping away. The road ahead divided into two; to the left the flat track, to the right the end of the snake-like track that curled its way up the mountainside. The pilgrims ahead of Kafia all merged left, Kafia embedded her heel in the horse's right flank and started the climb. Her horse plodded slowly but surely up the slope, at each turn the track became narrower and the horse trod more slowly. By afternoon she guessed she was halfway to the top. There was a gentle concave in the mountainside where Kafia decided to settle for the night. She sat and looked out on the land in front of her. The sleepy Sun's filtered rays brushed the earth below. Mount Or appeared like a tiny pimple on the horizon, Pashanka rolled out of her in muted greens like a ripple. She had never noticed the rippling effect from Mount Or; how the ridges rose evenly in an almost perfect arc. A bright green line marked the horizon to west of Mount Or and a golden yellow to the east; the jungle and the desert. Its beauty enthralled her but soon a deep sadness overwhelmed her and Kafia felt the grip of panic at the fragility of what lay before her. The disappearing Sun marked off another day, darkness and responsibility weighed down on her until she could hardly breathe.

The morning dawned dramatically across Goaero but Kafia awoke feeling fuzzy. She wearily saddled up her horse and sat heavily on him. She was ascending into the top half of the mountain where the landscape changed into a grey rocky land. The narrow path now widened but was covered in loose dark scree. The pink tinged mist fell around her like a curtain, making her feel clammy and chilled. By afternoon the way flattened out and Kafia supposed she had reached the summit. She still felt weak and queasy and shivered as the path led them into a narrow dark gorge sandwiched between two walls of rock. The mist was swirling smoke trails that seemed to chase each other, obscuring the way ahead. She began to see images within the dancing vapours and shook her head to clear her muddled mind. Her horse stepped uneasily over the unsteady ground as they entered the dingy chasm.

"HALT!"

Kafia's horse whinnied and bucked. They began to back out.

"HALT!" It was a woman's voice.

"Who goes there? Who stops me from passing through?" Kafia asked bravely in as loud a voice she could muster.

"It is I – the Guardian of Mortlock Range."

Kafia could not be sure but the rock wall to her left seemed to be moving; an oval protuberance appeared to be forming the words she heard.

"Then may I pass through, great Guardian?"

"You may...for a fee."

"What will I pay you?"

"If you guess and deliver you shall pass through, if you fail with your tale the mountain will eat you."

"Guess? Guess what?" Kafia was confused.

The rock was silent. She dug her heels into her horse's flank to move forward but at the first step a mighty crack opened up the path ahead. The horse was alarmed and stumbled back, again the track fissured behind them. Small jets of steam pushed through the opening which threatened to gobble her up. She dismantled to hold the horse still.

"If you guess and deliver you shall pass through," she repeated. "If you fail with your tale, the mountain will eat you. Fail with your tale...you want me tell you a tale, a story?"

Silence ensued. Kafia's knees were shaking. She closed her eyes and recalled the seven days she had spent in the Earth Chamber, the womb of Goaero. In there she had – finally – felt safe, cocooned. In that instant the fear left her and although she was weak and dizzy, she suddenly felt on safe ground. She took a deep breath and began.

THE STORY OF THE BONE CHILD

"A little girl stood on the edge of a turquoise sea. She wore a pale brown dress tied at the waist by a yellow ribbon. She stood on the shore looking across the water which lapped rhythmically at her feet. She did not sit or fidget from foot to foot, or smooth her straw-coloured hair that flicked across her face. Only her eyes moved; scanning east to west to east. There was plenty to see in the foamy waves; a school of

silver fish became acrobats of the air in perfect formation, a sea turtle slopped past, dolphins spouted and nose-dived in scattered joy and a pair of dragonflies glided on the currents of air. But the girl stared beyond. As the day drew on, a faint disc rose from behind the horizon and climbed directly upward through the sky. It was the Ghost Moon and only certain people could see it. The Ghost Moon took all day to reach the Sun and when it did, it gobbled her up and plunged the world into blackness. In the last struggling beams of the Sun, the sea washed up a small bone at the girl's feet. Only now did she stoop down to collect the bone. She added it to the other bones around her neck and went to rest.

As soon as the Ghost Moon released the Sun, her arrows of light woke the child who began her vigil all over again. The Bone Child led a simple life and all around her stayed the same except she who grew and grew until her dress was too small and her hair covered her newly curved chest. The necklace also grew heavier dragging her head down as if in shame, but still the sea spat one out at dusk each day.

One evening the clouds rumbled angrily across a red streaked sky and the girl loosened her string to add the latest bone. But it snapped and the bones tumbled down onto the sand. The sea reclaimed some, licking them back by her rippled tongue. The Bone Girl hurriedly scraped them back onto the dry sand. She sat and looked at them and her sudden weightlessness made her laugh out loud. She liked the sound. As the Sun came the next morning the Bone Girl did not stand at the shore; she got to work. Her busy hands crafted the bones into a boat. At dawn the next day she set out to sea. She had many protectors in the great ocean; fish, sea turtles, dolphins and a pair of dragonflies as she headed for the Ghost Moon at the edge of the world."

All Kafia could hear was soft hiss of steam rising from the tear in the earth. All of a sudden her horse whinnied and reared, his hoof caught Kafia on her temple and all went black.

Chapter 36

THE PEARL OF ANISHKA

"The king is missing," Mallory echoed the words of the soldiers. "My quest is to find the key to the king's voice but if the king is missing, what good is..." He trailed off, deep in thought.

Mallory was not sure how this startling news affected him. If Prince Encoda had given him orders he decided that he would carry them out until he received further news. Then, if the king was still unavailable to be reunited with his voice, he would also look for the king. Still the thought of a king-less country unnerved him; the behaviour of his old comrades showed some sense of order had been lost.

"Tell me again of the jewels that can make a man speak," asked Fifery. Fifery had spoken mostly the previous evening. Mallory had thought his own story was too complicated for this young unworldly Quill.

"Here, I'll show you the Bloodstone." Mallory carefully ripped open the pocket he had sown into his vest and pulled out the jewel. Its colour pulsated in the Sun's rays. Fifery touched it reverently. It reminded him of his Sand Diamonds and put his hand to his throat, suddenly remembering the ugly theft of his own precious jewels. His face contorted into anger and grief.

"What is it?" Mallory asked.

"Those soldiers, they stole my Sand Diamonds."

"You had Sand Diamonds?" Mallory shouted jumping to his feet, startling Fifery out of his mournfulness.

"Yes, that is what Guffer named them. He said it was unusual to have holes through them. I used to play with them."

"We have to go, NOW!"

"What? Why?"

"Because, Fifery, the third jewel is a Sand Diamond!"

Although Fifery was naive, he was sharp-witted. He jumped up and started to pack up the camp.

"First we need to collect the Pearl of Anishka," said Mallory, his arms frantically putting out the fire and folding his blanket.

"They have a day on us. We might catch them in Anishka but I expect those lazy lice are already on their way to Spode. Hurry!"

Mallory and Fifery stumbled through the bush until they came to a clearing that held the graceful columns of glittering purple. Mallory circled them, watching; contemplating; touching until he threw up his hands in exasperation.

"How do I know which one to open? None of them will budge."

"Wait, here…this might help," Fifery dug into his bag and pulled out the compass.

Mallory's jaw dropped in amazement. "Where did you get that?"

"The Blulupians. They asked me to give it to you. It found me in Blulupia, now it will help you find the pearl."

Mallory gently took the cuff and placed it on his wrist. He lovingly smoothed his finger around the face. The obscure marks waivered and came into focus. For a brief moment Mallory understood them, but its meaning was gone as swiftly as it arrived. He shook his head and watched the hands wobble before spinning around back and forth then finally snapping together. Fifery watched over Mallory's shoulder, barely breathing. Together they sped off in the hands' direction and almost crashed into a spire of gleaming amethyst rocks. The hands went slack and wobbled around, their job, for now, done.

Mallory placed a hand on the topmost oval but it would not move. He used two hands but the rock was stuck fast. Mallory picked up a flint and started to gorge at the join unsuccessfully. He bent low and tried to topple the entire column bracing his body against it. He tried to turn the top rock one way, then the other. He tried to climb on top of it to crush it with his weight. Sweat was pouring off him and frustration rising in him like a king tide.

Meanwhile, Fifery stood still and stared. His fingers moved imperceptibly along with his lips and he whispered something under his breath.

Mallory exploded. "Why don't you stop staring like an oaf and HELP ME!"

Fifery cowered, unused to angry outbursts, and backed away. Mallory raised his palms to Fifery and stepped back, "I'm sorry, sorry, I didn't mean to...I won't hurt you."

Fifery inched forward. "Six" he said quietly.

"Six?"

"Yes, each column has six rocks, look, six, six, six, six," he pointed to the neighbouring towers.

"Yes, I see, but what does that mean?"

"Six, six the number of truth

For by five it is held together,

See the joins and you shall find

The glue of human endeavour.

To touch the air and bow to the Sun..." Mallory joined in.

"To see her feathery rays,

To taste her joy and smell her fun,

Her praise rings out always."

They finished the child's verse together. The camaraderie of singing together made both men laugh. Fifery glowed with kinship; the shared knowledge of the rhyme made him feel part of the world for the first time. Mallory in turn was delighted that Fifery may have solved the riddle.

"It is the riddle of the senses. But what now?" asked Mallory.

"'To touch the air' comes first," suggested Fifery.

Mallory gently ran his finger along the join between the top stones.

"What does it feel like?" asked Fifery.

"Smooth. It feels so smooth, yet it looks gritty, like sand. It calls to mind...it calls to mind an egg! The egg of the sandpiper. She used to sing outside my window at dawn. She always sat in the tree. Her song would chime out above all the others. She would wake me from my slumber and force me out of bed for I always wanted to glimpse her. But she would fly away when the curtains twitched. Once I left them open but she was still gone when I reached the window. One cold day of the Sorry Season, I realised she wasn't singing anymore and my father found my sorry backside still in bed and kicked it until I ran howling from the house. Oh how I missed that bird! By now the leaves had left the tree and I could see a nest buried right in the centre. The canopy had hidden it all Sun Season. I climbed that tree to peek inside the nest. Lying right in the bottom, covered with feathers and straw sat a tiny egg. It was pure white with thin pink veins running through it. When I touched it with my small boy's finger it was the smoothest, most delicate thing I ever felt. Not only that; it seemed alive, warm, pulsing. My Ma always told me if you leave Mother Nature in peace, she will leave you in peace. From that day on I heard the sandpiper's chirp in my dreams and at daybreak I climbed the tree to check on the egg, made sure it was covered and warm. I loved that egg because my father didn't have to kick me out of bed again." Mallory paused.

"What happened to the egg?" asked Fifery.

"Shush!" said Mallory, his forefingers were still touching the base of the first stone.

"It moved."

As he gently lifted it off, he continued.

"One day, as the Sun was coming back from her sleep I found the shell cracked apart. The inside was as coarse as the outside was smooth. It was empty. I heard the sandpiper's call again but it was far away, next to another's window."

The top of the column revealed a dip where the stone had sat. It was even darker than the surrounding surface.

"'To see her feathery rays', what can you see?" asked Fifery.

Mallory sunk to his knees and stared deeply into the stone.

"I see...I just see a sparkling rock. Here, you have a look."

Fifery joined Mallory and gazed into the recess.

"Oh yes, I see the night sky, the night sky reflected in the ocean. Guffer used to say the stars loved the night because they could swim in the sea at night-time. He said that was what kept them so shiny and bright; their nightly wash in salty water. He said I would shine as bright as a star because I swam in the water every day." Fifery smiled.

"He called me Starshine most of the time, that's probably why I can't remember my true name."

"My memory of swimming in the sea was not such a happy one. I wonder if even the stars get taken by the Beach Eater," wondered Mallory.

They looked into the glistening rock deep in thought when they heard a small grinding noise. Mallory held his breath and lifted away the second rock.

Encouraged, they continued.

"'To taste her joy...'"

Mallory wrinkled up his nose. The rock had uncovered a pale disc of liquid on the top of the column. Bravely he dipped his finger in and cautiously placed it on his tongue.

"How does it taste?" asked Fifery looking at him intently.

Mallory, who still had his finger in his mouth, slowly removed it. He scrunched up his eyebrows, he rolled his tongue around his mouth, he looked up and away chasing memories. He closed his eyes.

"It sparkles upon my tongue, it's bitter yet has a buttery sweetness. DUCK'S EGG ALE!"

Fifery looked blank.

"It's a custom, when a young man comes of age. I remember when I had just joined the army my voice had dropped. The boys took me out to the forest. We made a fire in a clearing, the holy man came and made a circle of burning coals that represents a crown of light. Every man who was there wished for me. Some were crude – to do with women – some were for skills and strength, some for good fortune. After each had spoken the holy man showered me with Duck's Egg Ale, the yellow droplets represent Sun showers of luck. When all was said he handed me a chalice filled to the brim with ale. The ale is a special brew, only made for this ceremony and only the holy men know how to make it. They say it takes a duck egg to turn it yellow. It has a most exquisite taste; the glossy liquid breaks onto your tongue in bittersweet yeasty bubbles, then a tang of spirit is followed by the sweet spring sunshine gliding down your throat."

Fifery had an enchanted look on his face then set his eyes downcast. Mallory put a hand on his shoulder.

"When we are done, Fifery, when we have found the king's voice and your true name, I shall celebrate with you the gift of manhood. I promise."

Fifery smiled and nodded. The stones clunked and Mallory removed the third stone, as if by magic.

"Smell her fun," Fifery recited.

Mallory groaned.

"What is it?"

"I cannot smell, Fifery. I have never been able to smell."

"Just try," prompted Fifery.

Mallory put his nose to the rock and breathed in deeply, he shook his head.

"Nothing."

"May I?"

Mallory nodded. Fifery joined Mallory and inhaled. He sat up with wide eyes and let out a deep breath. He stooped down again and smelled. He stood up and paced, then rushed back for another smell.

"It's there but, but..."

"What? But what," asked Mallory frantically.

"I just can't place it."

"Try again, smell again!"

Fifery smelt and sniffed and smelt but try as he might he could not recognise the aroma in his head.

Frustration led the day into night. The two men sat disconsolately by the fire. Disappointment led night into sleep, and as the fire died down they both dreamt of stars and eggs and struggling in a deep purple glistening sea. The next morning Mallory made a decision. They would leave Anishka in order to find the Sergeant and retrieve the Sand Diamonds. Mallory carefully restacked the rocks and left the clearing, leaving marks so that he would find the place again.

ENCODA

E ncoda did not want Bravindo found. Already he felt as if his brother was a figment of his imagination. Breeda also saw her own brother, Beau, as a ghost, a ghost that had haunted her by day and night. Only the reassuring presence of the prince chased it away.

The caravan had travelled back towards Carbinia but the prince's presence distracted the party and the villagers they met on the way. Encoda was enjoying the holiday feeling; he experienced freedom and real life simultaneously. Goaerons actually spoke to him, admired him. And Breeda, well she inspired such feelings of tenderness in him that it was sometimes painful to bare. After ten days Encoda knew that he must return to the palace. People were asking about the king and Encoda knew that he could not dismiss his brother and forget about him entirely. Besides, he had an idea that if the king was missing for a whole season, he had reason to take the throne. He just needed to find the law and read the small print. He sadly farewelled his new comrades; they had shown him friendship, respect and belonging. But before leaving he discussed an idea with Breeda. They decided to start a guild that set out to find lost people. All the missing would be drawn up on a list and a group of investigators would be assigned to find them. Most of the gypsy group volunteered for the jobs and soon they were ensconced in their own offices in Carbinia with Breeda as their chief.

The palace was in a mournful and quiet state on his return. The ministers were busy keeping affairs in order, having no idea of either king or prince's whereabouts. It was with great relief when Encoda strode back into the palace and a meeting was called immediately. The ministers confirmed that Encoda's orders had been carried out and that groups of five soldiers had been despatched to all corners of Goaero. So far, they reported, there had been no word from anyone. Encoda privately rubbed his hands, if the king were to remain absent his ambitions would be realised, and all without spilling blood. He began to make surreptitious moves towards organising his coronation. He had been back at the helm for fifteen days when one of the courtiers interrupted him. He told of a messenger boy that had arrived on a horse, lathered in sweat and with threadbare hooves. The boy boldly refused to see anyone but the prince himself. Although the intrusion irritated Encoda, he bade him enter. The boy handed Encoda his letter, still warm from the safety of his breast. The prince raised his eyebrows in surprise, and then they dropped together in disappointment before scrunching into his brow deep in thought. The note from the Crone Agruella had suggested strongly the whereabouts of his brother and that the wench Kafia had set off to find him.

Prince Encoda dismissed the boy and called for his servant.

He gave him orders to saddle the fastest and freshest steed. Encoda decided to leave immediately, but not before finding Breeda and asking her a very important question.

He could feel the pull of the crown and knew there was only one person who he wanted beside him – Breeda. He sent message for her to come to him and waited, nervously, anxiously going over the words in his head. He waited and paced his chambers, still there was no knock at his door. He called his servant once again. The man came puffing into the room and like history repeating itself, said:

"Sire, Miss Breeda is missing!"

Encoda's face crumpled,

"What? Are you sure? Where? Where is she? Send me Elan!"

Soon Elan rushed in. He was Breeda's friend and assistant, and Encoda had also come to know him well.

"Elan, where is she? I saw her only yesterday, why did she not tell me she was leaving?"

"Sire," he bowed, "she left in great haste and agitation. In the night she had a dream, or a kind of vision…she really did not make much sense…she said she saw Beau, sensed him, he was alive but weak and was emerging from a vast water and had to find him. Sire, I tried to stop her, to accompany her with some others but she had to leave she said, right then."

"Where? Do you know where?"

"She would not say but she took warm garments, I do not think she knew herself."

"Why was I not informed of this? Why did she not seek my help?" Encoda was talking more to himself now and he recoiled in hurt and anger.

"Sire?" ventured Elan.

Encoda looked up from his confusion "Yes?"

"I have known twinship sire, in my village, of my age, they are a queer thing, almost one person in two, they are always connected, intertwined. I know it doesn't make much sense to the rest of us but I don't think the king himself could'a stopped her from going, with respect your majesty."

Encoda was not sure if he knew what Elan meant but the mention of the king brought him back to the present and he had no time to waste; he had to get to Bravindo before anyone else discovered him.

"There is one more thing, sire."

Encoda stopped and answered impatiently,

"Yes, what is it?"

"There are many missing, Sire. Since we set up the Guild of the Missing we have had hundreds of Goaerons here to report, and more pour in every day."

"You will have to deal with it Elan. We will confer when I return from my business. I shall be in Spode with the pilgrims. That is all."

Elan left to deal with the queue of people outside his office and the prince, in a fury, swept off into Pashanka.

KAFIA IN SPODE

A rough and ugly smelling tongue poked at Kafia's face. The horse, either in deep remorse or craving salt massaged her face and roused her back to consciousness. She let out a cry at the pain in her head and gingerly felt the large lump, congealed with blood. She winced and elbowed herself upright.

The slate walls of the gorge were silent and still, the path ahead was solid, the cool mountain air was whooshing through. Cautiously, Kafia got to her feet. Her head throbbed. She managed to slide her leg over the horse's back and gently nudge her heels into his flanks.

"Be gentle with me," she whispered as each jolt of hoof ricocheted around her head.

They cleared the towering peaks. The path continued along the ridge where she could see down either side of the mountain. The layer of scree led down to low alpine flowers, which blended into small tough trees before the path closed in under shining foliage of the well-watered valley. To her left she could see the town of Spode, her destination sitting snugly in the crevice of the three mountains. Soon she would begin her descent. Slowly Kafia's horse plodded down the winding path and into Spode. Her head nodded on each lurching step forward, barely conscious.

The woman who lived with her husband in the outermost house of town had watched Kafia's steady descent throughout the day. It was unusual for someone to enter the town by this route. Normally only regular visitors who had scores of tales risked the Guardian of Mortlock. The woman had tried to make out who it was all day long. She could tell it was not one of the taciturn pilgrims as they came on foot, and most traders had already arrived to take advantage of the town's busy-ness. By the last rays of the Sun, she saw it was a girl, and as the now dark outline reached her house, she also saw the girl was not in the best of health. Kafia finally arrived at the house, the woman put the horse's reigns over the gatepost and Kafia slid off the saddle into the woman's arms. She carried her into the house and laid her on a small bed under a window. The moon shone through onto her pale face giving her a silvery, unearthly pallor. A man emerged from the house and unharnessed the horse, gave him water and hay and tied him up.

Back inside they looked upon the girl.

"She looks like a bag of bones," the woman said.

"Bones," murmured Kafia, and she dreamt she was on a beach watching the waves take her memory in and out, unable to move but desperate to dive in to retrieve herself.

The woman, called Gretchen, gently stroked Kafia's hair off her face. She saw it was caught in a deep gash across the side of her head and drew in her breath at the severity. Her husband, Beaver, peered over her shoulder.

"She'll need that looked at."

Gretchen nodded.

"Lucky pilgrims are in town. Will you go?"

"Aye, better, she's breathing shallow."

Beaver left. The candles hissed in the silence, Kafia's small breaths hardly audible. Gretchen poured warm water into a bowl and gently cleansed the wound. She sang a lilting lullaby to the fragile girl.

"A wondering will will wander my sweet,

Wander my sweet, wander my sweet,

A wondering will will wander my sweet,

Home, home to me.

A flowering heart will flow my sweet,

Flow my sweet, flow my sweet,

A flowering heart will flow my sweet,

Home, home to me.

A lingering tale will live my sweet,

Live my sweet, live my sweet,

A lingering tale will live my sweet,

Here, home with me."

Gretchen's tears fell just as they had fallen a year ago while she sang the lullaby to her own lost sweet baby.

"I won't let you go, cross my heart," she whispered and she smoothed the sheet she had placed over Kafia.

Chapter 39

FIFERY, MALLORY AND THE SOLDIERS

The dull ache of failure and frustration sat heavily on Mallory and Fifery. Fifery was bewildered and felt guilty for letting Mallory down. Mallory was sullen. He was struggling with feelings of animosity towards Fifery, holding him responsible for the rift with his comrades and for not being able to identify the aroma from the rocks. Mallory was not comfortable leaving behind the pearl but he also feared the Sand Diamonds were slipping away.

They emerged from the dark bushes and headed back along the road that led into Anishka. Mallory consulted his map in which Fifery showed great interest. But Mallory's sour mood had stopped him telling how the Quills crafted them, he did not mention they were master Map Keepers and that Mallory was probably the only person in the whole of Goaero with a map. Fifery had never seen a drawing before, he thought it was beautiful. He could recognise the lines of the land; its language, he understood it. He saw Mallory trace his finger along an inky line that began at Anishka and curled through the mountains.

They set off again toward Anishka and skirted the town, eventually meeting up with the road that led west into the jagged mountain range of Mortlock. They walked along in silence; Mallory still stuck in an irritable hole and Fifery, who was anyway unused to social company and idle chatter. The road leading to the mountains was less busy than the one into Anishka but busier than usual with the town's holy men heading off on their Mid Sun Day pilgrimage.

"Mallory?"

Mallory jumped at his name, even though Fifery spoke it quietly.

"Yes?" he answered gruffly.

"Why did those men capture me? Why were they so cruel?"

Mallory softened. Of course, it was not this boy's fault. He berated himself for being so shallow, for using the boy as a scapegoat for his failings. It was him and his wretched nose that had always led him into failure.

"You are a Quill, Fifery," Mallory said kindly, "who I know to be fine people. But Quills no longer mix with Goaerons. Quills are not even considered Goaeron. They are a mythical creature both resented and scorned, both reviled and revered. No one really believes in Quills any more. There have been sightings but most are explained away as an eagle or such."

Fifery was beginning to understand.

"Maybe that is why I was sent to Shapeshifter Territory."

Mallory nodded and looked at Fifery.

"Fifery, I have stayed with Quills. Please do not be downcast. All will be well. I will take you to them but you must help me first. There is much happening in Goaero and I am on orders from Prince Encoda. Do you understand?"

Fifery now nodded.

"But...but what if the soldiers tell of me? What if others try to take me?"

"I don't believe they will speak of you...yet. They will be ridiculed and spurned. Besides, I will help protect you."

Fifery did not seem convinced.

"Believe me," Mallory added, "I know these men; you can not only outsmart them, but you can out-fly them as well," he grinned.

Fifery smiled back, feeling a little more at ease at both the encouraging words and the renewed camaraderie between them.

By now the road had run into the mountains. It was still wide and carved through the dank bottom of a valley with vast sheets of mountainside rising up on each side. The end of the valley was marked by another hill rising up steeply and the road swerved to the right to flow around it. Here the road narrowed and ascended over a ridge that joined the two peaks. They passed a solitary pilgrim who plodded slowly and intently. The road continued to rise and fall, twist and turn into a muddy track, kept wet from streams dripping down the slopes. After rounding another base, the road met a river and meandered alongside it. Mallory drew out the map again.

"Here, look," he said to Fifery, "we are still at least two days from the town. We need to travel faster so we can catch those scoundrels before they get there. I wish we had horses."

Fifery thought and said quietly:

"Maybe I could fly? I could carry you."

Mallory recalled his flight with Que. It was a good idea but he wasn't sure if Fifery was strong enough. There was also the risk of being seen. He, too, was worried that as soon as the soldiers reached town they would tell of Fifery's existence. Spode was full of strangers this time of the year and any talk of Quills brings forth a trumpeting of opinions. But, as much as Fifery's wings could get him into trouble, Mallory was sure they were also the key to keeping him out of it. He mulled over his choices, his fingers distractedly traced the edge of the compass.

"Fifery, I think I have a plan. It is the only one I can think of…"

"Go on," urged Fifery.

"There is too much risk for us both to fly, even if it were

possible. But if you fly ahead under the cover of dark, find them and show yourself..."

Fifery looked alarmed.

"Lure them back this way, towards me; they will surely follow. I will be ready to ambush."

"How will you know we are close?"

"I will know."

"Then I will do it," said Fifery.

Mallory calculated that the soldiers were a day ahead of them but as they were a larger group and probably injured, were moving slower. If Mallory and Fifery pushed on for the day and into the night, they would gain ground. At dusk Fifery stopped to rest before his night flight and waved Mallory off as he headed on determinedly.

When the moon was high Fifery took off and flew steeply up until he sensed the delicious wafts of the Eternal Mists. He breathed in deeply feeling energised with each inhalation, as if a fresh stream of life flowed to his wing tips and toes, spurring him on into the night. The dark bulk of the mountain slept below him and he felt disconnected from that world below and at peace. He began his descent toward the ravine Mallory was following. As he came closer to the mountaintop, he could see a faint glow rising into the sky from the other side and realised that Spode town lay at its source. He silently drifted down and saw intermittent specks of firelight as pilgrims camped on the wayside. He spotted a string of three fires, one bigger than the other ones, indicating a larger party than the individual wayfarer.

Fifery landed along a dark stretch of track free of camps and worked his way back on foot. He trod lightly upon the ground until he smelt the smoke of a dying fire. He crept onward and saw a small mound of glowing embers. Two quilted lumps lay snoring softly within its radiance. Fifery could see a white bearded face poking out of one of the quilts and he moved on. A little further a second fire burned brightly, a solitary figure sat prodding it with a stick, his head nodding in and out of sleep. Fifery clamped his cloak tightly around himself and sneaked past. The next camp was a longer walk but he could see it from a way off; the fire larger. He slowed cautiously. He sensed the Sun was stirring as the barest glimpse of light began to fringe through the sky. Fifery left the track and crept gently into the bushes at the back of the site, as he circled the camp he heard the dreaming, scratching and snuffling of more than one man. He stooped down in a position where he could see the men's bodies. He counted four by the fire. He inched down onto his stomach and lay in wait. As the dawn brought colour back into the world Fifery scanned the camp, one, two, three, four...where was the fifth? Fifery wondered if he had not found the soldiers but another party. Then one man stirred, rose, snorted and spat into the fire. He groaned, held his stomach and turned his head in stiffness and pain. Fifery noticed a bloody scab above the man's ear and with a peculiar feeling recognised his own fierce handiwork. It was Juke. Again, he could only see four men who were all beginning to wake and the absence of the fifth niggled him. Some sticks cracked behind him and a warm stream of liquid trickled onto his thigh. He turned over startled and looked up into the face of an equally shocked Mole. Fifery glared at him and backed away, and when clear of the bushes, stood up and pelted back towards the road before the stuttering Mole managed to alert the rest of the soldiers. Sarge yelled orders and kicked the slumbering men, hurriedly they packed away their gear and began to sprint along the road whilst pulling on breeches and slinging bags across their backs.

Fifery was running and thinking at equal speed. He had not meant to be rumbled so soon; he was hoping to have orchestrated his discovery thus giving him an advantage. Now he had to be extra cunning, he did not want the soldiers to guess he was leading them to Mallory. He did not know how far Mallory had walked or what he was planning to do when they met. Fifery's legs were tiring, he spotted a clump of trees ahead. He painfully ripped a feather from his back and dropped it on the road, then half flew, half climbed the tallest tree in the copse. Soon the soldiers ran past, puffing and kicking up dust. Sarge saw the feather, picked it up and urged his men to move faster. Fifery sighed in relief. He quickly jumped out of the tree and ran in the opposite direction and swept up into the air, only circling back when he was high enough not to be identified as a Quill. Soon he saw the men and in the distance the speck of Mallory moving toward them. He circled and watched until the meeting was imminent. Fifery landed some way behind the unit. He picked up two medium sized rocks and put one in each of his pockets. He found a branch, a little thinner than the width of his wrist and wedged it in his waistband. He flew back up into the air and watched as he winged on the breeze.

Finally, the soldiers and Mallory were within sight of each other. Sarge pulled them up, alarm bells now ringing. Mallory walked toward them unflinching.

"How unfortunate our paths have crossed again," he said.

"Where is it?" growled Sarge.

"I have no idea what you are on about."

"The Quill..."

Suddenly Fifery swooped down and tossed a rock at Juke's head.

"Right behind you!" he shouted as Juke dropped to the ground.

The men turned. Mallory did not hesitate and leapt onto Sarge's back pinning his arms behind him. Fifery flung the second rock at the cowering Ham who shrieked and fell unconscious. Sarge writhed and struggled getting an arm free which shot around to catch Mallory's temple. The memory of his father's beatings flashed, quickly followed by rage. Mallory yelled and swung the man around off his feet and tossing him to the earth. He leapt in the air, slammed his body down on Sarge and threw fist after fist at the man.

Meanwhile, Fifery charged down with the branch in both hands and belted Arnie in the chest knocking him off his feet. Mole squealed and ran in circles. Fifery landed on the ground in front of him and Mole shrank onto his haunches.

"Give me my Sand Diamonds!" he demanded.

"I...I...ain't got 'em," Mole cried.

"Where are they?" yelled Fifery.

Mole raised a shaking finger and pointed at his sergeant who Mallory was pummelling relentlessly. Fifery rushed over and pulled him off. He bent down to Sarge, swollen and bleeding.

"Where are my Sand Diamonds?"

Sarge coughed and managed to laugh.

"They're already gone," he spluttered.

"Gone! Gone?" Fifery said in disbelief.

The real value of the Sand Diamonds was suddenly clear in Fifery's mind. They were his only possession, and in that possessing he had had power, the power of choice. He had chosen to exercise his generosity and gratitude in giving them away. They were his, his link to the past, to his childhood, to Guffer, to Mutilin and now to his future with Mallory and the king. Those Sand Diamonds were everything to him and the theft of them violated him to his core.

"Gone where?" he interrogated slowly and menacingly.

Sarge spat bloody spittle into Fifery's face.

"Search them!" said Mallory.

Fifery and Mallory searched every man and bag. When they got to Mole, he let out a whimper and glanced back down the track.

"He knows where they are," said Mallory pointing at Mole. "Let's go."

Fifery, Mallory and Mole left the four men lying moaning on the road and moved off quickly.

"Spode is beyond that mountain," said Fifery. "A day's walk, no more, we can get there by nightfall."

"By which time," said Mallory, "Mole here will tell us where the Sand Diamonds are."

Mole swallowed and half ran to keep up with the striding men intent on the road ahead.

SAND DIAMONDS

The three men rushed along at full speed. Mallory needed to get as much space between them and the soldiers; he knew Sarge would be intent on revenge. They had been thoroughly thrashed however, which would slow them down. Mallory could not bear to think of his brutality; it made him feel hollow and queasy. He wondered why he ever joined the army; he abhorred violence and being a perpetrator made him feel sick. He turned his attention to Mole.

"Where are they Mole?"

Mole whimpered and panted as he tried to keep up.

"What? Are you still loyal to that bullying brute? C'mon Mole, you and I used to be friends..."

He gave Mole a moment to think.

"Besides, I am on direct orders from Prince Encoda himself; he will look upon you very favourably if you assist me with my quest."

Mole did not need long to consider his options, he was a simple fellow and would rather do what was required in the immediate moment than try to figure out his long-term prospects.

"He gave 'em to a pilgrim, for 'safe keeping'," he said.

"What was his name? What did he look like?" Mallory questioned.

"I dunno. He was an old slow traveller, strange coloured skin. He had three plaits, he was dressed 'ed to toe in a blue-green cloak with a dark blue robe under. Very similar to your trousers, they were."

Mole pointed at Fifery's legs, part of the ensemble gifted to him by the Blulupians.

"Good. Now, how long ago, and what instructions did Sarge give the old man?"

"Oh, only yesterday morn, he said he would find the old man in Spode in two days."

"And is that all?"

Mole nodded. "What'll you do with me?"

"You will stay with us for now, safer for you and us. But you will have to keep up and stop groaning."

Mole swallowed nervously. "Alright."

They hurried on in silence. By late afternoon they had rounded the squat base of the mountain and saw in the distance Spode glowing softly in the mountain's bosom. It was night when the men collapsed outside the town. They lit a fire and ate the last of their provisions before falling into an exhausted but nervous sleep. In the dead of the night, Fifery woke and silently flew up towards the peak and beyond. He bathed in the Eternal Mists of Life, refuelling himself for the day ahead, preparing for the vexation of town life.

The centre of Spode consisted of a large field that stretched from one side of the valley floor to the other. It was covered in a fine silvery grass which shimmered as the breeze blew across it. In the middle of the grass grew the Tree of Light. Every Mid Sun Day the pilgrims and townspeople gathered in the field to watch the tree. At midnight, the dark shadow of the moon rose to eclipse the Sun – as it did every night – but on this day the Sun was at Her closest to Goaero and a halo of golden light shone out from behind the moon. The escaped rays of the Sun came rushing down to touch the silver branches which rustled upwards to meet them and, in that moment, Sun and planet were united. The pilgrims would break out into a mystical chant which vibrated in the air with one continuous tone. All would be one.

Around the field, the town buildings were set in shallow steps up the mountain's foothills. In the dip between the three mounts the hub of the town housed the market, official buildings and some cottages. More homes spread either side of the field along the adjacent foothills.

As the three men entered the valley, they could see the silver sea of grass dotted with figures and the huge wide spreading Tree of Light, under which sat a solitary person. They had seen no sign of the green-cloaked traveller but as they drew closer, they could see that there were already many pilgrims camped in the field. There was a quiet air of reverence; most of the pilgrims sat in prayer with closed eyes. The three men, unwilling to interrupt, crept around them seeking a green cloak. Mallory nudged Mole and nodded at one pilgrim, he shook his head. After the fruitless search, they walked into the town. Here it was busier, noisier. Townsfolk scurried about carrying market wares, pushing carts and putting up colourful flags. Mallory stopped at a stall selling drinks.

"Good day, sir! A cup of berry juice for me and my two friends, please."

They drank the juice with relish by the stall.

"Tell me, sir, is there a place the pilgrims go other than the field?"

"Nah, mostly they stay put. Seem to go without food and drink half the time, til after Mid Sun Day...then they fill up," the stallholder explained.

"So, if I was looking for someone in particular and they were not in the field – but definitely here in Spode – where would you suggest I could find him?" asked Mallory, with slight desperation.

"Who is it you're after?" asked the man bluntly.

"We are here to meet a pilgrim..."

"Go on..." he urged.

"... a pilgrim dressed in a long blue-green cloak."

"'Is name?"

Mallory shook his head.

"What's he look like?"

Mallory nudged Mole.

"Oh...er, tall, taller then you, much taller than 'im," he said looking at Mallory who scowled back.

"Kinda blue looking..."

"Any more juice?" the stallholder asked.

Mallory sighed.

"Fill them up!"

He placed five times the value of the drinks in the man's palm.

"Sometimes they go healing, if someone's sick. I heard there's a girl on the brink of passing over in the outermost house of the north side."

"Thank you," said Mallory.

They moved off down the street that ran along the base of the northern mountain, and then climbed up until they reached the last house in the last row. A horse stood in the garden under the shade of a tree.

The three men strode up the path to the front door. Mallory knocked three times. Voices murmured within and the door swung open. A man looked at each of them in turn; he had never had so many strangers at his house.

"Can I help you?" he asked.

"Yes, I do hope so. Do you have a pilgrim with you?"

"Er...yes, we do." The man scratched his head.

"Do you mind if we come in and speak with him for a short time?"

The man nodded and let them pass. The door opened directly into a large room. To the right were a table and chairs and two comfy armchairs in front of the fireplace. In the far left corner stood a double bed and a small cot in a recess at the front. Next to the cot, a woman and a tall man in a blue-green cloak looked down at a young woman sleeping. The pilgrim was handing the woman a small bottle of golden hued water. As the party entered, the pilgrim turned and looked.

"Oh my Good Heavens and the Sacred Sun, praise to the Wandering Wisps and Wishing Willows, are my eyes deceiving me?"

Fifery's face exploded into a laughing smile.

"High priest Jacarando!"

They embraced warmly.

"You have become big and strong, my boy."

"We have both come a long way," replied Fifery. "And look who I found."

Jacarando bowed deeply to Mallory, he knelt at his feet, took his hand and ardently kissed his knuckles.

"Mallory, you may, or may not remember High priest Jacarando from your short, er, stay in Blulupia."

Mallory realised the pilgrim looked familiar, although he no longer had the wide-eyed zeal as he yelled 'Fire!' in his eyes. At that time he had been filled with such deep fear that he had dared not recall the events and a lingering distaste of all things blue had remained with him. He was quite taken aback to see a Blulupian who was both jolly and eloquent.

Jacarando continued:

"It is such great fortune, and an honour, to meet you, sir. On behalf of my people, The Blulupians, I sincerely apologise for our terrible hospitality. It was a grave misunderstanding. I hope you can, please, forgive us. You have, indeed, brought us great fortune and happiness."

"Oh, well, of course, yes, thank you," stammered Mallory unused to such respect and devotion.

"Do forgive me!" said Jacarando turning to his hosts, "how very rude of me. Gretchen, Beaver, it is extraordinary that these esteemed friends of mine have walked into your house. I wonder if we may intrude on you for dinner. We may then re-acquaint ourselves and tell our tales in comfort and privacy. That way I can also keep an eye on the girl."

The couple nodded vigorously; they had never had a group of such interesting and seemingly important individuals gathered in their home. Beaver had also noted the now unmistakeable outline of Fifery's wings under his cloak. Could he have an actual Quill under his roof?

"Please excuse me while I tend to the sick," he asked the men and turned back to the pale girl.

Gretchen gave him the bottle and he tried to administer a few drops into her mouth. She stirred, groaning, and reached out to the ceiling before slumping back into unconsciousness.

"What ails her?" Mallory asked, gazing at the fine-boned creature.

"We do not know," ventured the woman, "she arrived here on horseback yesterday, fell into my arms like a dead body. She has a deep cut on her head. The kind priest here has offered to help her."

They stood in silence for a time before sitting at the table on the other side of the room.

"Jacarando, I have a question. It is quite urgent, it is for this reason we sought you, though we knew not it was the High Priest of Blulupia we were seeking," Fifery began.

Jacarando nodded for him to continue.

"We have been led to believe, by this man here – Mole – that his companion gave you two Sand Diamonds for safe keeping."

"Ah, I thought you looked familiar," said the priest. "Yes...I suspected some dubious acquisition had taken place, but I did not peek inside the package, having given my word. I ask no questions and do as I am bid."

"Those Sand Diamonds are mine, stolen from me outside Anishka, where I was nearly taken myself, if hadn't been for my saviour here." He looked thankfully at Mallory.

"The Sand Diamond you bequeathed us, Fifery, has brought us great fortune and happiness. If I had known I had been handed your Sand Diamonds, its sisters...well, I suppose it has all turned out for the best."

Jacarando returned the Sand Diamonds to Fifery, who solemnly handed one to Mallory. Mallory took the Sand Diamond with great reverence and placed it on the table. He reached into his inside pocket and pulled out the Bloodstone and held it up, it subtly vibrated as a flash of light passed through it, he picked up the Sand Diamond in the other hand and felt their weight, absorbed their beauty and at that moment a shadow of light seemed to pass through Mallory. They all saw it and Mallory was somehow sharper, he seemed to be outlined with a sliver of light which stood him out against normal daylight. A strange sensation also came over Mallory from within. His senses became even more acute than before; he marvelled at the colours on Jacarando's cloak, he could hear myriad sounds outside the house, his clothes against his skin pricked and rubbed and an array of images of the silver field passed across his mind that were too fast and confusing to comprehend. After some time, Mallory put the gems away in his breast pocket and Gretchen started moving around to prepare food. Jacarando tended to Kafia, Mole and Fifery loitered around Mallory nervously, while he sat in silence, looking around him as if in a new strange world.

They spent the rest of the evening eating and telling tales, although Mallory remained quieter than usual. Jacarando regularly checked on the still sleeping Kafia, dripping more amber fluid into her mouth, followed by broth from Gretchen. Fifery could not stop glancing at the sleeping girl. Her peace moved him, her eyelashes lying delicately on her cheek touched him and her fragility made him want to wrap his broad wings around her for protection. Mallory took only one look at Kafia and it sent a pulse through his body that was new to him. He felt its aftershock for the rest of the evening as his senses seem to absorb her mere presence without needing the furtive glances of Fifery's. At the end of the night, when food, drink and words had run out, Jacarando said:

"Well, tomorrow is Mid Sun Day and we shall get no sleep. It's time to turn in."

With that, they all chose a corner or chair and fell asleep. None of them could hear the chatter of Jim and Jacarando's sprite, Jake, in the garden late into the night.

Chapter 41

MID SUN DAY

The next morning the entire town was busy with preparations and excitement. Many more pilgrims came pouring into the silver field. Only Kafia slept through it all.

Mallory felt tense. He was concerned that Mole would slip off and felt sure the Sergeant would arrive at any moment. He was itching to return to Anishka for the pearl and then back to Carbinia to triumphantly hand the three jewels to Prince Encoda. Much unsettled him; the disappearance of the king, his future position as soldier, his poor lonely mother. He was also conscious of the change that had come over him the day before, the power of the two gems made him nervous and his heightened senses also disquieted him. He felt as if he had been living in a haze all his life and now all was clear, until the clarity was so sharp it almost hurt. He decided to speak with Jacarando.

"Jacarando, I have a favour to ask of you."

"Go ahead sir, I would be honoured to be of assistance."

"The Pearl of Anishka, as I was telling you last night..."

"You were unable to solve the riddle."

"Yes, my useless nose...would you return with us and endeavour to name the aroma?"

"Of course! But it will have to be after the Mid Sun's Day festival."

Mallory smiled his thanks, though sighed inwardly; he was reluctant to stay in Spode.

"This year promises to be a special occasion, have you heard?"

Mallory shook his head.

"There has been a man meditating under the Tree of Light for forty days and forty nights. Nobody has seen him before. It is said he is the Wise One from the Sun and will deliver a message at midnight."

"We saw the man yesterday, why is he here? What does he say?"

"That is it, he has said nothing. The townsfolk have visited and left food, some pilgrims tried to converse but he was silent."

"What does it mean?"

"It means we have to be patient, Mallory; all will be revealed tonight."

Jacarando said his goodbyes and set off to prepare himself for the day and night ahead. Mallory listened to Kafia gently breathing. For a moment he yearned for her tranquillity before remembering he had to check on Mole again. Outside he found Fifery turning over the remaining Sand Diamond in his hand. He had been keeping an eye on Mole who was terrified of the Quill and dared not move an inch under his watchful gaze.

The Sun was as close to earth as She ever came, blasting down on Her beloved Goaero, checking in on Her teeming inhabitants and preparing to bask in the adulation they extended to Her on Mid Sun's Day.

As the light-filled evening drew on, the town's people withdrew to their homes to eat a celebratory feast. The same meal was cooked each year; roast pelican with summer vegetables followed by a rich pudding of giant yellow peach, flavoured with star anise and baked in a gooey pastry. They drank nettle mead which was made in the morning of Mid Sun's Day to be brewed and drank the following year. It came with a toast that remembered the events of the previous year.

The couple hosting Mallory and his companions baked this glorious meal for their visitors. As they made their toasts, they recalled memories of time past.

For Fifery it had been his last Mid Sun's Day with Guffer, who had made familiar in words the ritual Fifery was now enjoying. Mole and Mallory had shared their meal last Mid Sun's Day with the rest of their company and they laughed at how Dunstan had swallowed a bee. Having Mrs Buttle's home-made mustard vinegar poured down his throat as a remedy was almost as bad as swallowing the bee itself. Gretchen and Beaver remembered and toasted their lost child who had barely survived a week of life, having been buried the day before last Mid Sun's Day. They all agreed that a happier year should follow and toasted to that.

After supper the townsfolk made their way to the silver field. They congregated between the town centre and the tree, while the pilgrims sat in the field facing the tree in deep meditation. There was an excited buzz in town which was heightened by the strange appearance of the Wise One.

The Tree of Light was the largest and oldest tree in Goaero. It was fully grown before any man trod the earth. The tree had a broad smooth trunk with a thin bark that shimmered silver. The branches started high up forming a mushroom shape that was so large it was a miracle the trunk could hold it. The finer branches wove themselves together and sprouted wing like leaves which fluttered in the breeze like a thousand butterflies. Every Mid Sun's Day the buds erupted into bell shaped berries. The people of Spode declared if you listened at midnight the bells could be heard ringing.

The moon loomed over the southern mountain and the Sun burned brighter. They all perspired in the midnight heat and watched the dark blue orb glide towards the Sun. All was hushed. The townspeople hung their heads in reverence, the birds were silent, the breath of the pilgrims gently streamed through the field.

Suddenly a thud of footsteps and voices broke the silence. Mole drew in a sharp breath and nudged Mallory.

"Sarge is 'ere."

"Ah! A welcoming party,yYa shouldn'a gone to the bother," bellowed Sarge.

Ham, Arnie and Duke tittered nervously.

"You two take the north side, Duke and I'll take the south. Where are ya? Where's the pilgrim's got my gems?"

Mallory, still in sharp relief, silently crept out of the crowd and surreptitiously moved into the field's south side. Fifery took the north side, despite Mallory's frantic hand gestures to stay, while Mole, in true form, ducked down to hide amongst the legs of the crowd.

"'Ere he is!" Ham had spied Jacarando and called out to Sarge.

Sarge ignored the prayerful state of reverence and barged his way through the meditating bodies towards Jacarando. Fifery strode to meet him, but as soon as Sarge caught sight of the priest he made his move.

"Leave him be!" ordered Fifery in a voice that stopped Sarge in his tracks.

Fifery leapt up to Sarge. All eyes but the pilgrims' and the Wise One's were on them. He snapped the remaining Sand

Diamond from his neck and held it high. Sarge snarled at him, but the gesture had loosed the cloak from his neck which fluttered and flapped to the ground, revealing his two glorious white wings folded into his back. The wings opened and quivered in the wash of air and Fifery looked over his shoulder in alarm. The town's people shrieked and gasped and murmured in disbelief. Gretchen and Beaver looked at one another and moved closer to protect Fifery should anyone try to harm him. Sarge fumed that his secret was revealed. Mallory looked at Fifery and saw something in him that he had not seen before, a stature of a man, a commanding man, a play of golden light from the field whisked around his head like a...then he felt something, breaking Mallory's thought. The ground was vibrating.

The moon's edges kissed the Sun's, and a sudden silence prevailed again. The Sun's rays pulsed stronger still. The moment was building, the air grew fuller and the silver field reflected the bright Sun, showering the pilgrims from below with jets of light, causing halos to frame their bowed heads. She showered down sharp beams of heat, desperate to shine as brightly as She could before She was shrouded by the moon. Waves of fiery air broke over the townsfolk, until they could hardly stand. Mallory watched the tree and saw it sending out mirage-like ripples into the air, speaking with the Sun as She touched the shimmers and sent down yet more burning beams. Mallory could feel the vibration stronger now, he saw in his mind a horse galloping, sweat flying from its shanks, the rider urging him on. The rumble became deeper until he could hear it, feel it, taste it. He turned to the back of the field where suddenly his vision and reality merged into one. Thundering horse steps snapped the silence. Prince Encoda flew to the centre of the field, his black cloak flying behind him, his jaw set in determination. He pulled up his whinnying steed behind the outermost pilgrims. He looked directly at the Wise One, paused a moment and smiled.

All day and night he had ridden his steed ferociously. His neck stretched out, his eyes focused on the mountains before him, willing them to get larger. Earth and rocks flew from his horse's hooves as he took the corners around the foothills. He could taste the power soon to be his, he could feel the weight of the crown on his head, he could sense the presence of his queen at his side. Now once more he dug his heels into the flanks of his exhausted horse which reared and rolled its eyes back, snorting and spitting foam from its mouth. This 'Wise One' would die and no one would know it was the king.

Time stood still, the eclipse was in full power, absorbing the moment. The horse and rider tossed the moment aside and rose once more ready for their final gallop when suddenly a pale figure stepped out of nowhere into the path of the horse, held up a palm and a terrifying paralysis came over him. Encoda and his horse were frozen in mid-air, bound by invisible ties, even his face was frozen in an expression of fury and fervour. Again, the townsfolk shrieked and gasped and murmured. Questions filled the air, utter surprise and fear spread through the crowd for not all the people could see that

Kafia had appeared from nowhere. The town's people with no more words to convey their astonishment, just gaped and pointed, for they thought they saw a ghost; this young fragile girl dressed in a long white gown, the deep red gash standing out on her pale skin. Gretchen dug her fingers into Beaver's arms who restrained her from running to Kafia.

"Long live the King!" Kafia hailed and pointed at the Wise One with the other trembling hand.

The people now broke into a furore as the moon finally eclipsed the Sun.

"The Wise man is the king?" they questioned.

The king, the Quill, the magical girl – they had never seen any of these. They wanted to look closer at all three and began to surge onto the field, the crowd behind jostling for a better view. The silver grass was about to be trampled when the dusky twilight fell and in that instant the pilgrims opened their eyes, raised their arms to the Sun and chanted their low penetrating hymn.

"The ground beneath your rooted feet

Is swept by breath of honey sweet

And laced within her hidden core

The secrets of life are hidden before

The wind blows east and fires the name

That cradles dice to start the game

That we call life.

Life begins from your blessed seed

So we may grow afore we're freed

To join your body and be as one;

Children of the heavenly Sun."

The people stopped in their tracks and raised their now silent heads to the Sun whose halo radiated around the moon and fell in golden shafts. As custom had it, they too raised their arms and joined in the hymn so the chanting grew louder, vibrating every bone and branch. As the boughs shook they emitted a delicate, barely audible tinkle and a silver glow caught the Sun's rays. And for a time, there existed another realm altogether; the world in a suspended state of unity. The tree's fruit quietly emerged from the buds.

But time never stands still, and the moon began his farewell and moved on northward. As the moon and Sun pulled apart, dividing longingly like two drops of water, the pilgrims and crowd fell silent, and as the Sun again became whole they each made a wish.

The Wise One, the King Bravindo, whispered his wish and, finally after forty days and forty nights, opened his eyes. And there, standing before him in all the glory of the shining Sun, his wings glowing, his blond hair framing his handsome face, his chest beating, he stood, the granted wish of a king.

"Jesizeran!" he called out in a cracked voice.

Fifery turned his head, blood surged ferociously in his eardrums, his heart seized, his throat pulsated. The word, the word he had wished for a moment before, was at once so achingly familiar it enveloped him, yet so very strange he dared not repeat it. He faced the Tree of Light to see King Bravindo looking directly at him.

"My son."

As the magical moment passed the spectators and pilgrims broke out into bedlam. They did not know whether to look at the Quill, the king or the prince suspended in mid-air.

"Silence!" the king cried out.

Although his voice was weak, its message seemed to reverberate around the whole field. The noise ceased. He looked again at Fifery.

"Come!" he commanded.

Fifery nervously made his way to the tree. The king took Fifery's cheeks into his hands and bowed his head. He planted a long kiss on his golden hair and embraced him, murmuring;

"My son, my son, Jesizeran," as tears etched strips down his dusty cheeks.

He pulled away and looked at Kafia.

"You may release him."

Kafia nodded and lowered her arm. The horse tumbled forward and Encoda slid off the saddle, wide eyed and subdued. Before he could utter a word, the king spoke to all in a husky voice that seemed to whisper in each ear:

"Good People of Goaero, the time has come for you to know a truth. I am half Quill."

The crowd gasped, some exclaimed angrily, one or two even collapsed, others just gaped in shock. Encoda raised his head slowly, thoughts racing through his mind.

"One of my ancestors, the fine King Abalin loved a Quill woman named Quera. She bore a child who eventually became King. From that day on the second born son carries the mark of a Quill, as I do."

Encoda's mouth fell open, the story he told Kafia was a true one. In the Crypt of Manola he now realised he had seen the story; it was never a fabrication.

The King went on.

"I too fell in love with a Quill who bore our child. But the Quills discovered our travesty and were so angered they banished the child. As my punishment, as if I needed any more, they took away my voice, so I would never speak of it."

Bravindo now looked at Fifery and spoke.

"The last time I saw your mother, Jesizeran, we promised to meet at the Tree of Light at Mid Sun Day. I have come every long year in hope and now, now..."

He trailed off, tears welling again.

"I know now," he exclaimed, his thoughts overflowing, "only when we were united would I speak. Like a bee leaving its hive the truth is out, and so, many will follow. But like a bee, it will carry out good work, a labour that helps, that restores, that creates and that in the end rewards with the sweetness of life."

He paused.

"There was once a bee that strayed a little too far from his hive. Before he knew it, the wind took him and he was driven across an ocean and buffeted into a strange land. He landed on a flower and began to greedily suck the nectar to quench his dry dusty throat. Another bee, which was larger and differently shaped buzzed angrily toward him and stung him right between the eyes. The bee fell off the petal and dropped lightly to the ground whilst its spirit rose away. And the killer bee also fell to its death, right next to the small lost bee."

Bravindo paused again and allowed his eyes to scan the crowd. Each and every one felt he had looked directly at them – each one felt stung by that bee. Mallory stung with disappointment at the futility, Fifery stung with anger at the killer bee, Encoda stung with injustice, Kafia stung with compassion, each and every one of the crowd felt a pang of sorrow. Bravindo resumed and again they all felt the words were whispered into their own ear.

"There was once a bee that stretched his flight a little too far. The eager wind took him even farther away, across a vast ocean where he landed on a strange but beautiful flower. He begun to suck thirstily at the nectar, so dry was his throat. Another bee, with large wings and crimson stripes flew down to the flower and drank beside him. The crimson bee flew back to his hive and allowed the lost bee to follow. He helped turn the nectar into honey and stayed with the hive. From that day on the hive produced the most exquisite, sweet tasting honey in all the land."

Once more the king allowed his eyes, glistening with emotion to scan the crowd. And each one felt soothed, the sweet, warm hope laying a balm on the sting. Absolute silence reigned until the Sun had jauntily swished her skirts high overhead and settled herself for the drama unfolding below. The leaves on the tree gave a rustle that seemed to tinkle around the field.

Suddenly Kafia's legs gave way and she folded to the ground like a white handkerchief. Encoda was at least bred with chivalry and, being closest, went and swept her up in his arms. As he strode up to the king he hissed, as much to himself as to the fainted Kafia:

"How did *you* get here?" and then called out, "this girl needs help."

Gretchen came running from the midst of the crowd and held the small bottle of amber liquid to her mouth.

Encoda bowed low towards the king.

"Majesty, brother, I am so glad you are safe...and well,"

Bravindo returned the bow and held out his hand. Encoda took it and shook the dry hand of his newfound, new loud brother.

"Encoda we have much to discuss but first..." He didn't know how to put it and so beckoned Fifery to him again.

"This is my son, Jesizeran, heir to the throne."

Encoda swallowed and clenched his teeth, this was worse than he ever envisaged. Bravindo clearly knew Encoda's plans to become king. He also realised that, of course Bravindo had been initiated in the Crypt of Manola and had somehow looked into the right window without being consumed. He realised that he and all his ancestors were bred from a Quill, and although he did not bear the double pearl at the base of his spine, he too was half Quill and uncle to a full Quill standing here, right next to him. He stiffly bowed to Fifery.

"I am called Fifery, my friends call me Fifery," he said as he glanced at Mallory who had also stepped up to the king. "It was given to me by the only mother I have known, Clarissa Crowcrone," and he looked pointedly at the king for his own story was becoming clear and a force of anger was arriving with the clarity.

The king noticed the fire in Fifery's eyes and put his hand in a pocket.

"There are many things I can tell you and many things I cannot. One day, when you are ready my son, I will tell you what I can but for now take this; it will unlock all you want to know about your real mother." He placed a tiny silver key in the palm of Fifery's hand and closed his son's fingers over the top of it, holding his fist in his two hands. Fifery unfolded his fingers and the tiny silver key reflected the Sun off his palm. In minute writing, too small for the eye to read, a name was inscribed along its shaft. His mind reeled, his name, his father, his legacy all filled the empty space he had carried for so long but made as little sense as before and still lacked the thing he now knew he wanted most – his mother.

Before anyone else could speak, although all had fallen silent, Kafia moaned and fluttered her eyes open. The king, Encoda, Mallory and Fifery all looked at her. Gretchen held her head in the crook of her arm and Kafia struggled to sit up. She was weak in body but her mind was as bright as the silver grass and, as if she had dreamt of nothing else, she fixed her gaze on the king.

"Your majesty, I have to speak with you urgently."

"Speak my child."

"Not here, in private, for I have a grave secret and I am bid to speak with the king alone."

Encoda's fury boiled for was it not he who had discovered the wench, had taken her into his confidences? Mallory and Fifery gawked at her, so fragile yet filled with a spirit that thrilled them.

"Is there a place we may convene?" the king asked in his hoarse voice.

"Please your majesty, my humble abode is yours, and the young girl has been under my care, she will be comfortable there."

"Very well, lead the way," said Bravindo.

They walked through the parting crowd who bobbed and bowed at the scruffy king and stared at the Quill. Beaver had fetched Jacarando who was emerging from his trance and they followed. At the house they stopped at the front door. Gretchen opened it and hobbled in supporting Kafia who had no strength left. Outside the king turned and said:

"Jesizeran, Fifery you will come." Bravindo still spoke falteringly and Fifery felt his contempt rising.

"But the girl said she would speak to you only. I will stay here."

The king had never been defied and Fifery had never met a king before, especially one who was his father. Before Bravindo could respond Encoda barged in front of Fifery, being careful not to touch him.

"Bravindo, majesty, I should accompany you, after all I have been in charge since you lost...since you have been away."

The king's expression gave nothing away but he replied quietly,

"I shall speak with her alone, I will call you if I need to."

He turned without waiting for a response and entered the house, closing the door behind him.

Mallory turned to Encoda and bowed low.

"Mallory I see you have managed to fulfil your quest." Encoda did not sound at all impressed with that and Mallory sensed he was caught between the axe and the woodpile. Mallory himself was surprised that the king had spoken without the final gem, the Pearl of Anishka, but felt he *had* somehow managed to bring about the return of the king's voice. He now knew Fifery was the missing gem, the so-called thief. Mallory decided it was best to say nothing and simply nodded his head in thanks, but then said:

"I suppose I should return the compass." He took the bracelet off and handed it to Encoda.

"You may keep it, as payment. Well done."

Mallory puffed his chest with pride and stared at the shimmering cuff. The other symbols seemed to be clearer now. He looked up at the prince.

"Thank you, thank you sire. To whom should I report to now?"

"The king, of course!" boomed Encoda and stalked off.

Mallory sighed and turned to Fifery.

"There are strange things happening, Fifery. I know not where to turn."

Fifery nodded, he opened his palm and showed the key to Mallory.

"Can you read it? I cannot understand this, but even if I could make sense of the letters, it is too small."

Mallory looked at the key and knew with eyesight so keen and with a knowing so sure that he was amazed at his own clarity and assuredness.

"Quendi," he said.

"Quendi," Fifery repeated, "My mother?"

Mallory shrugged, "Probably. Ah, yes, I see now, yes, Quendi is your mother."

Mallory was finding the answers to questions flying into his mind. Then he wondered if he could hear what the girl was telling the king for he was now intensely curious. He turned his attention to the door and listened. He heard:

"In danger?" Bravindo's voice gained resonance with every syllable.

"Yes, in mortal danger, any day now the Beach Eater will find a way through, we must stop it."

"Tell me how you came by this knowledge." He rolled the words around his mouth slowly, savouring them.

"It started with Prince Encoda, I helped him out of the hole, the one through the Back Door. He told me I must spread word that you are half Quill, but I couldn't, see? I was a Secret Keeper, then you went missing and Prince Encoda went with some people to find you."

"Some people?" Bravindo was surprised.

"Er yes, it's a long story your majesty, anyway I came to look for you and I thought you might be here. But I wanted to be cured of Secret Keeping, it was making me sick, so I stopped at Arfan and they put me in the Earth Chamber..."

"In the Earth Chamber? And you survived? Ah I see, that is how you managed to freeze Encoda!" His voice reverberated around the room. Like a wine that has been cellared for many years, it poured out in a rich, earthy baritone that Kafia seemed to taste as well as hear.

"Yes, I think so, I am to become a Crone." Kafia could sense the king's power growing, regrouping, with every sentence.

"You will make an exceptional one."

"Thank you sire." If Kafia could have curtsied she would have. "In the Earth Chamber, Mother Goaero took away all my secrets but she gave me one back." At this Kafia turned even paler and sobbed.

"Carry on, be strong, my dear," the king said kindly, he was enjoying the use of tone now.

"Goaero will be destroyed," she whispered, "the Beach Eater will take us all, and I saw it happen, in my dreams, such horror, such cold ugly deaths." Kafia broke down into heart wrenching tears. "And then nothing, nothing left."

Mallory was shocked, he paced up and down the garden path, running his fingers through his blonde and white hair. He knew then, as he knew the grass to be green, that his next quest was against the Beach Eater and he could barely stop himself from bursting through the door.

That night the king slept in a bed for the first time in forty days. Mallory and Fifery sat next to Kafia while she dozed and felt a sense of peace restore them. Jacarando snored in the armchair muttering blessings in his sleep while the people of Spode and Anishka, Pashanka and Casino, Blulupia, Carbinia and the whole of Goaero celebrated through the bright night until what would have been dawn. It was only when the townsfolk of Spode emerged from their sleepy beds later the next day that someone noticed every branch on the Tree of Light held a double berry under a pair of joined leaves.

About the Author

Karen Peradon lives in Perth, Western Australia and has had a passion for words all her life, be it reading, writing or proofreading. She has conjured up the time, energy and courage to start a novel relatively late in life, having been far too busy travelling the world and raising her two children. After taking a creative writing course in 2009 this first novel wove its way out into the world.